Alone together

The meeting of lips— ... , the exquisite heat, th ... ised something more. ... tter sweetness of it, the ... hat electrified every se ... gainst her own, giving and ... me. His arms wrapped around her, ... her from her feet. Someone moaned—and Victoria dazedly recognized her own voice. The coarseness of clothing was torture against her skin; it demanded release and the balm of another body against hers.

Even as Raeburn's lips caressed her mouth and throat, even as he drew her ever harder against him—even then, she was alone. Alone as she had been for fifteen years. But now, for once, for just one night or even one hour, she didn't want to be alone anymore. . . .

Praise for *The Veil of Night*

"The next great romance author has arrived, and her name is Lydia Joyce. *The Veil of Night* is a stunning debut from a young writer who possesses remarkable maturity and style. Every page is charged with sensual energy and confident grace. It is a gorgeous, complex, absolutely riveting novel. If there is only one new author you will try this year, it must be Lydia Joyce."
—*New York Times* bestselling author Lisa Kleypas

"Intelligent. Passionate. Filled with dark secrets and illuminating love. This is what romance is about!"
—Robin Schone

"A powerful love story, compelling and beautifully written." —Alison Kent, author of *The Bane Affair*

"*The Veil of Night* is a lush, erotic historical Gothic romance, with just the right dark and mysterious hero and a strong heroine who can match him. Anyone who has ached for the Gothics of the past shouldn't miss this book!"
—Karen Harbaugh, author of *Dark Enchantment*

The Veil of Night

Lydia Joyce

A SIGNET ECLIPSE BOOK

SIGNET ECLIPSE
Published by New American Library, a division of
Penguin Group (USA) Inc., 375 Hudson Street,
New York, New York 10014, USA
Penguin Group (Canada), 10 Alcorn Avenue, Toronto,
Ontario M4V 3B2, Canada (a division of Pearson Penguin Canada Inc.)
Penguin Books Ltd., 80 Strand, London WC2R 0RL, England
Penguin Ireland, 25 St. Stephen's Green, Dublin 2,
Ireland (a division of Penguin Books Ltd.)
Penguin Group (Australia), 250 Camberwell Road, Camberwell, Victoria 3124,
Australia (a division of Pearson Australia Group Pty. Ltd.)
Penguin Books Indian Pvt. Ltd., 11 Community Centre, Panchsheel Park,
New Delhi - 110 017, India
Penguin Group (NZ), cnr Airborne and Rosedale Roads, Albany,
Auckland 1310, New Zealand (a division of Pearson New Zealand Ltd.)
Penguin Books (South Africa) (Pty.) Ltd., 24 Sturdee Avenue,
Rosebank, Johannesburg 2196, South Africa

Penguin Books Ltd., Registered Offices:
80 Strand, London WC2R 0RL, England

First published by Signet Eclipse, an imprint of New American Library,
a division of Penguin Group (USA) Inc.

First Printing, April 2005
10 9 8 7 6 5 4 3 2 1

Copyright © Lydia Joyce, 2005
All rights reserved

SIGNET ECLIPSE and logo are trademarks of Penguin Group (USA) Inc.

Printed in the United States of America

Without limiting the rights under copyright reserved above, no part of this publication
may be reproduced, stored in or introduced into a retrieval system, or transmitted,
in any form, or by any means (electronic, mechanical, photocopying, recording, or
otherwise), without the prior written permission of both the copyright owner and the
above publishers of this book.

PUBLISHER'S NOTE
This is a work of fiction. Names, characters, places, and incidents either are the product
of the author's imagination or are used fictitiously, and any resemblance to actual per-
sons, living or dead, business establishments, events, or locales is entirely coincidental.

If you purchased this book without a cover you should be aware that this book is stolen
property. It was reported as "unsold and destroyed" to the publisher and neither the
author nor the publisher has received any payment for this "stripped book."

The scanning, uploading, and distribution of this book via the Internet or via any other
means without the permission of the publisher is illegal and punishable by law. Please
purchase only authorized electronic editions, and do not participate in or encourage
electronic piracy of copyrighted materials. Your support of the author's rights is
appreciated.

ACKNOWLEDGMENTS

I have years of backlogged gratitude to express and not enough space here to do more than start the job poorly, but this, at least, is a beginning.

To my parents, Bill and Margaret, who suffered more than I did from all the rejections that came to their house while I was in college.

To my brother, Stephen, who will never read one of my books and yet is convinced that I am the most brilliant writer to have ever lived by sheer virtue of being his sister.

To my husband, who smothered his fears for the sake of my dream.

To my invaluable critique partners, especially Bekke, Mica, Larissa, and Daria, without whom this book would have had a very different shape.

To Serena Jones for being the first editor to ever believe and my agent Nancy Yost for supporting my career.

And finally, to Megan Boyle of Mobile, Alabama, wherever she is now, for first introducing me to the genre.

Raeburn Court
September 18, 1864

My dearest Lady Victoria,
    While your missive pains me, I cannot see how it changes the situation. Your brother owes me certain sums; if he cannot pay, the law must take its due course. I regret any embarrassment such a circumstance might cause your family, but I can see only one clear path.
    However, if you would like to discuss the matter with me, I shall be expecting you at Raeburn on the 27th of this month. Perhaps we can find a less unpleasant alternative together.

I am,
    Your faithful servant, &cetera,
    Byron Raeburn

Chapter One

Graceless and sprawling, Raeburn Court was a pile of mottled limestone atop the bald hill. Lady Victoria Wakefield spied it while the coach was still some distance off, and she watched it steadily as they approached the park gate; after all, there was nothing else in the bleak landscape to catch her eye. As they drew near, the squat manor house grew only more blunt and ugly, its saw-toothed crenellations pierced by random, unbalanced spires stabbing the slate-gray sky.

"A duke lives here?" Dyer's incredulous question echoed Victoria's thoughts.

"Best place for him." Victoria didn't bother to disguise her causticity in front of her lady's maid. After two days of traveling, first from Bristol to Leeds by train and then another five hours by coach, she was seething.

Her hands curled into fists at the thought of the peremptory letter tucked in her reticule, all but ordering her to Raeburn Court. She'd been sorely tempted to remain in the familiar surroundings of Rushworth Manor and let her brother Jack rot in debtors' prison, if it came to that. But the thought of the shame it would bring her family goaded her pride more than the duke's epistle had incited her anger. So she'd written ahead, packed a trunk, and driven to the Bristol train station, ignoring her mother's wails of protest and feigned fainting spells.

What her trip could possibly accomplish, she didn't know. In moments of dark reflection—and there had been plenty of time for reflection on the trip to Raeburn Court—she feared she was chasing a will-o'-the-wisp. Still, there was the faint possibility that she could persuade the duke to see reason. She tried to reconcile the possibility with what she knew of him. Rumor held him to be a man in love with darkness, an enigma, a pariah not because of the acts he committed but because of the conventions he failed to keep. Victoria shivered. Though she knew the Wakefields could weather the shame of Jack's insolvency, the thought of the inescapable whispers and knowing smiles that would follow them for years drove her onward. She had paid too much for respectability to have it taken away by her brother.

They reached the porter's lodge in silence. It looked even more derelict than the manor house, with missing shutters and ivy growing wild across the windows. Only a thin line of smoke curling toward the sky showed it to be inhabited. The coach jolted to a stop, and the guard opened the door, offering his arm to the ladies as they descended. He did not ask what luggage was theirs; the two of them had been alone in the coach since a farmer and his wife got out at Raeburn Court's manor village half a mile before. The guard swung the brassbound trunk and valise down from the roof, accepted Dyer's tip, and hopped lightly onto the coach again without a word.

As the coach rattled away, Dyer gasped sharply, and Victoria turned to see a bent-backed, wizened old man sticking his head out of the front door of the porter's lodge.

"Lady Victoria?" he demanded, rheumy eyes wavering from one woman to the other.

Victoria allowed herself a small smile at his uncertainty. Her carriage dress was made of fine black taffeta, but the unforgiving severity of its cut and its lack of ornamentation made it difficult to distinguish from the plain attire of an abigail. Her wardrobe had been marked by unrelieved austerity for fifteen years now, first from an excess of puerile anguish, then from self-abhorrence, and now partly from habit and partly from the intangible security such a uniform offered.

"Yes?" she said, solving his dilemma.

The porter fixed his gaze on her, blinking myopically. "His grace is expecting thoo at the house, my lady. Gregory shall fetch thy bags when he comes this evening."

"And how are we to get there?" Victoria raised an eyebrow and gestured pointedly at the half-mile drive stretching up the hill.

The porter laughed at her, a wheezing, reedy sound that shook his spare frame and ended in a wracking cough. Taken aback, Victoria could only stare as he tried to regain enough breath to speak. Still trembling with macabre mirth, he crowed, "Thoo'il walk!" and ducked back inside the lodge, slamming the door in their faces. Victoria heard the thud of the bar dropping into place, echoed in the sound of distant thunder rumbling in the limestone hills.

Victoria exchanged a silent look of amazement with Dyer. Then, with nothing else to do, she picked up her skirts and began the long trudge up the hill to the gray hulk of Raeburn Court. She glanced back once to make sure the stout abigail was keeping pace and saw the crooked, scuttling figure of the porter lugging their baggage into the lodge.

Thunder rumbled again, closer. A fat drop of rain fell squarely on her nose as a gust of wind caught the cage of her crinoline and sent it swaying wildly against the back of her legs, shoving her up the drive. She caught her balance, then steadied her bonnet with one hand and lengthened her stride in an effort to reach the hall before the storm broke.

Dyer puffed sturdily at her side, striving to make her short, thick legs match Victoria's long steps. Another drop splatted against Victoria's cheek, then another soaked through the fabric of her wrap and the gown beneath to wet her shoulder. She pressed her mouth in a thin line of displeasure, wishing fifty hells on the arrogant duke. Her carriage dress would undoubtedly be ruined, adding destruction of property to his growing list of sins.

Despite herself, she smiled at the absurdity of that thought.

They reached the door just as a peal of thunder shook the ground and the sky let loose, releasing a torrent of water over them. Victoria didn't pause to knock. She jerked the iron latch down and threw her shoulder against the battered door, half stumbling inside as it opened. Dyer staggered in past her, mopping her streaming hair from her eyes.

A great gust of wind wrenched the door from Victoria's grasp and flung it wide, and a sheet of water blew in to drench them. Dyer squeaked helplessly and lurched out of the way.

Biting back her brother's favorite oath, Victoria seized the door and wrestled it closed. She leaned against it for a second to suppress the traitorous thrill that tickled her belly and knotted in her lungs. She tried, as she always did, to be properly disgusted by the weather—for it truly was foul, she told herself sternly—but there was something in the madness of the wind and rain that caught at some dark corner of her soul and sent it spiraling wildly away from her.

When she turned, still gasping from her precipitate flight up the drive, she was startled to discover a plump, elderly woman hardly two yards from her.

"Pardon me," Victoria said with as much dignity as she could muster, knowing the pointlessness of the attempt even as she made it.

"Lady Victoria, I presume?" the woman said, her face folding into a thousand creases as she peered at Victoria in the light of the candle she held up.

Is everyone in this cursed backwater blind? Victoria wondered as the woman squinted at her, a touch of amusement returning. "Indeed."

Her cool confirmation was greeted with a toothless grin and a flood of friendly confidence. "His grace wasn't expecting thoo so soon, not afore Gregory comes back tonight with the carriage. How did you two come here?" The servant tutted reprovingly and took their rain-heavy wraps. "You must have walked, to be so wet. Imagine such a thing! Two ladies, walking in this weather—"

Victoria forced a smile. "I assure you, madam, that it was no decision of ours. That porter—" She stopped, struggling to find a civil way to frame her response.

The woman just shook her head and clucked her tongue. "The ninny. Silas will play his little games, I fear. Keep thissen right here, love, and I shall be back in a moment." She waddled away with the candle, still *tsking* and sighing to herself.

Victoria took the opportunity to survey the room. The vast, unlit chamber stretched before her—the manor's original great hall, no doubt—its deep shadows scarcely pierced by the gray light filtering through the filthy mullioned windows, which trembled in their frames as another peal of thunder cracked overhead. Ancient, moldering tapestries flapped like living things in the steady draft flowing through the room, and enormous cobwebs fluttered against the black rafters in the dim recesses of the ceiling.

"What a place, your ladyship! Gives me the cold clammies, it does," Dyer whispered loudly, craning to peer about the room.

Victoria shrugged off the chill that prickled the back of her neck and replied as sensibly as she could manage. "It's only an old run-down pile of stone. You needn't worry yourself so."

"Of course, your ladyship," Dyer murmured, but she hardly seemed reassured.

Victoria didn't blame her. There was certainly something unsettling about the place.

Victoria saw the candle flame bobbing in the darkness of the corridor long before she could make out the round form of the returning servant.

"There," the old woman said, beaming pleasantly, her homely, cheerful face a bizarre contrast to their surroundings. "If thoo'il follow me, his grace is waiting in the Teak Parlor."

Wordlessly, the women obeyed, Dyer following so closely behind her mistress that she kept bumping into Victoria's skirt. The servant led them back through the corridor she'd emerged from, then up a narrow staircase, through a series of rooms, and along a maze of hallways, chattering all the while. "It's so grand to have a young lord in the house again—not that his grace wasn't grand, of course not, I mean the old duke, of course—but it just isn't the same, is it? Mind the fourth step; 'tis loose. And such a pleasant air he has about hissen, and all, so regal and reserved, not at all like—" She interrupted herself with a surprisingly girlish titter. "But we mustn't speak ill of the dead. Not that his grace—I mean, the new one— isn't as hot-blooded as a young man should be. Certainly not. He'll be having house parties here, too, right enough, as soon as the hall's less of a shambles. The decline! I never thought I'd live to see the day! Well, thoo knows how those reformers are—Corn Laws, Rotten Boroughs, Reform Bills—what's next, I ask thee?"

She stopped and turned around abruptly, fixing Victoria with such a fierce glare that Victoria blinked and re- played the words in her mind, trying to find a coherent reply. But the old servant turned away again before she could answer, resuming her babble as she led the way down a wide, marble-floored corridor.

Momentarily suspended in bemusement at her sur- roundings, Victoria's anger returned in full force. How dare the duke summon her like a lackey to his tumble- down manor, to be insulted by one servant and accosted by another? She'd give him a piece of her mind—

Or rather she wouldn't, she told herself hopelessly. If she couldn't keep a civil tongue in her head, no matter the provocation, she might as well not have come at all.

"Here 'tis," the old woman said finally, stopping at a door. "The Teak Parlor." She opened the door, stepping aside to let the women through.

Victoria entered first. Though her eyes had adjusted to the dimness of the hallway, the duke was no more than a dark shape in a chair before the fireplace, a vague silhou- ette against the sultry glow of the coals in the grate. She heard a rustle of skirts and felt a nervous brush against her arm as Dyer crowded in behind her.

"Lady Victoria Wakefield!" the servant announced theatrically, and rather unnecessarily, Victoria thought with dry humor. She doubted the duke was expecting any other unfamiliar visitors that day.

Victoria drew in a breath, preparing her practiced conciliatory speech of introduction, but the man spoke before she could open her mouth.

"Thank you, Mrs. Peasebody. You may go. And take Lady Victoria's chaperone with you. She won't be needing one here."

Victoria was brought up short by the sound of his deep, rich voice. Somehow, she'd been expecting something different—pettishly spoiled, perhaps, or nasally querulous—not the unshakable self-confidence that echoed in every purring syllable. The door clicked closed, and she turned to see that Dyer had left with the servant without waiting for her dismissal. Victoria suppressed an irrational flash of irritation at her abigail.

Feeling that she had lost the initiative, she rallied her façade of imperturbability and strolled over to the nearest chair without waiting for the duke to offer her a seat. After all, he'd not stood when she entered, so there was no reason to believe he would suddenly begin to play the conscientious host.

She had thought to soothe the duke and pander to his ego, but now she quickly reassessed her plans. Raeburn might be as arrogant as her brother's diatribes would have, but there was a canniness in his preparations that made her hesitate. He'd done everything he could to make her feel like an intruder, setting the scene carefully and even stripping her of her attendant as soon as she walked in the door. If she had relied on Dyer's support, Victoria would have been made to feel very alone and vulnerable by the maid's rapid dismissal.

Well, she had never been the delicate type, but there was still something . . . disconcerting about the duke. He seemed to exude a kind of guarded watchfulness from his shadowed corner, a kind of physicality that made her want to shiver and rub her arms.

Victoria sat in the intricately scrolled chair, quirking the corner of her mouth in the expression of mild, non-committal interest she had mastered long ago. That the duke could see her face in the dim firelight, she had little doubt; he had carefully staged the encounter so she'd be left in no uncertainty as to who controlled the situation.

He seemed to expect her to break the silence, but she had a paltry hand and cared to show none of her cards before she was forced, so she waited for him to lose patience and speak.

Byron Stratford, Duke of Raeburn, regarded the woman with amusement, turning his tumbler of scotch slowly in his fingers. She was not what he expected—not from her letter, and certainly not from his acquaintance with her brother. Where Gifford was dark and dashing, she was fair and dowdy; where he was dandyish, she was austere to the point of severity; where he bore an air of extravagance, she seemed almost fiercely self-contained. He'd anticipated a mad tirade from the sister of the impetuous viscount, but as soon as she'd stepped into room, he'd realized the ridiculousness of imagining her doing such a thing.

He'd assumed that Lady Victoria was younger than her brother, but she had to be at least half a dozen years his senior. He'd thought her rash when she'd accepted his half-jesting invitation, but now he realized why she hadn't worried about scandal. Every line of her bearing declared that she was a respectable old maid, from her tight, pale blonde bun and her prim, haughty smile to the hideously unflattering carriage dress. No, she would be above suspicion.

He took a swallow of his scotch, savoring the slow burn down his throat. He would enjoy toying with her very much—would enjoy provoking her, if possible, until she forgot her steely control and showed herself for the hot-blooded Wakefield she still must be under her cool veneer. Then he would dismiss her from Raeburn Court with a negligent wave and leave her sputtering as she was hustled away. He smothered a quiver of conscience with another gulp of scotch. He was too old, too cynical for moral reservations, and besides, she was guilty by association. It was scarcely credible that she could share her brother's name and none of his character—or lack thereof.

She seemed disinclined to fill the silence, so he cleared his throat.

"My dearest Lady Victoria," he began in an insultingly intimate tone.

Her eyes narrowed, and he leaned back in anticipation of her priggish, insulted reply.

"My dearest duke," she returned instead in a throaty voice at least twice as suggestive as his own, going straight to his groin without consulting his brain.

Byron jerked upright before he could stop himself. His interest was sparked, and it had been a very long time since he'd felt that. Lust, yes; a man his age could not earn a well-deserved reputation for being a dissolute reprobate without frequently feeling—and almost as frequently indulging in—the urgings of lust. This, though—this was different. This was genuine interest. He'd become so jaded he'd almost forgotten what it was like.

"I suppose I needn't say why we are meeting here," he murmured, watching the lady closely. Was that a faint blush on the woman's pallid cheeks, almost invisible in the sullen light of the coals? He experimented. "Together. Alone."

The blush deepened minutely. It wasn't a flush of anger, though now that he was looking closely, he could see a hint of that, too. This was a purely physical, sensual reaction to his intimations, the slow spread of heat from the edge of the modest collar to her hairline. More than her voice belied her prudish façade.

"Your . . . indelicacy is hardly necessary," she said. Her strangely pale blue eyes flickered blindly over his face. "Your grace," she added, as if it were an afterthought.

More and more intriguing. He leaned forward in his chair. "I didn't think you'd come," he heard himself admitting.

Lady Victoria sniffed, an oddly prim gesture to be followed by such a velvety voice. "No doubt. Which is why I am here." She settled farther back into her chair, her muscles subtly relaxing.

Feline, sleek, and satisfied, Byron thought. She was digging in for a fight. Narrowing his eyes, he decided to change tactics and dove in bluntly. "I promised you nothing."

"Which is exactly what you'll get if you continue on this foolish course of action." She didn't raise her voice, nor did her words grow sharp, but Byron heard the steel beneath the velvet.

The cat has claws, he noted, obscurely pleased. "In what way?"

Lady Victoria smiled slowly, not the superior quirk of the lips that had been plastered to her face until that moment, but an honest if malicious smile.

It transformed her suddenly and alarmingly. Despite its cruel edge, it lit her face, erasing the hard, unflattering lines she had fixed it in. If it had been a happy smile, Byron might have almost called her . . . beautiful. The thought surprised him. He'd been democratic in his affections, bedding the gorgeous and homely alike when the mood suited him, but he'd always prided himself on his fine aesthetic when it came to judging relative merit. Lady Victoria was fashionably tall, yes, but her hair was limp and pale, and her body— He frowned. Byron could say nothing of her body except that it was slighter than was the mode, encased as it was in that ghastly frock and likely an equally ghastly corset. Somehow, though, he was not repelled by the thought of her hideous underthings but perversely curious.

She laughed once, a hard, artificial sound—he was convinced that her real laughter sounded as lush and rich as her voice—and tilted her head back so she was looking at him from under the pale lashes of her slitted eyes.

"My brother has no money," she said simply. "None. Father cut him off cold this month. If he wants even a paltry allowance, he must remain at Rushworth."

Byron sighed as if disappointed and let silence slip between them again. The woman didn't move—didn't even twitch. She just let the long seconds stretch out, her eyes shifting slightly under the fringe of lashes as she seemed to search out his face among the shadows. He watched her, tracing the firm line of her jaw with his gaze, studying the way her thin, delicate nose cast a shadow across her cheek. He felt an unexpected twinge of possessiveness, as if she were some exotic puzzle box or enigmatic cipher he wanted to own and decrypt.

Finally, he spoke. "I would say it is unfortunate, but I don't feel that it is. It is exactly as I had expected." He paused to let that sink in. "It is exactly as I had hoped."

Lady Victoria stiffened minutely. That got a reaction,

at least. "What do you mean?" she demanded. The control slipped from her voice, and Byron was pleased to note it was just as luscious as when she had been deliberately needling him. It would have been a pity to discover that such a fine instrument were a sham.

"I mean, my dear Lady Victoria, exactly as I said." He allowed some of the satisfaction he felt to seep into his voice. "I would have been disappointed if Gifford didn't default."

Now the woman was scowling. Byron rather thought it an improvement over the disinterested mask, but nothing, of course, compared to that fleeting promise of a smile. "You want him to be thrown in gaol?"

"A future peer of the realm, sent to debtors' prison? I doubt it's possible. But humiliation . . . yes, I want your brother to suffer humiliation so great it will stain his line—unto the seventh generation." He allowed himself a smile at that reference, enjoying the small blasphemy of casting himself in the role of a righteous God.

Lady Victoria, however, did not look amused. Lady Victoria looked like she wanted to throttle him. "Why?" she asked, her voice low and tense with controlled fury.

The question robbed Byron of the satisfaction of her reaction. "Because he took something that was mine." Every word was as bitter as gall. He spit them out at her, not knowing why he was giving her an answer when she had no right to any—much less a right to the truth. But what could it matter? What could she do about it? She was hardly in a position to take advantage of any knowledge. Still, the wound burned, even after three years. "Because he ruined it, and when he was finished, he expected me to take it from him, flawed, imperfect, and pretend it had never been touched."

Lady Victoria's eyes widened in surprise he doubted could be feigned. "A woman," she breathed.

"Yes. A woman. A paltry, mewling thing, but one I wanted. Gifford wanted her, too, but only as a toy. A wife of the heir presumptive of a dukedom or lover to an earl's son. Gifford made it seem so easy, I'm sure." *Freak. Unnatural monster.* He knew Gifford had called him these things in the wooing of Leticia; what else he might have said between his sweet blandishments, Byron could only guess. "Now I'll take my revenge. Better than a pound of flesh—I'll strip a ton from his pride."

She was silent for a long moment. Her face was unnaturally still, so perfectly composed he could read nothing from it. Finally, she spoke, her eyes somehow finding his in the shadows. "And so you brought me here to begin the humiliation. To start your revenge." She cocked her head as if expecting a response. He said nothing; the answer was patently obvious. "Then you have already begun to fail." An edge crept into her voice, hard and cynical and mocking. In a sudden revelation, Byron realized it was the tone of a woman who knew too much, who had seen too much, who had been stripped of her illusions years ago. She wasn't a bitter, dry old spinster. Not even a jaded sophisticate. She was an observer who'd sat in the shadows all her life just as he was sitting in the shadows now, disengaged and watching, judging. Was she judging him now? The idea was vaguely disturbing.

With a delicate sniff, she continued. "My brother would have to care for his sister—for her inconvenience, her honor, her person—to be humiliated by your treatment of me. And he does not. As for the rest? Jack shall flee to Paris or Naples or Vevey once he convinces my father to relent, and he'll live there in dissipated penury until he inherits. Since he cares nothing for his reputation, only the personal discomfort that beggary brings him will cause him a moment's pause."

The words falling from her mouth seemed out of some gross farce. To be deaf to insults, insensate to pricked pride, blind to degradation . . . Could such a man exist? Gifford had everything in the world that Raeburn had ever wanted; instead of skulking about the fringes of the aristocracy in a black cloak, Gifford could bask in society's light, smiling in the assurance of being accepted, even adored, while Raeburn's eccentricities were tolerated only for the sake of his title. And when Raeburn threatened to snatch it all away, Gifford's own sister blandly announces he wouldn't care? The pangs of his own injured dignity were so intense he could almost taste them.

Yet Byron felt in his bones that she was telling the truth. His only consolation—and that a small one—was that if revenge failed, Gifford remained a good investment, like the half a dozen other young dandies he'd secretly directed his agent to buy up for pence on the pound. But Byron could not accept the possibility that he'd failed—not yet. Vengeance might never have been more than a wistful fantasy, but if so, it was a sweet one.

"Then why are you here?" he demanded, stifling the urge to shake the smug smile from her face. "Do you dote on your brother so that you wish to save a name he does not value?"

"Dote? Hardly. He was putting toads in my bed when we were both still in the nursery."

"Then why?" he repeated, truly baffled.

She did not reply to his question, her expression remaining as frozen as if he had said nothing. She was a stranger, but he began tentatively feeling his way toward an answer as if he'd known her all his life.

"Because it is you who fear ostracism," he said slowly. "You didn't come for Gifford's sake but for yours."

Her eyes tightened, and he saw he had hit home. "I do it for the sake of my family."

"Of course. Such selflessness, to preserve your family's reputation—and through it, your own."

"What would you know of my motives?" Her eyes narrowed further to slits, and her words grew dangerously hard.

Byron relaxed as her control slid, and he began to invent a story, gauging her reactions and shaping it to suit. "And what would you know of mine? Gifford and I were once friends. He told me of you, bragged about how he could make you do anything for him. I privately thought you the cleverer of the two, what with your inconspicuous power reaching out through all the members of your family. Now I see that my estimation wasn't mistaken. As Gifford said, you would do anything at all for him—if it would save your own hide or advance your own interests." He leveled the words like a weapon. "You are selfish, my dear Lady Victoria, and you and I both know it."

Lady Victoria's face had grown more and more livid with each word he spoke, and by the time he had finished, she was sheet white and trembling with rage. She jerked to her feet and glared at him, blue-gray eyes flashing silver. "You clearly never had any intention of reaching a compromise, and I will not sit here and be insulted a moment longer. If it were my own pride I wished to save, I would better serve it by leaving. Good day, sir." Her back unnaturally straight, she spun on her heel and strode to the door.

Away from him.

The thought was jarring, and he called out instinctively to forestall her as she reached for the knob.

"You are not dismissed!"

She hesitated, anger and energy coiled in her muscles. Even across the room, he could feel her waiting for him to give her a reason to stay. A shock ran through him, surging through his lungs and belly to his groin. Did she feel it, too, that strange fascination that bound them? He had no idea what he might say, and he fumbled for something to delay her until he could produce a rational thought.

"There's a storm," he said, making his tone indolently reasonable, "and the next mail coach won't be by until tomorrow."

"Then you may lend me the use of your carriage, I'm sure," Lady Victoria replied icily, her spine growing straighter, if possible, in a show of indignant propriety. She began to turn the knob.

"If I were you, I shouldn't be so hasty to leave," he temporized, a bizarre desperation overtaking him.

"Oh?" There was no interest in her tone, but the hand on the doorknob froze again even if she didn't let go. From the back, not even the awkward lines of her unflattering corset could disguise the grace of her lithe figure, the unconscious seductiveness in the arch of her neck.

The prim dress and severe bun angered him suddenly. He saw them thrust between them as a barrier, keeping him beyond her spinsterish defenses. She thought she could defeat him so easily, did she? They'd just see exactly what her propriety was worth. He'd lost his opportunity for revenge—it had been gone before he'd started to plan it, had he only known. Was he so unmanned that he could not even keep hold of a woman? A pettish flare of anger hardened his voice.

"You want payment of your brother's debts forgiven. Impossible. I've put too much into buying them up;

they're quite a promising investment. But not demanding payment until he inherits—that isn't so ludicrous."

Lady Victoria released the doorknob, still without turning to face him. "What is it you want in return?"

Byron folded his arms across his chest. The daydream of vengeance, so dear to him only minutes before, was already fading. But if he couldn't have revenge, why should he deny himself the sister?

"You."

Chapter Two

Victoria whirled. "What?" she cried, torn between laughter and outrage.

"You." The voice came rumbling out of the shadows as if it were the most reasonable suggestion in the world, and for a moment, she was almost convinced of it. She shivered suddenly. The duke was most certainly a dangerous man.

"Your grace, I am not a bargaining piece." She'd meant to sound crisply offended, but the words slid out of her control and came out with a hint of invitation, as if she were only waiting to be persuaded. She cursed her tongue, behaving like an overawed ingénue of sixteen instead of a disillusioned spinster of two and thirty. She had faced unwelcome suitors before. Now was no different, and even if it were farcical for someone to propose a liaison at her age, she could see no other interpretation in his words, twist and turn them as she may.

Raeburn let out a short bark of laughter. Concealed by the folds of her skirt, her hands balled into fists.

"Everyone has a price. What's yours? Respectability? Money? Power?" He shook his head, a stirring in the shadows. "Allowing your brother's debts to be forgotten until his inheritance . . . for you, that could mean any one of the three. Saving face, preventing the loss of precious capital, putting you in the position of rescuer. How much would you pay to save Gifford? Yourself?"

She had the disturbing sensation that he was raking her with his eyes, examining her in every straitlaced detail from her knotted bun to her practical high boots with devastating intimacy, seeing under them—and, even more, beyond them, to the soul of the wind-mad woman who escaped the stifling parlors and drawing rooms of Rushworth Manor to gallop across the tenants' most distant fields. *Yet more impropriety*, she told herself, but something stilled her tongue as he continued deliberately, consideringly.

"I believe you already have paid with your body, betraying yourself every day when you lock yourself into your misshapen corsets and high-buttoned dresses." His voice softened persuasively. "All I ask for is a week—a single week of a different kind of self-betrayal. And who knows? You might find it to be your true self, after all."

"Your grace!" Victoria gasped, but more from reflex than horror, for she couldn't manage to put much distress into her tone. She had never been shocked by such suggestions, but now she couldn't even feel affronted. In spite of herself, she felt drawn to the mysterious, lascivious Duke of Raeburn, and mad as his idea was, it was more alluring than repellent. After all, she had come to rescue her family from the shame of her brother's penury, and that was exactly what the duke offered. And the price—the price was small, so small that the insignificance of it shocked her.

When had the intricate dance of society politics begun to chafe? When had her ambitions to direct an earldom become restrictive? She'd given her life to those aspirations, and now that she held them in her hands, they seemed so meaningless next to the untamed, aimless yearnings that had always moved quietly within her. Now those yearnings surged up, and she stood dumbly, stunned speechless by the sudden, fierce desire for . . . *freedom*. She shook her head. It must be the storm stirring the wildness in her, tearing through her years of experience to set free the impetuousness she thought she'd buried with her youth.

Raeburn continued, dropping his voice cajolingly. "Consider it. One week, and I shall allow Gifford to repay me at his leisure after he inherits. You return a heroine, and no one but you and I ever know of the bargain."

"And of that week, how much is yours?" She could hardly believe she was pretending to consider his ludicrous offer, whatever mad desires thrummed in her blood.

Raeburn chuckled richly. "Every moment is mine, but if you wonder how much of it will be spent in my bed— then the answer is however much I desire."

Victoria tried to suppress the heat that crept up her face. The unveiled hunger in his voice stirred an answer in her midsection and deeper, in her mind and imagination. She tried to hold back the reckless urgings that told her to seize this chance—not for her brother Jack or for Rushworth, but for herself. What would it feel like if the duke touched her? What would it feel like, to be in the arms of a man again after so long? Despite his reputation for debauchery, there were no whispers that a tryst with the duke was less than pleasurable, and surely she deserved a little pleasure to remember in her declining years. Or so she told herself, but that cynical thought had no connection with the way her heart was beating in her ears.

She'd made her choice, she reminded herself, stifling both the warmth and the restlessness that flooded her. But what if, just for a week, she could sample the alternative? She counted the days since her last courses; there'd be little chance of getting pregnant even if she were still seventeen. Not that any seventeen-year-old would know anything about counting days. She surely hadn't.

She knew the dangers and the rewards of what the duke offered—could lay them out neatly, logically, and weigh the benefits of each path. But still she hesitated, for how should she measure the strange, mixed impulses that swooped drunkenly through her mind?

"Come, my dear Lady Victoria," the duke interposed. "Do not be frightened. I shall hardly bite."

That decided it. Even though she couldn't see his face, the ironic, condescending amusement in his tone was unmistakable. He wanted to seduce her for sport, to privately mock her as he unfolded the secret mysteries of love to a foolish, aging virgin. Defiance flared within her. He'd have her, right enough, and she him, and then they'd see who was the most surprised. She raised her chin defiantly and tried to find his eyes in the shadows.

"Let me see you," she ordered.

For a long moment, Raeburn didn't move, and she feared he'd withdraw his offer. Then he stood slowly and stepped into the light, turning sideways to the fireplace so the dim glow from the coals was cast upon his features.

Her first impression was size. The duke was not the tallest man she had ever seen, nor the brawniest, but his presence filled the room so that he seemed to loom in a way her taller brother never could. She drew herself up in reflexive response and met his gaze squarely.

From his remarkable voice, she had imagined his eyes to be equally arresting—a brilliant blue or emerald green, or even a steely gray. But they weren't. They were a muted, muddled color, brown or moss-colored or somewhere between the two, and for a moment, she was almost disappointed. But the duke raised a slow eyebrow, challenging her bold stare, and his eyes lit with a hard, glinting humor. Victoria knew then that a striking color would have been mere superficial adornment to distract from the controlled power that seemed to course through every line of his body.

The lineaments of his face were bold and strong—almost crude, as if he'd been blindly carved of stone—but they were no less attractive for a lack of patrician daintiness. How old he was she could not guess: certainly younger than the roughened skin of his face suggested. It was not marked with the scarring left by youthful blemishes but with a deeper weathering, as if he had stood barefaced to wind and sun for a score of years. A massive brow, a heavy jaw, a body both broad and lean under a loose lounging suit.

His appearance was certainly unconventional, but it was also compelling, as if there were some connection between them that made his smallest movements stir an answer within her own body. He advanced a step, and Victoria had to catch herself to keep from backing away. She raised her chin as he stopped.

"Do I meet with your approval?" he said. The soft caress of his voice should have seemed out of keeping with his rugged appearance, but somehow it fused strength and grace, power and seduction. Victoria could not afford to lower her guard with this man.

"You shall suffice," she replied curtly. "Now let us draw up a contract—signed and witnessed—and the week shall begin."

Raeburn stared at her for a long moment, expression

unreadable. "A contract?" he finally said. "How . . . sensible."

He left her to wonder what that meant while he crossed to a small writing table. He lit a candle, drew out a sheet of paper, and began to write, the pale goose quill scratching and swooping across the page. His head bent over the sheet, unfashionably long hair curling over his collar. It was impossible in the dim light to tell if it was black or merely brown, but Victoria had the rather sensational suspicion that it was as dark as midnight. What was she getting herself into?

He finished writing with a final flourish and blotted the page before bringing it and the candle over to where Victoria stood. Lit from below, his face was even more harshly imposing, but she took the paper from him without betraying a tremor of uncertainty.

"Thank you, your grace." In the flickering light of the candle, she scanned the page. The language was indirect enough to obscure the exact nature of the bargain but clear enough to make a breach of contract unambiguous. "Clever," she granted him grudgingly.

Suddenly, the door burst open into the room, catching Victoria from behind and sending her lurching toward Raeburn. He caught her elbow and steadied her as the intruder apologized.

"Forgive me, thy grace, thy ladyship. I've brought up the lady's luggage to the Unicorn Room, and thy grace's order has been brought in from Leeds."

Victoria turned to face a tall, stooping man in a worn tweed jacket and pants that flapped around his knees.

"Just in time, Fane," the duke said. "I have a contract for you to witness."

Fane looked from Victoria to Raeburn as if sensing the

tension in the room for the first time. "Of course, thy grace."

The duke deftly plucked the contract from Victoria's fingers and guided her over to the writing table, still holding her elbow. His grip was neither gentle nor harsh, but firm and almost impersonal. It made Victoria feel oddly distant while at the same time stirring a twinge of desire that spread from her center to creep up her neck and face.

Raeburn dipped the quill and inscribed his name boldly, handing it to her when he finished.

Victoria stared at the words sprawled across the sheet. Once she signed, there would be no turning back. She thought of the touch of mouth on mouth, of body against body, and of the shame she would save her family through this, the greatest folly she had ever countenanced. She pressed her lips together, and before she could change her mind, she quickly wrote her name under his in her small, precise hand. Her heart beating in her ears, she passed the pen to Fane, who added his own prompt signature.

"Finished!" said Raeburn, snatching away the sheet and handing it to Victoria with a flourish. "Fane, show Lady Victoria to her room." Raeburn gave her a raking glance that sent shivers up her spine. "She looks like a half-drowned kitten. I expect to see you at supper, your ladyship—and in better form. Until then, good day."

And with that, he turned his back on her, radiating such a sense of feral triumph that her stomach lurched and she wondered if she'd regret her decision sooner than she would have imagined.

Trying to suppress the tightness that coiled in her gut, she preceded the thin manservant from the room. As she followed him through the dark corridors, she had the feeling there was more unknown in the room behind her than in all the rest of the sprawling, rotting manor house.

Victoria surveyed the bedchamber as the door clunked shut behind Fane. Her trunk squatted in the center of the floor, but neither Dyer nor her valise was in evidence.

It was obvious why the chamber was called the Unicorn Room: an ancient, fantastic tapestry with figures of svelte ladies and cavorting unicorns dominated one wall from the shadowed ceiling all the way to the flagstone floor. Victoria thought almost longingly of the neoclassical lightness of Rushworth, the jewel-box rooms lined with damask and broad windows. The chambers she'd always considered confining now seemed an image of airy grace compared to this cell.

The room was dark and cavernous, the gray limestone walls pierced only by the door and one slit of a window, and the newest of the spare furnishings was no more recent than the days of the Sun King. An unlit oil lamp on the night table was the only concession to modernity.

Victoria wondered which generation of the Raeburn stewards had ordered the blue plumes for the canopy and which of the Raeburn women had embroidered the flowers and mythical beasts across the bed hangings and counterpane. The chamber seemed as darkly secretive as its master, and suddenly, Victoria felt very alone.

What was keeping Dyer?

She suppressed that childishly plaintive thought— plaintive with more than an edge of fear, she admitted to herself. It couldn't be time for dinner yet, after all. She'd just have to wait, clammy carriage dress and shadowy ceilings or no. At least she had the oil lamp. If she'd been left with a candlestick or, God forbid, a rushlight or torch, she probably would have worked herself into a fine state of nerves before her abigail came.

Victoria crossed to the smoky fire sparking on the hearth, peeled off her kidskin gloves, and held her hands over the reluctant flames. As the stiffness left her fingers, she continued to study the room. It was very, very like the duke. Cold. Forbidding. Strangely beautiful . . .

Their meeting had been the most unsettling she'd ever had. She'd felt as if she were waltzing on quicksand, yet somehow, almost magically, she never actually became mired. It was fortunate that she had abandoned her original plan of flattery. The duke wanted no obsequiousness: he craved a challenge. Which she was more than willing to give him, she thought with renewed irritation.

Victoria sighed, ire dying at its birth. She'd made her choice, and a week in the duke's company still seemed more alluring than repulsive. Very soon, she would be in the arms of a man again, a man who, by all rumors, knew how to please a woman. A small shiver overcame her at that thought, a kind of queasy anticipation. If those rumors showed themselves to be true . . . But what of the others? He was certainly strange, and there were whispers of an inherited weakness of the mind or body, something not quite right that had haunted and misshaped him from birth. It all seemed far too grotesque and gloomy to her.

She wished that she had met him before, in the days when he haunted the parlors of London, but their paths had never crossed. He had run in the fast set with her brother, and she had stuck fiercely to her own more conservative circle. Even so, thus far she'd seen nothing more sinister in him than an instinctive arrogance and an inclination toward melancholy. She wondered illogically if he ever smiled, genuinely smiled, and tried to imagine his heavy brow softened and his shifting hazel eyes lit with pleasure . . .

She shunted her mind from that path, but it quickly hurled down another almost as disquieting. If the manor were one of the crumbling castles so ubiquitous in parlor novels, she'd be certain to find a hidden door behind the enormous tapestry, leading to a maze of secret passageways wending through the ancient depths of the dark fortress. For a long moment, she simply stood and stared at the wall, telling herself not to be ridiculous, but her sense of unease grew until there was nothing left but to check. She crossed the room, feeling foolish, her heel clicks echoing in the groin-vaulted ceiling. She faced the intricate hanging, trying to convince herself that there was nothing there. It was useless.

With a sigh, she pulled back the tapestry—and found a blank gray expanse of stone. She pulled back the other side—and nothing again. No outlines of a door, no suspiciously deeper cracks, no strange wall sconces, no discolored places. Nothing but a wall. Half disappointed and half relieved, she turned away.

Her wet dress, forgotten in the duke's formidable presence, was becoming increasingly uncomfortable. What *could* be keeping Dyer? Victoria tugged the bellpull by the bed, hoping that it would summon her lady's maid, or at least someone, from the depths of the house to help her undress.

She put the contract on the night table and settled herself on the padded stone window bench to wait. Even with only the faint light from the fireplace, it was difficult to see past the reflections on the glass into the dark, rainy courtyard. She could make out only indistinct shapes— the long drive that terminated at the porter's house with the distant smear of the manor village beyond, and moving along it, the dark box of a carriage.

A carriage? What would a carriage be doing, leaving Raeburn Court so late in the day? Victoria had the sinking feeling that it concerned her in a way that did not bode well. She watched as it rattled out between the gates and turned up the road toward Leeds.

It was too much to hope that it contained the duke, breaking his end of the contract and giving her victory through forfeit. She knew nothing of the man, yet Raeburn did not seem one to bluff. Rather, he seemed the type to exact every last pennyweight from any deal. She put a hand on her belly at that thought, feeling the same heady rush as when she balanced on the edge of a parapet, when the wind whipped suddenly between the trees, or when she galloped at breakneck speed across the fields. Moodily, she watched the carriage shrink in the distance, disappearing and reappearing as the road dipped and rose.

There was a light rap on the door, and Victoria started and turned away from the window.

"Come in," she called, composing herself.

Expecting Dyer, Victoria was surprised at the entry of a young and pretty brunette maid. The girl bobbed nervously. "My lady rang?"

"Yes . . . what is your name?"

"Annie, my lady."

"Yes, Annie. What happened to my abigail?"

The maid bobbed again, swallowing hard. "I thought my lady knew . . ."

Victoria's emotions, already strained, began descending rapidly into impatience. "You thought I knew what?" she prompted, attempting to project warmth and reassurance to calm the flustered girl.

It didn't work. Annie hesitated for a half a dozen seconds more before she managed to say in a strangled voice, "My lady's abigail just left, on orders of his grace. She's to stay in Leeds until thoo joins her."

The carriage! That high-handed, controlling bastard! Victoria spun, glaring at her reflection in the mullioned window, but in the darkening, rainy evening beyond the chamber, the road stretched long and bare. Alone!

Lightning flashed, and a peal of thunder ripped the sky somewhere close. The exaggerated melodrama of its timing amused her despite herself, and the anger that had threatened to overwhelm her subsided into a simmer again. She turned back to the maid and raised an eyebrow. "I see. And who is to attend me, pray?"

"I am, my lady." The maid all but whimpered.

Victoria looked at her for a long moment, then sighed. "Come along then, and help me dress. And stop shaking. I shan't eat you alive."

Annie gave her an uncertain look, beginning to relax only after Victoria belatedly remembered that she hadn't accompanied her comment with the comforting smile she had intended and managed to dredge one up.

"Aye," Annie said then. "Supper's at nine, my lady."

Victoria's smile turned humorless as she regarded her pale reflection in the window. "Two hours are more than enough time to make myself presentable."

If the Duke of Raeburn wanted a stiff spinster, a stiff spinster he would get.

Chapter Three

What the bloody hell did he think he was doing?

Byron sat in the darkness of the Teak Parlor, nursing his scotch and the growing sense that he'd just made one of the greatest mistakes of his life. He flipped open his pocket watch. It had been half an hour since he'd dismissed the last of the servants with their instructions — over an hour since he'd ordered Lady Victoria up to her room. By now she should be fluttering with nervousness or seething with rage or some combination of the two. And, by all rights, he should be gloating.

But he didn't much feel like gloating. In fact, he was having second thoughts.

Why couldn't he have kept to his plan of revenge? He was an inventive man. Even if his original plan was flawed, he surely could have found a way to make Gifford's life miserable for at least half a dozen years. And if he were clever enough, it would cost him just as little.

And yet . . . even though the thought of Gifford's suffering still held a good deal of satisfaction, Byron could not say it would heal his wounds. For it wasn't so much what Gifford had done that angered Byron as what it had shown him about himself. Things Byron had lived thirty-two years without knowing, things he could have gone happily to his grave in ignorance of. But now that Byron had been forced to face his ugly side, he couldn't forget it again, and he couldn't honestly say he wanted to.

He tossed back the final swallow of scotch and regarded the empty glass in the firelight, pointedly ignoring the decanter that sat waiting by his elbow. That was a way to another kind of hell, one fit for men too careless or too reckless to see its dangers. And despite the bargain he had just made, he was neither by habit.

The bargain! He scowled at the light glinting off the glass. The first new bit of skirt he'd seen in over a year and he lost his senses. But he knew that wasn't true. Though the offer itself had been impulsive, he'd felt quite firmly in possession of all his faculties—more so than he had in a long time, as if Lady Victoria's mere presence took his moldering wits and shook some life into them. She was an enigma he was determined to solve—but he had the suspicion that Lady Victoria might not be content to be deciphered without doing some deciphering of her own. Byron shrugged uncomfortably at the thought of the questions that could arise between them in the course of a week. She might have her secrets, but he had more than enough of his own to keep.

Still . . . he could be opening the door to a wolf, but after so many months of no company but a handful of servants and his own dark thoughts, the challenge of a wolf might be exactly what he needed.

Somewhere deep in the bowels of the manor, a clock struck nine. Each peal unrolled slowly, striking just off key in a way that raised the hair on the back of Victoria's neck.

The slouching figure of Fane—Gregory Fane, as Victoria now knew, the duke's unlikely steward and possibly valet and butler as well—led her down the twisting staircase, the candelabra he held above his head casting slanting, dancing shadows across the dark-paneled walls.

Finally, the stairs ended. Whether she was on the ground floor, some upper story, or even an underground level, she could not guess. Her own chamber was on the third floor, but she'd already realized that the various annexes of the manor didn't seem to be aligned by more than accident and that four floors in one section could easily be six in another.

Fane slipped down a narrow passageway, then into a wide gallery with a row of black windows looking out into the night. It was too dark to see past the rain-lashed windowpanes until a sudden stab of lightning illuminated a rocky declivity that ended in a rush of frothing water. Then the grounds were plunged into blackness again as thunder rumbled through the bare hills, and the room seemed even darker than before. Victoria suppressed the urge to ask her silent guide how much farther the dining room was.

The gallery ended abruptly, and Fane opened an unobtrusive door against the long side, dwarfed by the massive paintings that flanked it.

"Lady Victoria Wakefield," he announced to the dark interior, bowing.

Victoria composed her features and swept past the servant into the room.

The duke lounged along one long side of the table, his back to the fireplace again. Not one to quickly surrender any advantage, she noted. As before, he did not stand as she entered, and rather than match his discourtesy, she bowed her head in an exaggerated manner. He was not as well placed as he had been in the Teak Parlor; even in the shadows, she could see irritation flicker across his face, quickly replaced by amusement.

"Please sit, your ladyship," he said, waving his hand to the chair opposite his with inflated geniality.

As she moved to take the seat, a strapping young man, hitherto invisible, stepped away from the wall directly into her path. She resisted the urge to jerk away, but he only pulled her chair away from the table. So she sat, facing the duke across the narrow width.

"I see you have an . . . interesting domestic staff," Victoria said mildly as the duke rang the bell and a round-faced maidservant bustled in bearing a soup tureen. It was the first safe topic that came to mind.

He raised an eyebrow at her understatement. "My late great-uncle was an impoverished eccentric, and I inherited his staff and his debts."

"I see," Victoria said, though she didn't. "I'm sure you find it convivial, living here." She took a tentative sip of her consommé. It was bland but not unpleasant. Heartened by the discovery, she began to eat more vigorously.

Raeburn's jaw hardened. "I shall remain in this moldy pile of rubble only as long as it takes the Dowager House to be renovated. If not for a feeling of familial obligation, I should be happy to let it rot, but I suppose I shall soon have to begin the long process of making the manor house habitable again."

Victoria looked up, surprised. The thought that Raeburn liked the house as little as she did made him seem less forbiddingly remote. But that impression was shattered with his next words.

"Which is why I need the money from your brother."

He was mocking her. Victoria could see it in the lift of one corner of his mouth, in the glint in his fathomless eyes. She refused to rise to the bait and pointed out the flaw in his pretence instead. "Since you knew my brother would have no means to pay even the interest for years to come, you could not have hoped to exact anything until then."

Raeburn chuckled, and she was certain that he was fully aware of the sensual overtones with which he imbued the sound. "And he might not need to if you have anything to say about it, my dear."

She reddened, and she was angry with herself for doing so. "Exactly," she snapped and ate the rest of her soup in silence. Yet she couldn't help but be aware of the duke's nearness, the way he looked at her between sips and inclined his body in her direction. Strange that he should want to leave a house that seemed to suit him so well. Despite the trepidation that fluttered in her belly, Victoria's lips twitched at the thought of his "renovating" the Dowager House by adding dust, mold, and cobwebs.

The maid returned with a roast and some indefinable vegetable dish. After carving the meat, the manservant silently set a plate before her, the quantity heaped upon it more substantial than she expected for a second course.

"This is the rest of the meal," Raeburn explained, looking at her with an expression of amused condescension. "We eat simply here."

"I see," Victoria said, giving the two words ample significance.

The moon-faced maid curtseyed, and she and the manservant retired at Raeburn's wave, leaving them alone.

The silence spread between them, thin and tense, punctuated only by the hiss and spark of the fire on the hearth. Raeburn searched her face again with his too-personal gaze, though what he expected to find, she couldn't guess. Finally, out of sheer awkwardness, she tried to establish conversation on a more amicable level.

"Tell me, your grace, what is the history of the manor? It looks to be as old as the conquest."

"Older, though there's nothing remaining from those days. Ask Fane if you really wish to know." He looked at her, a forkful of meat suspended in the air. "I would rather talk of more interesting things." He took the bite. "Such as you."

Victoria blinked, taken off guard. "I assure you, your grace, there is nothing about me that is of interest to anyone."

He gestured with the fork before scooping up another bite. "That's exactly what you want them to believe."

"What is that supposed to mean?" she asked stiffly. She shouldn't encourage him, but she was curious despite herself. What could he think that he knew about her? Certainly not her mad streak, the wildness she kept so carefully hidden that not even her family had ever guessed its presence.

He chewed thoughtfully for a moment, then swallowed, his curiously shifting eyes never leaving her face. "Let me tell you how I see you, and you will know exactly what I mean."

She snorted indelicately. "You've already told me. A dull, aging spinster with a fondness for manipulation."

He chuckled softly. "You manage to make it sound so . . . well, dull." He set aside his knife and fork and leaned forward, studying her. "I see a woman who tries very hard to make herself unnoticed. A woman who sits against the wall by choice, not by necessity. The only daughter of an earl—one should think you'd find a husband easily. I see no obvious flaws."

She raised an eyebrow. "Then what are the less obvious ones?"

He chuckled again, leaning so close she could smell the cologne he'd used that morning, dark with spices and sandalwood. "Your flaws and perfections go so closely hand in hand it is impossible to separate them."

"Oh?" she said, trying to keep her voice even.

"Oh," he repeated teasingly. His eyes narrowed as he considered her. This close, they were more green than brown—amber-flecked emerald, she found herself thinking to her own bemusement. Yet the bemusement was detached because his nearness demanded almost all her attention. "Your face, for example—it is not beautiful."

"I never aspired to beauty," she said tartly, stabbing at a limp vegetable. "It incites neither my envy nor my admiration."

"Nor should it, for you are still a handsome woman, handsome in a way that makes mere beauty ashamed of its callowness."

Victoria smiled humorlessly. "'Mere beauty,' as you call it, has never envied me, either." Yet despite her reflexive cynicism, there seemed to be something honest in Raeburn's description that she hadn't sensed in anyone in a very long time. It intrigued her—and fed the warm flush that spread across her skin where his gaze touched her.

"It should," he insisted, his voice dropping on the last word. "Your forehead is high, but it is no flaw, for it balances your jaw, which shows a tendency to jut outwards when you are irritated. Like now. You should be more careful with that." He reached out, and before she knew what he was about, he touched her face, following the line of her cheek down to her chin and tracing it across. His touch was butterfly-light, but even so, she could feel the calluses of his hands, subtle and strong. She caught her breath, desire knotting in her center, and instinctively turned into the caress. In her mind whispered the words, *Too long, too long*, and she heard the dangerous, reckless rush of blood in her ears. "A strong jaw, but not heavy—stubborn yet feminine, like the thin thrust of your nose." He touched that, too. No one had ever touched her nose with such delicate inquisitiveness before. It was strange and somehow almost more intimate than a flagrant caress. He smiled as he surveyed her, his craggy face softening until it was almost gentle. But not quite. A proprietary gleam shone in his eyes, that of a lord surveying territory soon to be his.

Shaking off the mesmerism of his touch, she straightened abruptly and pulled away from him. "There is no need for courting and fine words. I am yours by word and by contract."

A mask slid across Raeburn's face. "Pardon me, your ladyship. I didn't realize appreciation would be so ill-received."

"Appreciation—perhaps!" she returned. "Flattery? I think not."

"My dear Lady Victoria, as you have so cleverly put it, I have little need for flattery with you." He stood abruptly, shoving his chair away from the table. "Come. We are finished dining for tonight."

She froze. "I am still hungry." The words came out cold and brittle as apprehension seized her in its grip.

Raeburn sat as suddenly as he had stood, seeming to melt into an indolently boneless lounge as soon as he touched the chair. The ire he had just shown all but evaporated, evident only in the slightly stiff line of his back, the too-casual tilt of his head. Yet she had the feeling that he had won some obscure victory through her admission: She had shown the first sign of weakness.

"Then, my dear Lady Victoria, please continue—eat," he said. "I would not like it said that I starve my guests."

Victoria's stomach was clenched too tightly to do anything but lurch threateningly at the thought of more food, but she cut off a tiny sliver of roast anyway and began chewing it slowly.

Byron watched her blatantly, amusement softening his irritation. Lady Victoria had been almost completely collected up until the moment he'd actually suggested that they leave—then came the crack in the façade, more obvious for the contrast with the smooth perfection of her earlier demeanor. She was flushed, flustered—exactly as he wanted her. She managed to be far too disconcerting when she was on her balance.

Actually, how he wanted her was out of that damned dress. It was more hideous than her traveling attire, though he wouldn't have believed such a thing were possible an hour before. Her hair, too, was even more tightly and unflatteringly plastered against her skull. He had the obscure conviction that it was a deliberate mockery, and he resisted the urge to reach out and pluck away the pins, one by one. Instead, he sat back in his chair and watched her pick at her food.

"So, your ladyship, if we are not to discuss you, what can we talk about?" he mused, more than half to himself. "Politics? Society? The weather?"

Lady Victoria looked up, her pale eyes slanted dangerously. "I've heard it said that every man's favorite topic is himself." She put a slice of roast into her mouth and bit down hard, her jaw muscles bulging slightly with the force of her anger.

"I am not accustomed to discussing myself," Byron said elusively, frowning at her sudden redirection. "We shall speak on something else."

"Oh, yes, your grace, I forgot," she said, her voice sweet with spite. "The Duke of Raeburn does not stand up to scrutiny. He desires to lurk in shadows, to wrap the fabric of dark night and darker rumors about himself." She raised her fork and waggled it at him as she spoke, and he felt an angry heat rush into his face as she smiled archly. "He only travels in a heavy-draped carriage, is only seen in society between the hours of dusk and dawn, and even rides under the cover of night. Everyone wonders, What does he fear? Why does he hide? Is he deformed? Unnatural?"

The white heat overtaking him, Byron snaked his arm across the table and seized her hand, stilling the fork at the end of its swing. How dare she mock him? How dare she come, an old society maid, and march into his life to make judgments on subjects she knew nothing about?

A small piece of him realized that he was being irrational, but he didn't care. Her hard-edged expression reminded him of all the other faces that had gaped at him over the years—speculative ladies whispering behind fans, children gazing at him with the bold curiosity of youth, and, years before, the half-pitying, half-fearful looks of his own nursery servants and the image of one young face set in an expression of such horror and revulsion that another quarter century could not begin to erase a single detail from the picture burned into his mind. The memories flooded over him, as if the prying, judging eyes of his thirty-four years were staring at him all at once, and he shoved them away with vicious desperation.

"What do you know of me and my reasons?" he rasped out. "What right do you have to make such ignorant pronouncements?"

Lady Victoria kept her silence. Her hand felt cold in his, small and frail. He could crush it with a single squeeze. He could feel the weakness in her bones, and when she looked up across the table to meet his eyes, he could read in her expression that she felt it, too.

But there was no fear in those blue eyes, no shrinking

away from his strength, his control. Instead, they were lit with contempt, and a sneer curled her lip when she spoke.

"Let go. You're hurting me."

Each word was leveled as an accusation, more damning than the most furious diatribe. He released her as if burned. *Monster. Beast.* The words could not have hung more piercingly between them if she had spat them at his face.

Byron sat back, exhaling sharply. "And so what do you think?" he said, shifting the conversation back toward its original course. A form of morbid self-flagellation, he knew, but he had never earned it more than today.

"About you?" Lady Victoria sat back, too, her eyes hidden by a pale fringe of lashes as she regarded the play of light across the surface of the fork that she twirled idly in her fingers. She looked at him meaningfully and set it down across her plate with exaggerated care. "Your grace," she demurred, "as you say, I should hardly dare have an opinion about you."

Byron snorted. "I don't believe you have ever 'not dared' to have an opinion in your life."

A flash of humor passed across her face, and a rag of surprised laughter was torn from her, a sound that thrilled up his spine and left him hungry for more. The expression was gone in an instant, but when it disappeared, it took with it the hint of malice that had tightened her eyes and made her face seem older, harder.

"Such unexpected levity, your grace. For that alone, I must consider." She tipped her head to the side, examining him, and he found himself uncomfortable under the intrusion of her gaze. It wasn't that she seemed to see beneath his clothes—he had given and received plenty of those looks in the past and enjoyed both thoroughly—but she seemed to look through his skin, too, to the sinews that bound his muscles to their bones, to the surface of his brain where his thoughts were read as they flashed fleet-ingly across. Could she also see the hidden debility, the one no doctor could ever understand? He almost believed anything was possible for her.

Finally, Lady Victoria spoke. "I think . . ." She paused. "I think everyone is right, in a way. I think you like the shadows: both the drama and the anonymity. But I also think that you're as frightened as—well, as you accuse me of being. The cowardice behind the bravado." She twisted her mouth ironically in something too bitter to be a smile. "There's something we have in common: We each think the other's a coward, and we each think the other is wrong about ourselves." She raised her glass, still half full of wine. "To the belief in cowardice, then, in all its bold forms."

"A queer thing to toast," he said, but he raised his glass as well, and they drank.

She took a few more halfhearted bites and then set the fork down.

"I've finished eating," she said almost casually, lean-ing back in her chair. "Won't you lead the way?"

Byron marveled at how fully she had regained her composure. Her face was perfectly smooth, and her long-fingered hands lay still upon the edge of the table. No twitch, no tightening betrayed any nervousness. Only a sliding away of her eyes when his gaze met hers showed that she was not as sanguine as she appeared.

"Of course," he murmured, standing. Lady Victoria re-mained seated until he circled and pulled her chair out for her. Then she stood gracefully, took his proffered arm, and walked with him from the room as regally as a queen.

Chapter Four

Victoria could hardly hear the rustling of her skirts and the scuff of Raeburn's boots against the floor, and even the sound of the rain lashing the windows was almost drowned in the rasping of her breath and the pounding of her heart. Vainly, she tried to maintain some pretense of calm, but her heart and breath only spiraled more wildly out of control. Her only consolation was that she need not fear that the duke could hear her; if he could, he would have surely already given her one of his sideways, too-knowing looks. Cursing herself silently, she fought to pull herself together. She was no shrinking violet or blushing debutante, and she had no business acting like one.

Even more distracting than her rebellious body was Raeburn's closeness. Pinned to him as she was, she could not miss the muscular hardness of his side, the restrained power in the arm that held her to him. He was deeply attractive—and just as deeply frightening. What had she gotten herself into? she wondered belatedly. She could hardly claim ignorance or inexperience to excuse her outrageous bargain. In another woman, she would call her behavior recklessness, but that her years of restraint could be so easily shattered was nonsensical. Canny, reserved, politically astute—all these she knew herself to be. But which trait could account for the mad contract that even now nestled in the drawer of her night table? It was the storm, she told herself as thunder rumbled across distant hills. Storms had always made her feel itchy and queer, as if her skin were too small, her clothes too tight.

They had passed through the door to the gallery, and the duke closed it behind them, leaving them in utter darkness. Though her eyes had adjusted to the flickering dimness of the dining room, now she could make out no more than the vaguest forms. But Raeburn did not pause to find and light a candle—he didn't even slow his pace, but strode confidently through the blackness as if he'd walked that route blindly for years, as if he'd been born to darkness. Victoria gripped his arm tightly, trying to match her steps to his so she would not stumble against some unseen obstacle. *Deliberate perversity and melodrama,* she thought, resisting the instinct to start when a statue loomed too suddenly before her. Yet she couldn't keep from feeling unaccustomedly helpless as she plunged into the darkness on the duke's arm.

Raeburn's stride changed. "Stairs," was all he said, but he spoke in a silky murmur that sent a shiver up her spine even as she lifted her foot higher to accommodate the first step. Whether it was the same staircase that she had descended an hour past, she could not guess, but she was certain they climbed much higher than her room had been. They passed through a series of interior rooms— Victoria felt the cold fingers of a draft against her face and the sensation of space as their footsteps echoed hollowly with every pace—and into a corridor so narrow her flaring skirts brushed against the wall. Then they went up again in a tightening spiral until Raeburn stopped abruptly.

Victoria stood, uncertain, blind, and breathless. She heard the susurration of fabric against fabric and realized the duke was reaching out just as a latch clunked. A rapidly widening sliver of gray appeared against the void, and the muted sounds of rain grew to a nearer rush. The sliver quickly resolved itself into a doorway, and before she could react, the duke strode through, pulling her in his wake.

The darkness beyond was a few shades brighter, and she could make out a circular wall enclosing the room, pierced with half a dozen broad mullioned windows around its circumference. Raeburn released her, and she crossed to one of them in a show of nonchalance. The storm's fury had subsided into a wind-flung wash of rain, and through it, she could make out the roofs and peaks of the manor house a story or more below, no more attractively or felicitously arranged from a height than from a distance. But though Victoria looked over the Romanesque crenellations and Gothic gargoyles, only a fraction of her attention was tuned to them—the rest was held captive by the duke.

She heard him cross the room, his heavy steps unfaltering, and then he stopped and there was a soft creak as the room lightened minutely. She turned to see him throwing a measure of coal into a small ceramic stove. In its light, she could make out the furnishings of the room—there was not a bed, as she had more than half expected, but the floor was layered with rugs and strewn with piles of opulent pillows, and three oriental divans marked the circumference.

"I should hardly be surprised if your manor were scattered with such boudoirs," she said, hiding her nervousness behind causticity. "They seem quite in keeping with the dissolution of the architecture."

Raeburn looked up at her, face inscrutable. "And its master?" He swung the stove door closed again, shutting out the light. "This room was an eccentricity of my predecessor—and one of the few that could be returned to a habitable state on short notice. The morbid claim that he used a tower chamber like this one to imprison his wife."

"Do they?" Victoria said weakly. She imagined some ethereal damsel going slowly mad as she passed her days and nights in solitude with no more company than the rooks that built their nests on the ramparts below.

The duke broke in on her thoughts with an undignified snort of what Victoria could only guess was derision. "He had no wife." His shadowy figure straightened, then loomed close as he crossed the room over to her. "Let that be a lesson in credulity: people will believe anything if it is sufficiently romantic or dramatic."

Victoria bridled. "Trust me, I need no such lessons." He was so close now that she could smell him—the scent of his cologne and beneath it, his personal odor, as carnal and intoxicating as she would have imagined it to be. She caught herself sternly before the urge overtook her just to close her eyes and breathe it into herself.

She felt his hand touch her arm, then he was guiding her to one of the low couches and pulling her down next to him.

"Tawdry," she pronounced chillingly, trying to still the warmth that Raeburn's nearness brought.

The duke stiffened, and for a moment, she thought he was angry. But when he spoke, she heard suppressed mirth instead. "Indubitably."

She could feel the pressure of his leg against her hoops, could hear the whispers of his movements over the wash of rain and patter of her heart. She realized he was trying to intimidate her, to make her feel small and weak and helpless. Even more chafing, he was not completely unsuccessful. She sat rigidly, but he made no move to touch her.

Finally, when the silence had drawn out longer than she could bear, Victoria cleared her throat. "I should appreciate it if you would light a candle."

Again, a sudden stilling beside her. And again, provokingly, there was humor in his voice when he spoke. "I am certain you should, but I prefer darkness tonight."

She shook her head and sprang to her feet. Raeburn's hand snaked out and grabbed her by the wrist before she'd gone two strides, bringing her up short. She overbalanced all at once and landed half-sprawled in his lap in a tangle of skirts, her elbow meeting something soft and her head something hard. Raeburn grunted.

"That was my head," she snapped, rubbing it.

"That was my chin," he replied, pain in his voice, "and my stomach."

"Serves you right," she muttered, discomfiture making her childish.

She tried to wriggle off his lap into a more dignified position, but while he let her straighten, he held her fast against him.

"Your grace," she protested, "I am hardly accustomed to being—being *manhandled* in such a manner." But already awareness of his body was penetrating her outrage, and to her chagrin, her voice lacked the bite she'd meant to put into it.

"Your ladyship," the duke replied, his mouth very close to her ear, "must I remind you that we have a contract?"

"No, indeed, your grace." The taut dignity of her words were betrayed only by the shiver that ran up her back.

His arms were implacable iron bands around her, and she was sure that his lips were as hard as his voice, as hard as the rest of the body she was pinned against. She should be angry, her conscience whispered. She should feel imposed upon, if she were a decent lady. But no decent lady would have made her foolish bargain with the duke, and she could only feel strung tight with anticipation and something else, a strange kind of lightness in the knowledge that propriety had no place here.

Victoria relaxed unconsciously against her captor, and he chuckled, low and suggestive. "There's my girl," he murmured. She stiffened immediately, and he laughed again. "The delicacy of your pride must always be watched, mustn't it?"

"No more than yours," she shot back.

"Touché." With his arms still about her, he leaned forward until the stubble of his cheek rubbed against her neck. Victoria stifled a gasp as his breath blew warm and damp against her skin, but he did not kiss her as she half feared—and half hoped—he might. "No perfume," he observed. "Not even a hint of toilet water. There is something . . ." He breathed again, deep, a hairsbreadth from her skin, and she fought a sudden wave of dizziness. "Practical lavender, no doubt to keep the moths away from the clothes. You don't disappoint." She could almost feel his lips brush her neck with every syllable.

"I have no idea what you might mean," she said, sounding more breathless than stern.

He was close, so close! His wrists were brawny under her hands, his body lean and warm. He stirred old needs within her, needs she had ignored for so long but that would not be ignored that night.

"Your dissimilation," he explained. "It has no cracks—at least, you believe it to have no cracks. The bloodless, undesirable maiden aunt you play must not intrigue men with rare and exotic perfumes, so you wear none. In my experience, however, the desperation of age causes foibles even more extreme than mere scents and paint."

Raeburn lowered his head a fraction of an inch, and his lips came to rest in the hollow of her collarbone, barely exposed by the neckline of her modest dress.

Victoria caught her breath. Tension coiled hard in her center as a warning spike trickled up her spine until her limbs felt heavy with it. Soon, the mouth would move— to kiss her, taste her, tease her.

But after a long moment of stillness, the duke pulled away. A small moan of disappointment escaped her as frustrated anticipation wound tighter in her center, sending a shiver thrilling across her inflamed skin. She felt everything with exquisite sensitivity—the rough brush of stiff silk against her arms, the coarseness of her dress's seams, every individual bone in her corset and each thread in the weave of the duke's jacket, bunched under her hands. Most of all, she could feel the duke, burning with heat through the clothes that separated them. When he laughed, the soft gust of breath against her skin was like a gale.

"What you don't know," he whispered, "is that all the scents of a perfumery could not be more titillating than the raw smell of your flesh."

He released her, and dizzy as she was, she clung to his wrists for a moment before realizing she had been freed. She dropped his arms and stumbled to her feet and across the pillow-strewn floor to a window. There was the sound of a match flare behind her, and the room brightened minutely.

She fought the duke's pull from sheer instinct, clutching at the arcs of stone between the leaded diamonds of glass, seeing nothing, only feeling him furnace-hot behind her, only hearing him approach with footfalls like a giant's. Her hands tightened on the stone as he grazed her hair with his fingers, her head tilting back into the feather-light caress from some obscure impulse of its own. Inside, she was drawn tight and thin, waiting—

"What do you fear?" Raeburn whispered, the words shivering in the air between them.

"I am not afraid of you," Victoria said tightly. She didn't turn to face him.

The hand traced slowly down the bare length of her neck to rest on her nape. Victoria could hear him breathing now, too hard and fast, as if he'd just climbed three flights of stairs, not crossed a small tower room.

"No," the duke said, and Victoria heard a strange kind of gravity in his tone. "No, you wouldn't be. But you are afraid."

His hand moved; there was a twist, a loosening, a breath of air, and Victoria realized he had unfastened the first of the long row of buttons down her back. The tightness within her uncoiled suddenly, lashing her with fire that surged from her center through her limbs. Her dimmed vision faded to almost nothing, and she turned impulsively, too light-headed for thought, and pulled the duke's head down to meet her own.

The meeting of lips—the strange softness of the skin, the exquisite heat, the alarming dampness that promised something more. Victoria had almost forgotten the bitter sweetness of it, the mingled hunger and completion that electrified every sense. When they met, Raeburn's lips were unresponsive under her own, but only for an instant. Then they hardened, giving and taking at the same time. His arms wrapped around her, holding her tighter against him than her instinctive inclination had pressed, half lifting her from her feet. Someone moaned—and Victoria dazedly recognized her own voice. The coarseness of clothing was torture against her skin; it demanded release and the balm of another body against hers.

The fabric encased her, isolated her in a cocoon of silk and linen. Even as Raeburn's lips caressed her mouth and throat, even as he drew her ever harder against him, and even as a rush of heat suffused her at his touch—even then, she was alone. Alone as she had been for fifteen years. For once, for just one night or even one hour, she didn't want to be alone anymore.

The duke's tongue pushed against her lips. *Closer, closer.* She opened them and let him in, tasting him as he explored her tongue, the ridges of her front teeth, the roof of her mouth. When he retreated, she followed. He tasted of wine and of himself, rich and intoxicating. She could drink him forever, and then, some part of her mind whispered, she'd never be alone again.

Finally, the kiss ended. Victoria drew back with a sigh and opened her eyes. The duke regarded her evenly. Though his expression was impossible to read in the light of the single candle he'd lit along the wall, his scrutiny was unmistakable.

"You are full of surprises," he said, his voice hoarse and slightly winded. "If you were a courtesan, you could make your fortune in that kiss alone."

Victoria laughed unsteadily, too conscious of his arms around her, the gaping buttons in her dress, and, most of all, the overpowering desire to kiss him again. "By all rights, I should slap you for that remark, but I find that I have no desire to do so."

"I should hope not. But it makes me wonder: How much more have I underestimated the Wakefield spinster?" His hands traced up her back to the highest of the fastened buttons and slowly began to undo it.

"No more than most," Victoria said, and then he lowered his head to meet her lips, ending speech.

This time, his fingers did not still in their work but sped up, moving with increasing dexterity from one button to the next, all the way down the length of her back. Victoria's fingers curled in his thick hair; she slid her mouth away from his and burrowed her face in his neck, tasting him, breathing his scent of spice and masculinity. She slipped her free hand under his coat—four buttons, and the waistcoat below was open.

By now, her dress was hanging open, only the sleeves and the flaring of her crinoline keeping it from sliding off. Rough and strong, the duke's hands moved beneath it, across her bare upper back, trailing heat across her skin as he pushed the gown from her shoulders. She let him tug her arms through the sleeves, first the left one, then the right. As each arm came free, she twined it again about his neck, but when he finished, he pushed her back at arm's length and surveyed her.

Victoria should have been embarrassed, she knew, what with her bodice bunched around her waist and only her corset and chemise between her body and the duke's gaze. Yet she wasn't. Not even the faintest flicker of self-consciousness stirred as Raeburn folded his arms across his chest and leaned back, perusing her slowly. His gaze only sent a wave of heat through her, another surge of insanity. She wanted to go mad for the night, for once in many more years than she cared to count.

"Well?" she demanded, returning his look levelly.

"I was right," he said. "Your corset is hideous." Before she could do more than open her mouth in surprise, he pulled her toward him again. "But you most certainly are not."

She freed herself and laughed, surprising herself even more. "I think I am flattered," she said.

Raeburn reached for her again, impatiently.

"Not yet," she admonished brazenly. "Take it off." She motioned imperiously to his waistcoat and jacket.

The duke stood impassively, and for a moment, she thought he would take umbrage at her orders. But then he seemed to make a decision, and he rapidly peeled his clothes off, tossing them to the floor.

Victoria began to approach, but he stayed her with an extended hand and unbuttoned his shirt and collar with rapid ease, slipping off his braces and dropping the shirt and undershirt on top of the other garments.

He was splendid, even in the dim candlelight. His muscles bunched over his arms and across his chest, and his stomach was a hard plane, his wide shoulders narrowing to a neat waist where a dark line of hair disappeared into his trousers.

"Oh," Victoria said involuntarily.

He chuckled languorously, pulling her to him. This time, she did not resist. He reached efficiently through the open waist of her dress to the ties that held her petticoat and crinoline in place. A few tugs and they loosened—a final pull, and she was standing in her deflated skirt with her hoops puddled at her feet. The duke lifted her free. His chest was hard and smooth against her, the feel of his skin thrilling her searching hands. So long, so long . . . For a moment she felt other hands against her body, remembered words of ardor whispered in another voice. When her feet touched the ground again, she snaked her arms around him and bent her head to bury it against his body, just breathing the essence of him, exulting in the touch of flesh against heated flesh. She tasted him, running her mouth slowly up his chest, across the hard line of his jaw to his mouth. What matter whose touch? What matter whose mouth? His hands, which had been busy loosening her corset, stilled and drew her against him. He was like a wall of fire, solid and burning, engulfing her. She could not taste him enough, touch him enough, breathe him enough . . . His lips, his eyes, the line of his throat—all were beautiful.

Raeburn was the one to finally pull away, gasping.

"My God," he said. "And to think I planned to teach you a few tricks!"

"Someone once told me the best tricks are the ones no schooling can teach," she said through the memories that swam up in her mind. "He said they are guided by desire and tempered by passionate intuition."

"And is this passionate intuition?" His finger grazed her flushed cheeks, her swollen lips.

"No," she said frankly, "merely animal lust, as I'm sure we both know."

He resumed his work at her corset laces. "You are an enigma, Lady Victoria."

She swallowed hard, aware of the enormity of what she was about to do—to forget a decade and a half of self-discipline, forget everything she had paid and everything she had gained. But alone in the dark with the duke, all that she had lived for faded into trivialities. Respectability, social influence, familial power—no longer did being the hidden hand of Rushworth hold any attraction. Instead, the years of personal privation and self-denial crowded in on her. Loveless, friendless, with only the distant acquaintances that polite society allowed. Passionless. Heartless. Safe.

She looked up at Raeburn. His expression was hidden

in shadows, but she had memorized his face with her fingers and her lips. Strong, remorseless, wonderful. Forehead damp with desire. He wanted her with a sheer carnality that took her breath away, perhaps as no man had ever wanted her before, and the knowledge of his need brought another wash of heat across her skin, leaving her tingling and near-trembling in its wake.

He had finished loosening her corset, but he paused, watching her, searching her face.

"You are thinking," he said.

She laughed, but the sound was high and artificial. "I do that at times, your grace, but I always repent."

"And of this, too, will you repent?" She could not tell if there was merely curiosity in his voice or if, perhaps, there was a hint of regret or even guilt.

She shook her head, her hands spread across the smooth tautness of his chest. "My soul is not pure enough to allow for such twinges of conscience." The bitterness of the words was unexpected but genuine.

Again, he scrutinized her. "And what precisely do you mean by that?"

"Nothing," she said, pressing herself against his bare chest, willing him to let the matter drop.

But he would have none of her distractions. He caught both her wrists and pushed her away. "We have all the hours of darkness for that—enough even for you." Though she couldn't see his face, she was certain he was glowering.

She tried again. "Your grace, I didn't know what I was saying. It was the foolishness of the moment. It means nothing; there is nothing to talk about."

He released one of her hands and began stroking the other gently, teasingly, as if to assure her that he hadn't forgotten the business of that night. She felt a flush creep up her cheeks; for once, she was grateful for the shadows in the room.

"I have found that we reveal our most profound natures in our most thoughtless comments," he said.

"Then I doubt you ever reveal anything, your grace; you are so nice with your words." The edge in her voice was not spite but a resentment at his prodding and a desire to deflect his attention. But she knew it was no use. Frigidity . . . oh, where was the wall of frigidity she once lowered so effectively between herself and the world? It had melted in the darkness of the gaudy tower boudoir.

"Not often. Not now," the duke said, and he lapsed into silence, raising her hand to his mouth almost absently and kissing her fingers slowly, one at a time. She shivered. His tongue played between them, his lips traveling their length leisurely.

He wanted her. She could feel it in every tense line of his body, in the twisting fire that his need stirred in her. She pursued her advantage. "Come, let's not talk." She stepped closer to him until their bodies met, tilting her face up mere inches from his.

She could feel his smile against the back of her hand. "There will be time for everything, I promise you. From dusk 'til dawn."

Victoria pressed her lips together stubbornly.

He must have sensed her recalcitrance, for he sighed in an exaggerated manner. "Must you be so difficult?"

"Yes," she replied without hesitation.

He chuckled. "I shouldn't have asked." He reached out and touched her face with his free hand, caressing the length of it.

She leaned into the touch, savoring the physicality of it. *Keep it here,* she thought. *In the touch of skin, the caress of fingertips. Let all the rest be forgotten, just for tonight.* But she knew better than to speak her thoughts aloud. Indeed, he was already continuing.

"What I can't understand is how you can be so brave yet so frightened. Why the disguise, Lady Victoria? Why the bluster? Why the façade?"

He did not seem to be teasing her; his voice was subdued and grave, almost as if he were musing to himself. Victoria bit back her facile answer. What could be said? There was a long moment in which there was no sound but the constant wash of rain against the roof and the wind among the eaves. The duke stood there, determinedly inquisitive and yet . . . not threatening. Not comforting, certainly, but not intimidating, either. He was almost familiar, as if she had known him in some other age or as if she herself was in him, distant and distorted. Two like spirits, caught in unlike bottles. She spoke on that thought.

"You of all people should know. I know nothing you don't—the cipher's key is locked in here." She brushed his forehead with her fingers. "You look inside and tell me. Why?"

Raeburn caught the hand on his brow and pulled her against him.

"You can't shift things back to me so easily," he said.

She laughed, trying to sound carefree, but she feared it came out rather strangled.

But the brush of his bare chest against her naked arms soon dispelled her lingering sense of gravity, and she let it whirl away in a return of carnal need. She could feel his manhood pressing hot and hard through his trousers and was neither ashamed nor frightened; it was as it should be, she thought, a man desiring a woman in the darkness, the woman turning to the man to hold back the night of the mind.

Chapter Five

Byron tugged the dress over Lady Victoria's head hurriedly, dropping it to the floor even as he began to unhook the metal fastenings down her corset busk. Lust made him impatient, but even more—far more, he admitted to himself—he feared what she might say if she were not distracted. *You look inside and tell me. Why?* How could she think she knew why he hid? How could she hope to understand the despair that plagued his days and haunted his nights?

He slid the corset from her shoulders and pulled off her chemise in almost the same motion.

Brazenly displayed before him, Lady Victoria faced him straight on, head tilted high and chin jutting out as if daring him to make a disparaging remark. High breasts, full for her spare body and firmer than most women her age; soft, sloping shoulders; smooth skin; slender waist—all consummately desirable. She held herself with a natural, sensual elegance, and he had the sudden conviction that this was a woman born to be loved. No wonder she hid behind ugly clothes and a cold smile. She had to embrace extremes just to counter her inherent erotic attraction.

The thought of taking her in his arms, crushing her bare flesh against him and taking her mouth in his, sent another spear of desire into his groin. Yet he did not reach out for her, though his body cried out for release. She was bare to the waist, but it wasn't enough.

"Take down your hair," he ordered.

"What?" she said, her voice tinged with surprise.

"Your hair. Take it down."

After a moment's hesitation, she complied, her breasts lifting tantalizingly as she reached behind her head for the pins. She plucked them out swiftly and began to uncoil the tight bun. Then, looking at him measuringly, she stopped and shook her head one, two, three times until her hair tumbled down across her shoulders.

Byron immediately saw the reason for her hesitation. Her face framed by a mass of pale waves, Victoria seemed suddenly younger, less certain of herself. The lines of her face, so severe before, now softened into delicacy, and even the set of her chin faded from belligerence to mere stubbornness. Without the armor of her tight bun, she was transformed into a creature both rarer and more vulnerable.

Byron reached out and took a lock between his fingers. It was silk-fine, like fairy tresses, but the ends were unmercifully shorn at a length that fell just below her breasts.

"You've savaged it," he accused, holding up the blunt ends as evidence.

"There's no one to ever see it," Lady Victoria replied, but her eyes slid past his.

He shook his head. "No." The lady before him was too complex for such reasons. Like her clothing and the cold manner she adopted, her hair was part of the disguise that kept the world at bay. "You cut it because you hate it.

Because it's striking and beautiful, and beauty is danger-ous." He lifted the ends to his lips and kissed them as Vic-toria watched, her eyes riveted on his hand. "I will find out why it's so dangerous before this week is up," he promised softly. "I will fathom your secrets and under-stand you, Lady Victoria."

Her gaze never wavered. "Not before I uncover your own."

He kissed her then, silencing her, pushing back the fear that she was right. Her mouth was ripe and sweet, her nipples brushing provocatively against his bare chest as she leaned into him. His hands tangled in the wild waves of her hair as he pulled her harder against him—one lock caught in his mouth, and he laughed and pushed it aside and kissed her again.

"You are still wearing your shoes," he said when they separated. She was a tall woman—her heels brought the top of her head above the bridge of his nose.

"Yes," she agreed breathlessly.

He dropped to his knees, examining them more closely in the dim light of the single candle. "They have buttons," he said reproachfully.

She laughed, and the sound had a reckless edge. "Yes. Many, many buttons."

He snorted. "We'll just see what's to be done about that." He stood and swept her into his arms in a single, deliberately dramatic movement. She gasped but did not squeal in surprise as another woman might have done, and when he had deposited her on the divan, her next words were full of reproof.

"You might have warned me."

Byron shrugged, taking one narrow ankle into his lap. He unbuttoned the shoe efficiently and slipped it off, then took her other foot and repeated the process. He stopped and looked at her where she lay stretched along the length of the low sofa.

Victoria's expression was expectant, her lower lip caught between her teeth. The air of lingering youth and fragility still hung about her—he could not think of her as a tight-laced spinster when she looked like that, nor even as a sophisticated woman of the world. Not child-like, certainly not, but vulnerable in a way that he never would have guessed when she first walked into the Teak Parlor.

Vulnerable—and wanton.

Byron was still holding her left ankle, so slender he could encircle it with one hand. He slid his hand slowly up her silk-clad calf, watching her closely. Her breath caught, then quickened. He paused at the curve of her knee, then untied the ribbons holding up her stocking and rolled it, ever so slowly, down and off. She shuddered slightly as his hand touched bare skin, and he lifted her leg to his lips, tracing it upward with his mouth to the crease of her knee. The skin was smooth, downed with soft hair. He smiled at her sigh and removed the other stocking. A tug at the pantaloon strings, another pull, and she was lying naked before him.

Her legs were shapely, narrow at ankle and knee and full at calf and thigh, impossibly long, leading inevitably to the triangle of pale curls where they met. Too thin for fashion, he objectively knew, but at that moment, they seemed perfect.

"I feel rather at a disadvantage," Victoria said, a tiny quaver in her voice. "You know, with me . . . like this"— she gestured at her nakedness—"and you . . . like that." She waved at his dark trousers, still fastened firmly around his waist.

Byron laughed quietly. "Safest way to have you."

Then he leaned across her body, brushing his lips against her stomach, the valley between her breasts, her neck, her mouth. Her arms slid under his as he reached her face, her hands encouraging him as their lips met. Soft palms and delicate, curved fingernails thrilled across his back as Victoria escaped his mouth and began an assault of her own, licking, teasing, nibbling, kissing every inch of his face, his neck. Her mouth was impossibly hot against his skin, as hot as the arousal that strained at his trousers.

He rested his weight on his elbows and captured her face in his hands, cradling it he explored her mouth slowly, thoroughly. It was damp and sweet and inviting, soft and willing, like her body. Under him, she shifted, freeing her trapped leg so she held his hips between her thighs. He groaned and pressed his erection against her inviting heat, gathering her against him and devouring her mouth.

Finally, their mouths separated, and he spent a long moment just breathing into her web-fine hair that lay softer than silk against his cheek.

"I could get drunk off you," he muttered.

Victoria didn't answer, but a moment later, he felt her fingers working nimbly at his waistband. He hardened more, if possible, as her hands brushed against his arousal in their work. The first button loosened, and then the next. He groaned and pushed off her, stepping away from the divan as he stripped off his shoes and socks, trousers and drawers. Victoria watched him, her eyes glittering and hooded.

"Better?" he demanded.

"Better," she agreed. She opened her mouth again but stopped, a blush so crimson even to be visible even in the candlelight creeping up her chest and across her face. She seemed to shake it off, and she spoke: "Come—come to me."

Byron chuckled. "With pleasure." But instead of joining her on the divan, he knelt beside it near her feet. He began at her ankles, kissing, licking, teasing, then worked his way up the insides of her calves to her knees where he paused at the sensitive crease. She shivered delicately as he caressed the skin with his tongue and teeth. He passed more slowly up her thighs, where the flesh was softer, hotter. Her legs loosened, opening to him as he moved upward, closer to their joining. He paused at her nest of curls, as pale as the waves that spilled across her shoulders. He could hear her breath quicken, feel the muscles in her legs tighten against his shoulders in anticipation. He looked up. She was watching him intently, one hand gripping the back of the divan, the other balled at her waist.

"Are you? . . ." she asked, surprise and anticipation mingling in her face.

As an answer, he closed the space between them. He found the soft folds among her curls and licked slowly, experimentally. Victoria gasped, and her hands seized his shoulders—not pushing or pulling, just gripping hard. He tasted her again, and this time her gasp had a sharp, sibilant edge.

"More?" he whispered, knowing she could hear him even over her own ragged breathing.

"Yes," she moaned. "Much, much more."

He laughed and probed harder with his tongue, sliding between her folds into her hot softness. The hands on his shoulders tightened suddenly, her thighs widening and loosening as she arched her hips toward his mouth. He moved his tongue within her, her body exquisitely attuned to his rhythm. He adjusted his speed to her reactions, her rasping breaths, her clinging hands, her ankles tight about his waist. Absorbing himself in her, he sought the perfection that would send her plummeting—

And found it. With a choked sound, Victoria went rigid and arched against the cushions of the sofa. Byron didn't stop, didn't even slow as she began to tremble, then almost convulse with every stroke of his tongue. She tried to speak, but the words mingled with inarticulate noises and emerged as nonsense. Still he pressed on, pushing deeper into her hot slickness as her hands constricted on his shoulders and she rocked and moaned.

Finally, she collapsed, panting, and he pulled away. But the hands on his shoulders reached under his arms and urged him up as her hips tilted harder into him.

"Now," she said, the word ground out between clenched teeth. "Please, *now!*"

He came to her, but taking his own time, pausing to circle her navel with his tongue, to kiss her breasts as she shuddered under him. Finally, his mouth came even with hers. She pulled his head down, taking him with her lips, demanding, hungry. He was light-headed with need for her. It rushed through his veins, throbbed in his ears, centered in a single surge of blood and desire. Her body moved beneath him, hot and supple, begging for the release he held in his power.

Once more, he took her swollen lips, returning in full their passion, tasting her mouth, her tongue with his own.

"This will hurt a little," he managed to warn her, but she only shook her head, half laughing as she gasped for air. He could not wait to interpret her response—denial? amusement?—as his need seized him. He took the invitation of her tilting hips and slid into her slick tightness, almost losing control as he buried himself in her heat.

There was no barrier, no stronghold of virginity to

interrupt his entrance. Once again, he'd misjudged this strange, contradictory woman, he thought, but even that realization could only distract him for a moment.

Victoria moaned and pushed against him until they met. He started to move within her, but she tightened her grip on his arms.

"Not yet," she said hoarsely. Her face was strained, but she seemed to savor the anticipation of it, the enjoyment of expectation heightening the glory of the moment. She closed her eyes, going somewhere inside, away from him.

Byron realized suddenly that it was not enough for there to be pleasure given and taken. He wanted Victoria to be aware of him, as aware of him as a man as he was of her as a woman. She was beautiful like that, he realized—beautiful with her face drawn in the grimace of lovemaking, beautiful with her slight curves laid out beneath him, beautiful with her tightness clasping him intimately, as if she would turn them both into one marvelous animal. But he did not want her to plunge into ecstasy alone. He wanted her with him as she went over the edge—he wanted to be a part of that beauty at its climax.

He kissed her forehead, her eyelids, her lips.

"I'm here," he whispered. "Look at me. Remember— I am with you."

She opened her eyes and met his gaze. "For now," she agreed, a wry smile twisting her lips.

He kissed them smooth again and began to move slowly, surely within her, long strokes that carried him from the edge of her entrance until they met, again and again. She gasped with every thrust, a sound of mingled pleasure and need.

"For tonight," he agreed, and after that, there was no breath left for speaking.

He quickened his pace as her hands urged him on, until he reached a rhythm that sent her quivering and gasping against him. He could feel the trembling in her thighs, the goose pimples that crawled across the flesh of her arms as she tightened them about his body, pulling her harder against him. She clung to the apex for half a dozen strokes, a dozen, and then he abandoned himself as they fell together, the hot rush of release leaving him weak and heavy-limbed as they slowed, slowed, stopped.

Finally, after a long moment of stillness, he pulled away. Her hands reached out, as if from some instinctive need to bring him back, but she let them drop as soon as they brushed his skin.

He found a piece of clothing—his shirt, he realized. He shrugged. In the name of chivalry, nothing was too great a sacrifice, he thought ruefully. He cleaned himself, then reached between Victoria's legs as courteously as he could and repeated the service for her.

He looked up at her as he set the shirt aside. Her hair was tangled madly around her head, her pale blue-gray eyes enormous in her delicately boned face, with a touch of gratefulness there that oddly stirred him.

He was spent like he hadn't been in years with any woman, but suddenly, he didn't want to send her packing off to her room. Not yet.

He arranged some of the pillows into a semblance of a bed, then pulled a coverlet off the back of another of the divans.

Wordlessly, he returned to Victoria's side and bent to scoop her into his arms. She held on as he carried her over to the pillow bed and lay her gently upon it. Then, still in silence, he lay down next to her and pulled her firmly against him, his chest to her back, her buttocks snugged against his groin. Then he pulled the coverlet over them both.

He drifted off to sleep with her warm length against his, and his dreams were haunted by the ghosts of lavender and black-clad sylphs.

Between dreams and waking, Victoria had the strange sensation of levitation, of movement through darkness and half-glimpsed rooms. But she was not afraid. Around her, in her waking dream or sleeping wakefulness, were strong arms, and she knew instinctively that they would not let her fall.

Chapter Six

Victoria woke to sunlight and a timid rap on the door. After a moment of confusion, she realized she was in the Unicorn Room, tucked snugly under the blankets. After another, she realized she was naked, and the events of the night before came rushing back. She lay still, dazed by the memory of it—wonderful, terrible, frightening. What had she done? And what would she give to do it again?

She bit back a curse as the knock came again, more insistent.

"Come in," she said, levering herself up against the pillows while keeping the counterpane tight around her shoulders.

Annie the maid slid in and closed the door behind her, looking even more frightened of Victoria than she had the first day.

Victoria stifled a frown. That was not a good sign.

"His grace thought thoo might like to eat in thy room whilst thy wardrobe was being finished," Annie said, cringing behind a heavy-laden tray.

"My wardrobe . . ." Victoria repeated stupidly, looking around the room for her trunk. It was gone. "My *wardrobe*!"

Annie flinched, rattling the teacup against its saucer. "His grace promised that thy original clothes would be returned to thee when thoo leaves." The maid hesitated.

"But . . ." Victoria prompted, her unease growing.

Annie had the look of a trapped rabbit. "His grace—that is, his present grace's great-uncle kept three seamstresses at all times for his lady guests. His present grace has set them to sewing curtains and linens and the like for the Dowager House, but now he's having them make a few dresses for thee." She sucked in a breath, as if to steel herself for the next confession. "And there's the corsetry. His grace had some ordered from thy spare garments when thoo came. It ought to be up from Leeds by noon."

"He has ordered *corsetry*?" She almost sprang out of bed before catching herself. The gall of that man! Stealing her clothes while he reordered her life to his satisfaction, effectively imprisoning her in her room with no more deserving target for her ire than a shrinking girl-child. As if the events of the night before had given him some obscure right over her!

No, an insidious little voice reminded her, *she* had given him the right when she had signed their agreement. But to think that just hours ago, she had almost trusted him, and then he had almost immediately taken advantage of her. That was a mistake she'd never repeat.

She controlled her voice before Annie fainted dead away from sheer terror. "Please bring me the tray, Annie," she said. "Then you may go. It appears I will need no help dressing this morning."

Byron sat in the study of the Henry Suite, wading through the nightmare of ledgers and diaries and scraps of paper that were his predecessor's financial records. Though he had lived in the manor nigh on two years, Byron could still not think of the chambers as his. They had been inhabited far too long by other men who had left their impressions upon it more indelibly than he could ever hope to. That was the secret of Raeburn Court, he had finally decided; it always made one feel a stranger.

And yet he did not hate it. That was what never ceased to amaze him. He grumbled about it, railed against its in-adequacies, but he could not actively dislike it. The first time he'd seen the building, summoned to his great-uncle's side at the impressionable age of twelve, he'd seen the hideousness of it, the sprawling wings of every imaginable age of architecture appended to the main mass of limestone at haphazard angles. Yet even then, it had called to him. Even then, it had whispered of secrets and darkness and ancient passions burned into the rock. So when his great-uncle, in one of his rare lucid moments, had lectured him on his duty to restore the building to its former grandeur, he had been honestly able to promise to do as much as he could in his lifetime. The man had seemed feeble then. Who knew that it would be nearly a quarter of a century before Byron set foot in the manor house again?

And now here he was, trying to do the impossible by turning this derelict ruin into a house suitable for the seat of a duchy. As heir presumptive, he had been given free rein with half a dozen other estates and had turned them into profitable enterprises, and now he found himself pouring the fruits of the last two decades of labor into a project that would take his lifetime.

Still, he was hardly poverty-stricken, whatever he might have told Lady Victoria. Even with the capital tied up in various investments, he had a neat five thousand a year to live on. Hardly extravagant, but manageable. Damn Gifford, anyhow. Byron remembered the man's smug smile shot over the head of Byron's betrothed at Lady Kilmaine's soirée. That smile told Byron that Gifford knew exactly what he was doing; it had been a challenge, a mockery, a prediction of the future, all wrapped into one. And all the while, the faithless, fickle Leticia had leaned toward Gifford with her wide green eyes gazing up at his inattentive face.

The quill bent dangerously in Byron's hands, and he loosened his grip with effort. Gifford would pay. Perhaps not as Byron had hoped originally, if his sister kept her end of the bargain, but if nothing else, the man was a good investment. The gouty earl would die soon, and Gifford would spend the rest of his life in debt to Byron.

Byron sighed and shunted his thoughts along more pleasant paths. Such as Lady Victoria, who had probably just finished dressing. She was doubtlessly more than a little peeved at him for the replacement of her wardrobe, but he'd be damned if he'd spend the next week with her trussed up like a mournful crow. Still, he hoped she wouldn't throw anything at Annie. The girl would surely have a fit of hysterics and would have to be carried down to the servants' hall, such as it was.

Usually the chase of a woman drove him, the consummation of a successful seduction merely the concluding paragraph of the tale of pursuit. But Victoria was different. Conquest only made her seem more elusive. Conquest! He snorted. It would be best to first ask who was conquering whom. He'd had women who were desperate for him before—and even more women who had pretended to be—but Lady Victoria's hunger had seemed to encompass him only by the felicitous circumstance of their coinciding presence. Still, it wasn't until the mo-

ment of consummation that he had realized that her experience extended to more than a few stolen kisses.

He shook his head and glanced at his pocket watch in
the low light of the oil lamp. Time for dinner. He stood
and strode to the dining room, darkly anticipating the
meeting with Lady Victoria, looking forward to counter-
ing her anger with an offhand word, a dismissive wave
that would send her into a fit of rage and make her lose
the iron control she seemed to value so highly.

When he arrived in the room, she was not there. But
Mrs. Peasebody bustled in with an important expression
on her flushed face, and he knew the news would not be
good.

"Yes?" he prompted, taking his seat as the housekeeper hovered with self-conscious deference beside his
chair. Even Mrs. Peasebody's silences seemed to be
louder than those of other people.

She cleared her throat. "Thy grace, I hardly wish to be
a bother. I know how busy thoo must be, with the records
and accounts and renovations and that. Why, thy grace, if
it was just me, I shouldn't say naught. Never one to put
missen forward, me."

"*Yes,* Mrs. Peasebody," Byron interjected, knowing
that she could go on in that vein for another five minutes
if she weren't redirected. "Your humility and discretion
are an example to us all. What is it?"

"It's only her ladyship," the woman fluttered, oblivious to irony. "Why, I hardly know how to tell thee. I
thought of ordering Cook to hold dinner, but I know thoo
is so very par-*tic*-ular about when thy meals are served,
and then I thought, 'Senga, my lass, thoo'd best go to the
duke and tell him, and let him decide.' So that's what I've
done." She beamed at him proudly.

Byron reminded himself that snapping at her would be

like beating a spaniel for whining—it would be inexcusably brutal and would only serve to make matters worse. "I see that, Mrs. Peasebody, but what you've yet to tell me is what exactly is to be decided."

"Oh, thy grace, that's why I've come. Her ladyship won't be coming down to dinner as she's still being dressed. Why, I gave Annie a right good scolding for her sloth, but there's naught to be done about it."

"I see," Byron said, frowning at the white expanse of tablecloth before him. He'd pegged Lady Victoria as the efficient type, not one to hover around the dressing table for half a day. She must be doing it to spite him. He considered holding back dinner, but he'd eaten the cook's food cold before and had no desire to repeat the experience. After all, Lady Victoria was no reason to inconvenience himself. "Have a tray sent up for her, then, and tell her that I shall be joining her as soon as I am finished with my meal." If that didn't inspire her to faster efforts, he didn't know what would.

"Oh, thy grace, does thoo think it wise? I mean to say, she *is* a lady, and to enter her room while she's in dishabille"—she pronounced it dis-*ha*-bil-lay—"why, it couldn't be proper." She opened her mouth to say more, but she must have caught the expression on Byron's face, for she shut it again and just nodded. "I shall just go and tell her," she said in a whisper that was loud enough to travel fifty feet. Then she bustled out, passing the kitchen maid, who bobbed to the housekeeper before setting a hot meat pie before Byron and leaving out again.

Byron picked up a fork. With Mrs. Peasebody's usual inefficiencies, Lady Victoria's food would be tepid at best by the time it reached her, and he was not above feeling a small surge of satisfaction on that account. He realized belatedly that he probably should have at least informed her of his plans for her attire, but he shrugged off the tug of guilt. She'd signed the contract. She'd known what she was getting herself into. A week in his company, a week in his power—if it was dissatisfactory, there was nothing keeping her at Raeburn Court.

With that thought, he took a generous bite of beef pie and settled back in his chair. He'd see Lady Victoria again soon enough.

Byron rapped perfunctorily at the door to the Unicorn Room, then opened it without waiting for an answer.

Lady Victoria was alone, perched on the edge of an enormous Elizabethan chest with a tray balanced awkwardly on her knees. The lavender silk he'd selected for her morning dress was perfectly suited to her, he saw immediately; it brought out a golden cast to her hair and gave her pale eyes a clear depth that was muted by black. Her hair—that was another change. He was surprised and pleased to see fashionable curls in an arch around her face and a neat whorl at the back of her head. But when she looked squarely at him, he suffered a less pleasant revelation.

Her cheeks and lips were heavily rouged, her eyelashes and brows darkened in almost comic relief against her fair skin.

"Your grace," she oozed sweetly, her usually sensual voice transformed into something high and rasping. "I hardly expected you so soon."

He crossed to the window and pulled the heavy drapes closed before turning to glare at her, folding his arms across his chest. "Of course not, your ladyship," he said in a voice he knew stated the exact opposite.

"Why, I was *hoping* to come down and join you for dinner, but I fear Annie hadn't finished dressing me." She fluttered her hands at her hair. "You know how *important* it is for a lady to look her *best*."

"Wash it off," he said flatly.

Her eyes widened in false innocence. "Your grace?"

"Wash it off," he repeated. "Now. Or I'll do it for you."

She tittered. "Why, your grace, I thought you'd *appreciate* my efforts. After all, it was you who sent down to Leeds for underthings more suited to a wharf-side doxy than a respectable lady." Though a saccharine smile remained pasted to her face, her last words were acid-laced.

Byron frowned, foreboding growing within him. "Whatever do you mean?"

Her eyes narrowed and the smile fell off her face. "This," she snapped, pulling up a corner of her skirt where her stocking peeked above her sturdy boot.

Red didn't do the color justice. Scarlet, flaming, even crimson—all of those better described it. Byron looked up to her face again, a white mask of fury under the ridiculous paint, then at the offending ankle.

"My dearest Lady Victoria," he said firmly, determined not to laugh, "I can assure you that I sent no specifics to the corsetiere. I merely made a list of items and asked that they be suitably attractive." His voice wobbled on the last word, but he plunged bravely on. "The corsetiere and my late great-uncle evidently had very different . . . tastes in corsetry than you—or I, for that matter."

"You mean to say this"—her wave encompassed the hidden parts of her underpinnings as well as the terrible stockings—"was accidental?"

"Yes," Byron said fervently. She still looked at him skeptically. "If you disbelieve me yet, please take into consideration your lovely morning dress. For your dresses, I left much more detailed instructions." Her expression began to soften. Byron leaned back against the wall and quirked an eyebrow at her. "If you would like, I shall allow you to dye my drawers any color you please in retribution."

That did it. Incredulity warred with amusement on her face, and finally she burst out laughing. The sound thrilled up his spine—beautiful, musical sound, every bit as luscious as he had imagined it to be. He raised his other eyebrow, surprised at the freeness of it coming from this restrained woman. Images of the night before flashed across his mind. *Not that restrained,* he corrected himself.

"Bring me the facecloth," Lady Victoria said when she could speak again.

Wordlessly, he wet it in the room's washbasin and handed it to her. She scrubbed the paint from her face, her expression carefully bland. With a hard look, she gave the cloth back to him.

"If you try another trick like replacing my wardrobe, your grace, whatever the outcome or intentions, I shall dye your entire wardrobe colors you never imagined existed."

"I consider myself duly warned," Byron said gravely.

"Good," she replied, then smiled, her face lighting brilliantly. Her pointed chin and sharp features gave her a strangely impish appeal, and Byron found himself watching the transformation with fascination.

"Stand up, your ladyship," Byron said when her smile had faded again. "Let me see what the seamstresses have done with you. It could hardly help but be an improvement."

Lady Victoria's expression turned wry, but she set aside her tray and stood. She turned with exaggerated slowness for his inspection. Though he knew she meant to goad him, he found it almost titillating as she exposed first one angle of her body, then another to his sight. First her face, with its clear gaze, then the length of her neck, the swell of her breast, the arch of her nape, her other ear peeking like a shell among the whorls of hair. She looked years younger than when she arrived—certainly not girlish, but closer to girlish than withering and half-spent, as she dressed to be—and there was a native sensuality that permeated the air about her now that she no longer imprisoned it behind walls of whalebone and black taffeta. When she came around to face him again, the expression in her blue-gray eyes was worldly yet dryly amused, intriguingly at odds with her delicate, porcelain complexion, and Byron had the sudden certainty that, shorn of her somber disguise, she would have been the kind of woman who incited devotion among the ranks of callow youths and dotards alike.

"Well?" Victoria demanded. "What now? You could examine my teeth. Or I could prance up and down the room—go through my paces—if you wish."

"But I saw your paces last night—most thoroughly and enjoyably," Byron pointed out. She colored slightly in response, and that faint flush of heat was enough to send him over the edge. "Come here," he ordered roughly.

Victoria paused for a moment, as if to show that she obeyed by choice, not because she had to, then stepped forward.

Byron closed the remaining space between them until her skirts pressed against his legs, but he did not reach out for her. Instead, he stood regarding her blatantly for a long moment, almost nose to nose. Victoria neither flinched nor leaned away, and her jaw was set in the

recognition of a challenge issued, stubborn yet feminine.
And challenging in its own right.

Byron seized that chin between his thumb and forefinger. Victoria stiffened, and she was still frozen in surprise
when his mouth came down on hers. But only for a moment. Her lips opened under his tongue as she pressed
into him, slipping her hands under his morning coat and
bunching the fabric of his waistcoat in her fists. Her
mouth was hot and welcoming, slick under the slow
strokes of his tongue. A jolt of desire went through him,
straight to his groin. He kissed her with his eyes open,
watching the color creep up her cheeks, drinking in the
look of pleasure and the pain of longing that knitted her
fair brow and made her moan into his mouth. Her hand
found the hard bulge of his arousal, stroking it through
the fabric of his breeches, and it was all he could do not
to strip off her crinoline and throw up her skirts right
there.

With a sound of regret, he drew away. She sighed
piteously and opened her eyes.

"Why?" she whispered.

"Because, as much as I'd prefer to dally here, I have
duties to attend to today," he replied dryly. He cupped her
face in his hand and tilted it up. Her skin was silken, frag-
ile under his rough fingers, and he could feel her pulse
fluttering at her throat. He cocked his head to the side.
"What made you, Victoria? One moment Alecto, the next
Circe." He referenced the mythological Fury and en-
chantress without a trace of humor.

She jerked away, stepping abruptly out of the circle of
his arms. Her gray-blue eyes were wide and calm, but
there was still a flush of passion on her cheeks and her
swollen lips. "Your grace, I promised you a week," she
said hoarsely. "I did not promise my confidences."

"Have you given them to anyone?" he mused coolly, rocking back on his heels.

"Not for a very, very long time," she said, her voice hard, her eyes dark with old memories. "Wisdom comes with age and cost."

He could almost feel her secrets, vibrating in her voice even as she tried to shunt the conversation toward generalities, but he could not read them, however hard he tried. Was she a scorned lover? There were nuances of loss and disillusionment, certainly, but somehow, that did not fit. "One might think that naïveté would be a happier condition," Byron said, softening his voice, hoping to prod some revelation from her.

Her reply was unequivocal. "Then one would be wrong. For the naïve, the pain of learning merely has not come." She seemed to shake herself, and the moment was lost. "Let us speak of something else," she said, her face closing.

"Of course, your ladyship," Byron murmured, letting the matter drop. Almost regretfully, he checked his pocket watch. He should go soon—in fact, the carriage was probably already waiting for him at the front door. But to leave Victoria now, when he could almost taste her secrets . . . He knew what would wait for him when he came back—the collected spinster, all memory of their exchange erased from her cool features. He'd come too far to allow her to slip back into her old role. Better to keep her with him and off-balance.

"How would you feel about a short trip this afternoon?" he asked, snapping his watchcase closed.

"To hell and back?" she replied with false lightness.

He quirked an eyebrow. "Actually, I was thinking of the Dowager House. I go most afternoons to examine the progress that's being made with the renovations. *From hell and back*, if you like."

She smiled tightly. "My time is yours."

"But of course," he replied, and extended his arm as if they were descending to a ball.

Giving him an exaggerated nod, she took it and let him lead her from the room.

Chapter Seven

Victoria tightened her grip on the leather loop as the carriage jolted again. She could sense Raeburn's presence as a shape in the blackness across from her, but she could see nothing of him, for the carriage had no windows.

She fought a sudden feeling of being impossibly alone, surrounded by insane servants and their even more insane master. *He travels in darkness . . .* That was one rumor that proved to be truer than she would have imagined. What other strange stories might have a basis in fact?

She heard Raeburn shift as the carriage hit another rock. Tension radiated through the darkness. He was waiting, she realized—waiting for her to ask the question on the tip of her tongue. *Why?*

She remembered his expression as they went through the main doors of the manor to find the carriage sitting there like a great black coffin. When she had cast a surprised look his way, she found him already watching her. His expression seemed to challenge her to make a comment, but behind the bravura was a defenselessness, as if she'd just seen some shameful and infinitely embarrass-

ing secret. Before she could make anything of it, the
footman had opened the door and lowered the steps and
it was time to enter the carriage.

Since then, they had ridden in silence.

It was ridiculous, Victoria thought. The night before,
they had shared something. Something more than just
their bodies. She had looked at Raeburn and had seen
something she recognized in herself. Now, although attraction still thickened the air in the closed box of the carriage, he was as remote and forbidding as when she'd
first arrived.

It seemed like an eternity before the carriage stopped.
Victoria squinted against the flood of light as the footman
opened the door. Raeburn paused to turn up his coat collar, tug his silk scarf higher about his face, and pull his
unfashionably wide-brimmed hat over his eyes—the
only odd note in his smart attire. Then he stepped out of
the carriage and thrust his arm toward her, more a demand than an offer.

Victoria took it, steadying herself as she stepped onto
a wide gravel expanse in front of the house. She tried to
pause to take it in, but Raeburn pinned her arm to his side
and hustled her up the walk to the door, his head down
and steps swift. Despite her long legs, Victoria had to
break into a half trot to keep pace, and her attention was
so taken with the effort not to stumble on the rough path
that she got only a fleeting glimpse of the house—an impression of herringbone red brick, white plaster, and long
black oak beams. Then they were inside.

As soon as the door shut, Raeburn stopped dead as if
he'd been in no hurry at all.

"I'm bringing a master pargeter in to restore the ornamental plasterwork on the upper stories," he said with
studied casualness. "Some of it was lost when repairs

were made on the west-facing gables about a century ago, but the designs can be recreated easily enough."

"Oh," Victoria said, at a loss. Her question still hovered unspoken between them, but Raeburn's jaw was set forbiddingly and his hazel eyes bore into hers, daring her to ask it. She could not find it within her to take him up on the challenge.

A heavyset, middle-aged man trundled into the room, covered in dust and with an apron about his waist.

"Your grace!" he exclaimed heartily. "Grand news, grand news! The woodwork is finished on the ground floor, and the addition is back on schedule."

Raeburn smiled dryly. "So nice to find that things are going well for once."

The man nodded as if taking the comment in stride. "Of course, of course. But come! You must see what we did since you last visited."

"I'll show myself around, if you don't mind, Harter. And her ladyship as well. I'll find you again when I need you."

Harter gave Victoria a preoccupied half bow as he rubbed his hands on his apron. "I see. In that case, thy grace, my lady, I'll just be off . . ."

And with that, he was gone, passing through a doorway from which the sounds of hammering filtered into the room.

Raeburn released Victoria's arm and moved deeper into the room. "Poke and prod at whatever you'd like." He cast a wry expression over his shoulder. "Nothing here is dangerous, you know."

Victoria realized that her uncertainty and disconcertment were written on her face and schooled her features into a more bland expression. "I've never been bitten by a rug before, but since this house is yours, one can not help but be cautious. Unpredictability appears to be the most fundamental element of your character."

Raeburn just snorted without turning around from his examination of the paneling on the opposite wall.

Victoria gave a mental shrug and decided that she might as well "poke and prod" if he was going to ignore her.

She stood at the midpoint of a long, narrow chamber, once a hall, now divided by furniture and rugs into two distinct parlors decorated in tones of scarlet, purple, and umber. *Like a Yorkshire sunset,* she thought, remembering the dazzling view as she stepped off the train at Leeds.

The room's scale should have been intimidating, yet there was something oddly comfortable and intimate about it, a well-worn feeling that lingered despite the pristine furnishings and the gleaming, newly polished oak wainscoting.

She crossed into the parlor opposite the one that Raeburn was examining, noting the heavy, simple lines of the furniture and the archaic paintings that hung on the walls. But the most striking feature was the narrow stained glass windows that flanked the fireplaces at the ends of the hall, four jewel-toned glowing pictures of slender, long-faced women with intricately draped robes and tumbling hair. They were also the only unobstructed source of light for the room, for the other windows were all close-swathed.

"It is very different," she said. That was certainly an understatement. "Most people would have made the house lighter, more delicate. This seems positively medieval."

She turned to face the duke in time to see a humorless smile flash across his face. "Delicacy doesn't suit me.

This does." He paused as if deciding whether to add more before speaking again. "I met a young architect by the name of Webb two years ago. He's idealistic to a fault, believing that he's part of some artistic revolution, but I like his work. Simplicity, naturalistic beauty, and medievalism are the guiding principles of his little group— the Pre-Raphaelite Brotherhood of architecture and design, I suppose they could be called. I am too cynical to be excited by their ideas, but I hired his company to design a house, not to inspire me."

"How practical," Victoria murmured, vaguely disappointed and only half believing. But what had she been expecting? An enthusiastic endorsement of his personal aesthetic? Still, feeling that she was shortchanging the house, she added, "It is beautiful, though. Not what I would have expected, but beautiful nevertheless."

Raeburn made no reply as he walked a circuit of the other parlor. "Harter was right," was all he said when he finally spoke. "It is finished." He waved toward the wide doorway opposite the front door. "Let's see the rest."

Victoria led the way and emerged between two more rooms, mirrors of the last, but this time set up as a salon and a dining room in rust, gold, and midnight blue with a dozen heavy-draped windows along the back wall. Small fixed transoms held more stained glass, this time curling with flowering and fruiting vines. Victoria had the strange feeling that they were as much for light as for beauty, as if Raeburn expected the curtains of the large windows below to stay drawn. There was a closed doorway at the end of the dining room, and another opposite it, bright with sunlight, through which a skeleton of raw beams was visible—the addition.

Raeburn stalked a slow perimeter of the rooms while Victoria watched, puzzled. She had the growing sensation that the house was a portrait of the duke, done in such precise detail that every idiosyncrasy in his nature was laid bare, if only she knew how to look at it.

She shook her head, giving up as Raeburn returned to her side. He escorted her to the staircase that ran up the long wall of the salon.

"Naïveté," he said musingly as they mounted the first step side by side. Victoria stiffened and pressed her lips together at the reminder of their earlier discussion but said nothing. "I doubt I've ever had such a luxury. I have suffered frustration but never disappointment."

"If one's expectations are low enough, one can never be disappointed," she returned tartly, "though that is no way to live."

Raeburn cast her a sidelong glance. "Lady Victoria, you surprise me. I thought all your optimism should be dead by now."

She smiled coldly. "Optimism, perhaps, but not expectations."

He made an incredulous noise. "To have expectations is optimistic."

He was attacking her with crude philosophy, trying to sneak under the door when hammering down the walls would not work. Victoria's eyes narrowed. Two could play at that game. "Then not even you can claim to a true pessimist, for you are too practical a man to have embarked on such an ambitious project as this house unless you expected it to come to completion."

Raeburn did not deign to reply. They reached the top of the stairs in silence, and he released her and took the lead.

There was dust in the air, and the sounds of hammering were loud and close. Raeburn strode down the central corridor without pausing to see if she followed, stopping at every doorway to look in, exchanging a few words if there were any workers within or surveying the room with a single, penetrating glance if there were not. He acted as if Victoria had disappeared, and she took advantage of his rather studious inattention to proceed more leisurely, guessing at the functions of the rooms as she went by.

The first was a wide, windowless room with a doorway that went through a series of two small rooms to another large room that overlooked the back garden—the bedchambers for the duke and duchess. The nursery suite was equally recognizable. Then there was a series of rooms all in a row—bedrooms, probably, and two adjoining rooms that could only be the schoolroom and governess' chamber.

Had it been designed with Raeburn's unnamed ladylove in mind? And was he still hoping to use it for his family? The thought was strange to her, the image of the duke surrounded by cherubic children ludicrous, almost impossible. And yet the undeniable reality of the floor plan confronted Victoria not only with the possibility that he had entertained such a vision but with the certainty of it.

Victoria caught up to Raeburn at the far end of the hall, where two small chambers sat empty with pipes jutting out of the walls.

"I've had two years of hip-baths," Raeburn explained, suddenly choosing to acknowledge her presence once again, "and come spring, I hope to have my last."

"Water closets?" Victoria asked. Her family's town house in London had such luxuries, but at Rushworth, they still had to make do with chamber pots and bathwater hauled up from the kitchen.

"Indeed," he said. "A small indulgence." He turned. "And now I must check the progress of the annex."

"What are they building there?" Victoria asked, curious despite herself.

"There's to be a sitting room, a library, and a study. It will mirror the kitchen wing on the other side, except the sitting room will have French windows leading out to the terrace."

French windows—another bit of proof that the house was not being prepared for him alone. Raeburn's expression was closed, but Victoria thought she saw a flicker of pain pass over it, if only for a fraction of a second before he turned his face away. It awakened an echoing pang within her, one she did not dare examine too closely.

"This house is very important to you, isn't it?" Victoria asked softly. "You might have found the young architect Webb to design it, but he designed it as much *with* you as *for* you, yes?" She spoke slowly, working through the thought as she went. "It's important because you put so much of yourself into it—even your dreams, although you didn't realize it until too late."

Even at a quarter profile, she could see the tightening of his jaw. "And?" he prompted tightly, as if inviting a blow he knew was inevitable.

A blow she had no intention of delivering.

"And I like it," she said, feeling almost shy.

He turned to face her, surprise passing over his face, followed by a flash of a smile that tugged at the corner of his lips—not the dry grimace she'd seen before, but a real, if infinitesimal smile. For once, his shifting hazel eyes lost their hard, self-mocking glint and shone warm and green.

"It pleases me to hear you say that," he said, and he seemed almost as surprised at making this confession as she was hearing it. But he regained his equilibrium first, covering his moment of openness with a devilish grin. Taking her gloved hands in his, he pulled her to him.

Victoria felt the blush creeping up her cheeks, and panic welled up from somewhere deep inside to choke her. Seduction, yes—she knew where she was with seduction. But his eyes still held a warmth that was not entirely sensual, and it left her feeling tongue-tied and stupid. And afraid.

She jerked her hands back. "Your grace, I did not say it to please you. I said it because it's true." She turned and strode away, back down the length of the corridor.

Raeburn caught up with her at the head of the stairs. He grabbed her elbow, and she whirled to face him.

His gaze was hard and speculative. "Now I am beginning to understand," he murmured, his voice barely above a whisper. He brushed a stray strand of hair from her face with a calloused finger, and she shivered.

"Let me go."

"All in good time," he countered, but he released her immediately. As they descended the stairway side by side, he turned the conversation back to the renovations as if nothing unusual had passed between them, his voice dropping back into a casual tone so easily that it left her feeling lost and disoriented.

At the base of the stairs, he stopped and looked at her, an ironic twist of his mouth telling her that his thoughts were in a very different place than his words. Victoria hesitated on the last step, returning his gaze levelly—or rather, at a downward angle, for with the advantage of the stair, she was a good two inches taller than he. But when he spoke, his words did not match the challenge in his expression.

"I must talk to Harter now, your ladyship. I will meet you at the carriage."

And thus she was dismissed.

Victoria glared futilely at his broad retreating back. He probably expected her to go out to the carriage now and wait for him. Rebellion stirred within her, and she strode across the width of the room to a door placed in the exterior wall. A small push opened it, and she was facing the back garden of the Dowager House.

Or rather, what might have once been the garden. Now a tangled, trodden mass of weeds reached up to the door, and Victoria could barely make out the shape of a neglected fountain among the mass of furze that choked it. Beyond was a tangle of brush where a copse of trees had gone wild. The sound of hammering and sawing was loud, but the workmen were out of sight around the corner of the house, and the stillness of the garden made it seem as if the noise was coming from another world.

Holding her skirts high, she stepped tentatively to the ground. Her scarlet-clad calves above her shoes were immediately soaked by the dew-weighted grass, but abruptly, Victoria didn't care. The rain-heavy wind touched her face, teasing her, and suddenly she wanted to run across the ruined garden, dash into the coppice, and shimmy up the nearest tree trunk as if she were ten again.

Madness. She knew it was madness, but she let it take her anyhow, laughing and twirling across the weeds, disregarding the damp and her fine skirts in the sheer exhilaration of unchecked movement. Raeburn's fine skirts, she reminded herself, her smile broadening. If he wanted to watch out for them, let him. She stopped and reached her hands toward the overcast sky, took in deep draughts of sweet air damp with the promise of rain. How long had it been since she'd done anything so spontaneous, so unrestrained? Except her daily rides at Rushworth, explained away by their constitutional benefit, she could not remember a time when she had just let herself *be*.

She ripped off her gloves, tore off her black bonnet, and threw them to the ground, turning her face to the sky to catch the first drops of rain. For fifteen years, she had been unassailably respectable, and what had it earned her? She'd had power of a sort—to shape the running of the earldom, to make and break social careers through a timely change to a dinner party list.

But influence at what price? Watching every word, every smile, staying in the shadows, hiding from unwanted suitors under grotesque dresses—unwanted not because she had become sexless but because she dare not indulge in even the most tame courtship. Knowing that she was a ruined woman, and that any whispered word might hurl her into infamy . . .

She clutched her skirt in both fists, the soft pastel silk bunching under her hands—the first of its kind she'd worn since the . . . travesty that had nearly torn her life apart. She couldn't call it a tragedy; it was not noble enough for that. She felt the fabric pull taut, and she paused, uncertain whether she wanted to revel in its sensuousness or shred it with her bare hands. She dropped the skirt. For six more days, it wouldn't matter what she wore. For six more days, it wouldn't matter what she did—except to Raeburn.

"Lady Victoria."

Abruptly, the duke's voice broke into her contemplation as if summoned by her thoughts. Victoria turned to face him, and she felt herself blush, abashed and chagrined to be caught traipsing bareheaded among the weeds in a private moment she'd meant for no one else to share.

But there was no censure in his expression as he stood, close-wrapped, in the doorway. There was desire, and amusement, and something akin to sadness or envy, but no condemnation.

"I thought I might see what progress you had made in the garden," she offered as an excuse.

Raeburn nodded, not in acceptance of the claim but in acknowledgment, and motioned for her to join him. Suddenly subdued, she scooped up her bonnet and obeyed. She realized this was the brightest light in which she'd ever seen him, and she took the chance to study him as she linked her arm through his proffered arm and stepped through the doorway. His face seemed older than it had in the shadowed rooms of the Dowager House and the even darker chambers of Raeburn Court. There were deep lines down the sides of his cheeks, and the skin across his nose was rough. From his avoidance of the sun, Victoria would have expected his face to be smooth and pale for his years, but instead, he looked as weather-beaten as any shepherd. Oddly, it enhanced his idiosyncratic attractiveness instead of detracting from it and accentuated the contrast between him and the parlor gentlemen she was used to associating with. Certainly no parlor gentleman's arm had been as strong, no step as sure as his was. But he made her feel neither small nor weak but energized, as if his vitality were a challenge and an inspiration wrapped into one, and at the same time strangely attuned to him, both as a man and as a person. That discovery should have troubled her, and she knew it would when she considered it later. But at the moment, she floated in a bubble of calm, and she did not want to prick it too soon.

They walked through the house side by side, and at the

front door, she stopped to tie her hat primly on her head again.

"No," Raeburn said, lifting away the bonnet as soon as it touched her curls. "No. I like you better without."

Victoria started to remonstrate, paused, and thought better of it. It seemed ridiculous to worry about such a small point of propriety when the entire week was a massive breech of almost every rule polite society had ever known. So she dropped her gloves into her bonnet and allowed them both to hang from the crepe ribbons as the duke escorted her into the waiting carriage.

This time when she settled back into the darkness, there was no feeling of awkwardness between them. The carriage rocked as the footman climbed onto the back, then jolted as the horses stepped forward, away from the Dowager House. A house that had been planned for the footfalls of children, for the comforts of a husband and wife and their blooming brood.

"You planned the house when you still wanted to marry her, didn't you?" Victoria said softly.

"Yes," the duke said. His answer was brief but not abrupt.

Victoria allowed the silence to stretch between them.

Finally, Raeburn sighed. "We were to be married as soon as it was finished. She did not like the plans, I fear—she thought the house too modest for a duchess, and she never cared for the sensibilities of the aesthetes. I did not know how much she disliked it, though, until it was far too late, and even then, I never had the desire to change it. It seemed right somehow."

"You must have loved her very much." To love and lose—wasn't that the way of the world?

His laugh was bitter. "Leticia? Never. She was—is—beautiful, and I admired her, certainly, in the way a man might admire a fine piece of art. 'For earth too dear . . .' But no, I didn't love her. I loved the idea of her, perhaps, or her image, but not the woman. I don't think I've loved anything as concrete as a woman for nigh on a dozen years."

So he had loved, once. Victoria wondered what had happened. Now, though, he seemed to want to pretend he was incapable of emotion. And Victoria could not believe that.

"You love the house," she pointed out, the easiest defense. "It is hard to find something more concrete, even if it is inanimate."

"Houses do not judge, nor do they despise. It is easy to love a house." His manner was offhand, but there was a pain beneath the words that cut her.

Impulsively, she reached out and found his hands in the darkness. They were cold through his gloves, but his grasp was sure.

Though Victoria's action had been ingenuous, his grip's solidity in the blind void of the carriage was so potently sensual it sent a sliver of warmth shimmering through her, followed by a sudden tightening awareness of his body, invisible but so close. She heard Raeburn catch his breath as he felt it, too. For a single, breathless moment, they sat frozen, hands clasped, and then Raeburn pulled her to him.

Blindly, their mouths met. Victoria's crinoline flattened against Raeburn's legs, but she ignored it. There was only room in her mind for the stubble-roughened cheek under her hand, for the hard-softness that were his lips on hers, for the warm taste of his tongue teasing her mouth. Her forehead bumped against the brim of his hat, and she pushed it back impatiently. Her fingers snaked beneath the silk scarf to twine in the dark curls on the back of his neck. They were fine and silky, like the locks of a child, and Victoria made the comparison with the feeling of one who'd had a revelation.

The carriage jerked to a stop. Victoria allowed her momentum to push her back into her seat, but she did not remove her hand from Raeburn's even when the footman opened the door and let down the steps. The duke twitched his scarf back into place and adjusted his hat, then he let her go—was it her imagination, or was he reluctant?—and stepped out of the carriage into a misting drizzle. Victoria followed, taking his arm, and he led her quickly across the three paces into the manor.

There, the lingering, tenuous sense of affinity was severed by the approach of the housekeeper.

"Yer were gone such a time!" she cried as she bustled up, a drably clad maid in her wake. "Did thoo keep thy hat on, thy grace? Only thee knows how I do worry, silly old woman that I am." She threw her hands up. "And look at her ladyship! The skirts! The bonnet! What has happened to yer both?"

"Nothing at all, Mrs. Peasebody," Raeburn said dryly, handing his coat, hat, scarf, and cane to the maid.

"Peg, thoo ought to have seen to her ladyship first," Mrs. Peasebody scolded, taking Victoria's bonnet from her hand and tugging the wrap off her shoulders without waiting for Victoria to give it to her.

"It's quite all right," Victoria assured her, but the woman continued scolding the maid as they both retreated into the inner recesses of the house.

She stood awkwardly next to the duke, nothing remaining of the tie between them but the awareness that it had been there, half relieved and half regretful that it was gone.

Raeburn raised an eyebrow, his expression perfectly

neutral. "I have work I must do. I fear there is little in the way of diversion in this house, but if you summon a maid, I'm sure she shall be most happy to show you to the library."

"Thank you," Victoria said, for lack of a better reply.

He frowned. "You can find your chamber on your own?"

Victoria wondered what he'd do with her if she lied and claimed not to, but she answered truthfully enough. "Yes, though it is, perhaps, the only room about which I could make such navigational claims."

Raeburn nodded curtly. "Then I shall send Fane to escort you to supper. Until then, Circe." He turned on his heel and left.

Chapter Eight

Byron knew he was close; so close he could almost taste her secrets. Just a little more time, and the solution for the puzzling woman might be in his grasp.

And yet, did he really want to know?

He glared at the door in front of him. If Victoria's character could be explained away by some dull tale from her past, if all her complexities were given a simple solution, he would be . . . disappointed. Once there was no mystery, there would be no reason for interest, and the remaining days of her stay would stretch out into pleasant if routine debauchery.

But his curiosity was not diminished by that possibility, only stimulated by the chance that there was more to her than could be reduced to insignificance by whatever old pain she held inside, more to her than the embittered consequences of a drama that had played out years before.

But it was not a desire for entertainment that had caused their last conversation to haunt him all afternoon, that had now driven him to her door, unable to wait to see her until the evening. He felt something between them, a connection that was different from lust and growing stronger with every hour in her company. It was a feeling entirely foreign to him, but one that he was becoming accustomed to of late.

For more than a decade, he'd haunted every seedy pub, attended every questionable party, and patronized every dingy brothel of London's fast set. He'd kept a succession of mistresses in a little flat on Baker Street, and he'd dressed and behaved with the flamboyance of a born reprobate. Mysterious rumors surrounded the heir presumptive of Raeburn, as he'd known they inevitably would, but instead of shying away from them, he deliberately exaggerated them until his long cloaks and eccentric hours became as much a part of his image as his roughened features and black hair. Until Leticia had shattered his world.

He'd told the truth when he'd said he hadn't loved her. That was the most ironic part. No, it was not passion but insulted pride that had caused his furious, precipitate flight from London, riding hell-for-leather north for three nights without so much as a single manservant for company. Then, still half-mad with fury, he'd sent the rash letter that dismissed his entire staff . . .

He shook his head to clear it of those memories and knocked.

"Come in." The reply was immediate, and Byron pushed open the door.

Victoria was sitting in the window, holding a piece of paper up to the light of the drizzling afternoon. The sharp features of her face were softened by the tendrils of hair that had escaped during their trip to the Dowager House and now curled in a wispy halo around her face in the gray, oblique sunlight that filtered into the room. Sitting, without the advantage of her height, she looked less solid, more delicate, but just as damnably desirable as she had been in the blackness of the coach. She straightened when he crossed to her, as if sensing her vulnerability.

Byron said nothing as he reached past her and twitched the curtains closed. He caught her sideways look, but she kept her silence for a few long seconds. Then she sighed in the dimness and waved the paper.

"My mother," she said. "She wrote it the day I left."

"Oh?"

She shrugged. "The usual response when I have done something that she doesn't like but that her sense tells her is for the best. Apologies tempered with a splash of indignant self-pity." She hesitated, then passed it to him. "There is nothing private, and you might find it amusing."

He skimmed the letter, his eyes well accustomed to reading in partial darkness. *My most darling daughter . . . I should not have remonstrated so strongly . . . I am an old woman, you know, and sometimes we are a bit silly . . . We all miss you terribly . . . your loving Mamma.* When he reached the end, he gave a snort, but when he raised his gaze to meet Victoria's, he found that she was smiling softly, almost tenderly, at the piece of stationery.

"You really do love her, don't you?" he said with a pang of envy. His own mother had been kind but distant; he hadn't spoken to her since his great-uncle's funeral, when he assured her that her income and house would remain intact for her lifetime. His father he could scarcely remember.

"She's my mother," she said simply. Then she added, with a brittle kind of lightness, "She's not in half the need of me that she pretends, but I think it's her own way of consoling me, of giving me a purpose since I never wed."

"And why didn't you?"

Victoria gave him a sharp look, but he returned it

levelly, keeping his rising sense of anticipation carefully locked away. This was it: the moment when she would confess all or shy away, most likely for good.

"You of all people should know," she said finally.

Byron sat on the stone bench built into the wall across from hers. All he wanted to feel at that moment was the excitement of a challenge, but the expectancy that thrummed through his every muscle had no edge of thrill in it. Instead, he felt a sympathetic kind of tension, as if the forces that had held Victoria captive for however long now seized him, too, and the only way to dispel their power was to know their source.

He reached across the space that separated them and touched her cheek. Her eyes were round, luminous, and filled with a pain that went into his gut.

Victoria closed her eyes, leaning into his touch—grateful just to let herself go, if only for a little while. He brushed his thumb across her cheek. The caress had no hint of seduction in it, yet she felt her body respond to him, and for once, she was glad of its disobedient impulses, of its freedom that broke past every restraint. If only this moment would never end . . .

"Who was it?" Raeburn asked softly. "I know that you want to tell me, whether you choose to acknowledge it. You invited this subject too blatantly for me to believe otherwise. So tell me, who was first?"

The world came crashing back, jarring Victoria from her false repose. She jerked back and opened her eyes, looking into Raeburn's unreadable face.

Lord, but he was right. She wanted to tell him—to tell someone at last—but it was so, so hard. The old bitter caution took advantage of her vacillation, seizing her tongue before she could stop it. "First, your grace? How delicately you put it. How many lovers do you think I've had?"

"Who was it before me, then, your ladyship?" The title held a scornful note, mocking her formality.

"It's of no consequence." No, she did not want to tell him, she decided abruptly. Perhaps someone, someday, if she must, but not this cold duke whom she hardly knew.

"If it's of no consequence, you shan't mind telling me." His voice grew deeper, softer, and she saw a hint of compassion creep into his eyes. "I won't betray you, Victoria. Trust me."

She opened her mouth to refuse him again, but then she shut it because she realized that she did trust him, however strange it might seem. Finally, she sighed. "His name was Walter. He was the oldest son of an earl, and we were very much in love—or at least, we thought we were." She smiled slightly and shook her head. "In retrospect, it was as much self-absorbed infatuation and lust as anything."

Raeburn traced the line of her nose, resting his finger briefly on its tip. "You loved the way you felt when he looked at you, when he touched you, when he whispered into your ear."

Victoria looked up at him ruefully. "Aren't all young passions painfully the same? I loved him as much as I was able, I suppose, but I fear it wasn't the kind of love it should have been. He was twenty and I only seventeen, and although our parents had reservations about an alliance at such a young age, we still became engaged. Once we were betrothed . . . well, the wedding was only two months away, and parents tend to turn a bit of a blind eye once a betrothal has been announced, so one thing led to another, and we became lovers in every sense of the word. We met in gardens, in back parlors, even once in a stable. Then, only two weeks before the wedding, Walter rode out to his family estates because his father was ill."

"And he found another woman."

Victoria shook her head. "Nothing so romantic. He had a cold when he left, and it turned into pneumonia, and he died the day before we were to be wed." She snorted. "Something so . . . banal to destroy one's life, don't you think? How much more suitable to have a sufficiently theatrical hunting accident or some freak mischance abroad. Instead, I was bereft by a cold."

"You can't tell me that your heart never recovered."

She smiled at the memory of her younger self. "At the time, I thought I would not survive. But though I was left heartbroken, or as broken as such a self-centered heart could be, the more indelible result of the liaison was the unhappy fact that I was left ruined, as well." She looked at him obliquely. "I miscarried our child a month after his death. No one ever knew."

"And since then—"

"The armor, as you called it. Yes. I didn't want to go out into society again until I was nineteen, and even then, I dressed in mourning. Mourning for Walter, but even more—though I'd never have admitted it then, not even to myself—mourning for me. I was young and resilient and might have been back dancing and laughing the very next season, but I had lost my only chance at marriage, because now I had a secret: I was unmarried and no virgin. I comforted myself by pretending privately that I really was Walter's widow who had buried her love with her husband, but there was a more ugly truth. Few men would take me as I was, and I did not have the courage to risk ruination by confessing my past to those who might have. And so I became the Wakefield spinster." She shrugged slightly. "There is nothing brave or glamorous in my story, and much that is cowardly and tawdry, but I have accepted it. It is mine."

Raeburn traced the line of her jaw with one rough finger. "And do you miss him at all?" There was a strange note in his voice, of regret or even pain, and Victoria tilted her head to look squarely up at him.

"Walter? Goodness, no. I still feel for him, that his life was cut so short. But for me?" She smiled humorlessly. "He was a good boy who would have grown into a fine man, but we were both too callow to have the depth of feeling that would result in a lifelong grief. He was in another life, one that I lost. I've made many choices since then, and the ones I made with him are too distant to rue."

"And what about now?" Raeburn asked, his voice hardly above a whisper. "Will you rue this choice?" His hand descended to cup her breast through the silk of her dress.

Victoria's breath caught. "Ask me in another fifteen years."

Then Raeburn's mouth met her own and ended the need for speech.

When they finally separated, he took her hand and squeezed it once, then stood, his eyes hooded with something she could not decipher. "I will see you tonight."

And then she was alone.

Once again, a clock somewhere struck nine as Fane led Victoria through the echoing hallways, but this time, he traveled up instead of down. The rooms they passed through seemed vaguely familiar, as if she'd seen them in a dream or another life, but it wasn't until she was facing a door at the top of a spiral staircase that her suspicions bloomed into certainty.

It was the tower room.

A surge of emotions battled within her—disappointment, resignation, titillation. After what had happened in the Unicorn Room that afternoon, she had expected some sort of change from the night before. She didn't know whether she was angry or glad that there appeared to be none.

Opening the door, Fane announced her as decorously as if she were entering a grand salon. Raeburn looked up from a low table in front of the little stove, dismissing the servant and inviting her in with the same wave.

Branching candelabra sat at the center of the table, bathing the room in a soft glow. The hard planes of Raeburn's face were strangely gentled by it. He leaned back on his hands as he regarded her, his unbuttoned waistcoat falling open. His coat lay on the floor beside him, and his shirtsleeves were rolled up and his collar unfastened, revealing the shadowed hollow of his throat. His bearing was both indolent and tightly coiled, like a half-slumbering panther, and he radiated a hungry sensuality that seemed to bridge the distance between them to brush against her skin.

She crossed slowly toward him, feeling like she was wading ever deeper into an oriental fantasy. The room looked even more exotic and garish than it had the night before, as if it had been taken from the fevered imagination of an illustrator for the most risqué translation of the *Arabian Nights' Entertainments*. In the light of the single candle, there had only been a feeling of Eastern extravagance, but now, the riot of red, blue, green, and gold was revealed. Out of the score of pillows mounded on the floor, the dozen rugs, and three divans, not one repeated a pattern.

"Join me," Raeburn ordered, stretching his long legs out in front of him as he tilted his face up toward hers.

"Though you might want to leave that contraption behind"—he waved to her crinoline-rounded skirts—
"since I doubt it will be anything but awkward when
eating like a Turk."

"I shall manage, I'm sure," Victoria said, matching his
light tone and ignoring the small thrill of anticipation and
dread that shot through her. Was there some trace of
recognition of the confidence she had shared with him
that afternoon? She couldn't tell. She dropped one of the
pillows on the other side of the table and positioned herself over it before sitting carefully as her skirts billowed
around her. "Am I to be honored with your personal attentions tonight instead of the flawless service of your
most excellent staff?"

The corner of Raeburn's mouth quirked, acknowledging her jibe, but he responded coolly. "Their lack of pol-
ish is as much my fault as theirs, and as much my
lamented great-uncle's as mine. Two decades of senility
do not lead to excellent domestics. He left me a score
when it would take at least three times that number to
keep the house." He uncovered one of the dishes, revealing cold tongue, pallid boiled vegetables, and some
sort of potatoes that looked grayish and unappetizing.
But the smell that wafted out was at least wholesome, if
not tantalizing.

The mundane nature of their conversation and repast
seemed at odds with the gaudy surroundings and the sensual awareness that tensed the air between them, but it
was obscurely reassuring, too. "And you've done nothing
to rectify the matter in the year you've been duke?"

Raeburn shrugged, removing the lids of the other three
dishes. "I've devoted my time to renovating the Dowager
House and attempting to make the place profitable
again." His lips twisted as he served her a generous

portion from each dish, and he headed off the obvious question. "My own cook went back to Essex to tend to her mother, my butler married, and I dismissed the rest of the staff at my London town house." His tone did not encourage her to inquire why.

Victoria took a forkful of assorted boiled vegetables to cover the awkward silence that settled between them, fumbling for a new subject before the conversation foundered entirely. It shouldn't matter if it did; after all, the embarrassment properly belonged to her host, and she had nothing at stake to make her feel chagrined. But somehow it did matter, so she rescued the discussion with all the grace she could muster. "I shouldn't think that it would be hard to make a profit from such extensive lands."

Raeburn shook his head, but the tightness dissolved from his face, and Victoria felt a sympathetic loosening in muscles she hadn't realized she had tensed. "I can't even find tenants for two tracts, and I've had to cut the rent on the others. There's not the money in wool there used to be, and the Raeburn flocks are poor at best. I've brought in some merinos from Spain to improve the long-haired flocks and Irish rams to improve the short-haired ones, but it will be years before I see the results." His face darkened. "Meanwhile, Stoneswold and Weatherlea are half deserted because the weaving is all done in factories in Leeds. The weavers' families have all left or been reduced to menial labor."

Victoria realized that he cared—not just about property and income, but about the common villagers, too. There was perhaps something medieval in his concern, but if it was stained with feudal overtones, it had a certain chivalric element as well and was rather touching. "Oh," she said and took another bite of the vegetables. They dissolved unpleasantly on her tongue, and she made a face despite herself.

Raeburn raised an eyebrow. "Still not accustomed to plain Yorkshire cooking, I see," he said.

Victoria smiled ruefully. "No," she agreed, thinking wistfully of the French chef at Rushworth. *Rushworth.* Its cool, orderly limestone façade seemed like a dream now. Much more real was Raeburn himself, twirling his fork idly and watching her with half-lidded eyes. A ghost of a smile played about his lips, and she wondered what he was thinking as a trickle of warmth slid up her spine. Not that it mattered. What mattered was that they would enjoy each other again that night, without fears or regrets, and after five more nights, they would part ways forever. And she could forget whatever confessions she'd made in a moment of weakness. Just a week of carnal indulgence and a reward at the end, and back to society as if she'd never left. The thought should have been comforting, but instead, it stirred a coldness in the pit of her stomach that leached away even the heat of Raeburn's presence.

She shook her head to dispel that thought and took another bite of the over-boiled food, followed by a long draught of wine. "At least your cellar cannot be faulted," she said, attempting to keep the conversation light when she felt anything but.

Raeburn didn't seem to notice her unease as he held the dark red liquid up to the candle flame. "I should hope not. That's the one thing I did send for from London, and it took a month of settling before everything was drinkable after it arrived."

Victoria slid gratefully into the new avenue of dialogue, beginning a discussion of vintages and transport methods that lasted through the rest of the meal. She had wanted to distract her own thoughts as much as keep

Raeburn to safe topics, but when she set down her fork after the last bite, she knew that she had failed. She felt troubled by the man who reclined so nonchalantly across from her, and she didn't know why, which was the most disturbing thing of all. She could have told herself it was Raeburn's sheer physicality that was bothering her, or the hideously overdecorated room, or even the confidences she had made, but it would not be the whole truth.

"Filling, if not palate-beguiling," she remarked, setting her napkin down beside the plate.

Raeburn smiled mysteriously. "There's still more." He gathered the plates and dishes and set them aside, and from the darkness beside the small stove, he produced a final dish with new plates and silverware. With a flourish, he uncovered the top.

"A crumble?" Victoria asked in surprise, looking at the pastry-topped fruit dish between them.

"The best peach crumble north of Manchester," he agreed. "And it happens to be the one thing the cook makes well."

Victoria looked at him doubtfully as he put a generous scoop on her plate. He chuckled at her expression and dipped his own fork into the dessert.

"Try it," he coaxed, bringing the fruit to her lips.

Victoria hesitated a moment, sensing again that strange tension within her that had everything and nothing to do with the flutter of warmth his gaze kindled in her belly. Raeburn's expression turned amused, and she automatically met the implied challenge by opening her mouth.

The cinnamon-rich syrup flowed onto her tongue, and when she bit down, the firm peach flesh yielded in a rush of juice. "Oh!" she said when she'd swallowed. "That's lovely." The taste of it lingered, sweet and enticing. She reached for her own fork, but Raeburn put a restraining hand on her wrist.

"No," he said. "I shall do it for both of us." Watching her with hooded eyes, he raised a forkful of the crumble to his mouth and took it slowly between his teeth in a way that made her catch her breath and blush like a girl of half her years. A smile quirked the corner of his mouth at her reaction.

That was enough to swamp her uneasiness in a wave of pricked pride, goading her into outdoing his performance when he brought the next bite to her lips. She ate it slowly, luxuriantly, curling her tongue around the peach slice before taking each bite. Raeburn's expression grew sharper, and when she licked away a bit that had dribbled from the corner of her mouth, it turned to raw hunger and his hand tightened around her wrist. An answering warmth spread from her center to suffuse her body, and she was suddenly conscious of the calluses on his palm against her skin, of the constriction of her corset and the texture in her dress.

"If you continue in the same manner, I fear you shall not finish Mrs. Macdougal's fine dessert," he said with an underlying intensity that belied his light tone.

"Who says that would be a bad thing?" Her voice caught slightly and tumbled out high and strained.

"'Twas never I."

Victoria's sensation of strangeness returned with full force, disquiet mingled now with a feeling that was almost like pain. Impulsively, she disengaged herself from Raeburn's hand and lifted it to her mouth. She held it there for a long moment, fingertips to lips, as if she could breathe the essence of him, isolate it and dissect it into its components and so discover what in him was troubling her so. She pressed her lips to his palm, brushing her tongue across it, learning every fold and crease of his skin as his breath grew fast and ragged.

It was useless. There was nothing there but mute flesh—suggestive even in its uncompromising bluntness but devoid of the answers she sought. When she released him, he curled his hand closed as if catching her kiss.

"Fortune-tellers claim they can read a life from the lines and creases on a palm." Victoria shook her head and smiled slightly. "I can read nothing except that you must not wear gloves as often as gentlemen generally do."

Across the table, Raeburn's expression was both distantly amused and strangely sad. "What would you read? My fate is hidden from such blatant sciences. They say I carry mine in my blood, which no one can read."

"Secrets upon secrets, like the little Russian dolls that sit inside each other. I'm sure that even Mrs. Peasebody has her own dark shadows in her past, if only we knew them."

Raeburn's lips quirked. "You puncture my self-importance so skillfully."

"And remind me that my own is misplaced." Victoria stood abruptly and turned away, more discomfited by the train of thoughts that followed her reply than she cared to show. She had allowed herself to believe, on some basic level, that she mattered, that her small story made some minute difference in the world. And looking at Raeburn's smile, she knew that she had fooled herself.

She crossed to one of the arching windows that looked outward, away from the buttresses and balconies of Raeburn Court. Through her own reflection, she could make out the stony declivity encircled by the hedge and the white scar of the drive that led up from the lane. The moon shone through wispy clouds, turning the pools of low fog to opalescent fleece. It was desolate but eerily peaceful, not at all foreboding as it had seemed in the midst of the storm's fury. Yet a niggling sliver of intuition warned her that she had been much safer the night before, when she could be carried away by madness and blame it on the wind and rain.

Victoria turned back to face the duke. He was watching her, his expression inscrutable in the highlights and shadows of the candlelight. He lounged carelessly, one leg cocked, the other straight, and she could see the outline of his muscles where his shirt was pulled taut across his chest. If there had not been a glimmer of something human behind his haughty mask, Victoria could not have controlled the iciness that crept over her. But there was something—wry sadness? poignant self-mockery?—and it dissolved the knot of coldness into nothing.

She took a breath, surprised to find it slightly unsteady. "We are two old frights, aren't we?"

Raeburn's mouth creased in a frown, and he began to shake his head. But then he paused, seeming to catch himself, and shrugged. "Perhaps. Are you always so direct, your ladyship?" His tone was teasing but not without some exasperation. "It seems that not even one's closest and most precious delusions are safe when you are nigh."

Victoria smiled thinly. "I am better at self-scrutiny than self-pity, I fear, and I tend to extend it to others. I've lost the habit of mercy, if I ever had it."

"And forgiveness?" Raeburn's stare was suddenly too perceptive.

Victoria shook it off. "There is no one to forgive. If I bleed, then I put my hand in the way of the knife." She leveled a pointed look at the duke. "I am rarely cut twice."

"No," he murmured, his expression softening. "I suppose not."

He stood and skirted the table, stopping in front of her. Victoria held herself stiffly, tilting her head up the necessary two inches to meet his gaze directly. The lines across his forehead and the grooves down his cheeks were thrown into shadow, making him look older than his years. Older, and sadder, and she realized with a shock that some of the sadness seemed to be for her.

She felt like she had been taken up and shaken. Being dismissed, manipulated, taken for granted, even admired or desired—all those things she was comfortable with; all those things were almost impersonal reactions to the way she chose to present herself to the world. But there was nothing impersonal in Raeburn's gaze now. It seemed to bore straight through her, into the most secret corners of her heart, and far, far worse, it seemed to ache for what it found there. Never had she felt so exposed, and never again did she want to—much less in front of the haughty duke.

Raeburn reached for her, grasping her by the elbows, but she jerked back and turned her head away.

"I do not need nor deserve anyone's pity," she rasped. "Least of all yours."

Raeburn wrapped an arm around her waist tightly enough that she'd have to fight to break free. She didn't, for he captured her chin in his other hand and tilted her head to face him fully, and the intensity of his expression sent a bolt of pain through her that robbed her of her ability to resist. If there had been even a hint of mockery or censure or condescension, she could have tossed her head and pulled away with a cold laugh. But there was only the same sadness, and she found she had no defenses against it. Awareness of him trickled involuntarily through every inch of her body, more poignant than uncomplicated carnality, burning her and weakening her at once.

"Look at me and tell me you do not need it," he said tensely. "Not pity. I think of you too highly to offer that. Sympathy, kindness, compassion—tell me you don't need those."

"I can't," Victoria whispered, the words dragged from her. Why couldn't she lie to this man, as she had to so many others? Why couldn't she just turn away? Maybe she had seen too much, felt too much of him that day through the house he was building. Whatever it was, she could not find it in herself to shut him out. "But still I do not deserve them."

A painful, lopsided smile flitted across his face. "Heaven preserve us from our just desserts."

He lowered his head, and realizing what he was planning to do, Victoria jerked hers away.

"Kiss me, dammit," he growled, catching the back of her head in one broad hand.

Victoria tried to shake her head even as he held it fast. She felt like her mind had been scraped raw, her walls undermined while she had been watching the gates. She could not stand to be touched now, not while she was still reeling.

"Give me a minute—half a minute!" she moaned. Time enough to rebuild the holes in her defenses and mount another guard. But her pleas were smothered as their lips met.

Her breath caught and was snatched away by Raeburn's mouth on hers, and with it went her resistance. The dark heat in her midsection erupted through her like molten silver, searing every nerve and dissolving every bone until she seemed to pour through her own lips in pure sensation. Raeburn's tongue pressed against her teeth, and she welcomed it in, thrilling with sheer sensation. The rhythm of his mouth, of her body in his arms, of her hands twisted in his waistcoat pulsed with her heartbeat in her ears. She tried to retreat into the bliss of it, to forget everything but the feel of flesh on flesh, but every touch and every taste kept her rooted in the moment—and rooted in the knowledge that it was not just *a* man but Raeburn, shadowy and dangerous Raeburn, who held her. The kiss, his touch, her need—they were mind-brandingly euphoric, but even as she burned his taste into her memory, her euphoria was mixed with the bitterness of despair and, even deeper, the taint of desperation and soul-clanging emptiness.

A sound tore from her throat at their separation, half moan, half sob. For a moment, she just stood, too shaken by the rush of sensation to move, fighting down emotions that had lain quiescent for so long she had almost forgotten them. The quiet despair of habitual loneliness: that she was used to, that she could conquer. But not so this much more personal pain and the knowledge that she was here—and there, across the bridge of air and breath, was Raeburn, offering an ephemeral surcease she'd be mad to accept.

"Don't do that again," she finally said. Her voice was perfectly collected and rock steady. She wished she could say the same for herself.

"And why not?" His tone was as sober as his face.

She pressed her lips together. "Because I bargained with my body, no more."

"I can take nothing else that you do not freely give me." His hands slid down her back, finding the buttons at her waist and undoing them quickly. He slipped his hand in the gap, and with two tugs, the first of her petticoats loosened. A moment later, her crinoline slipped from her hips to pool at her feet.

"Must those always go first?" she asked, seeking vainly to recapture the lightness of two minutes before.

Raeburn raised an eyebrow but answered her anyway. "They are always the most in the way." His hands slid down to encircle her rear, and he half pulled, half lifted her against him. His expression remained intent and grave, and she knew she had not succeeded in redirecting his thoughts, wherever his hands might be roving.

She tried archness next. "I am standing on my crinoline."

Raeburn didn't even dignify that attempt with a remark, merely lifting her off her feet and swinging her in a half circle. He did not set her down immediately but held her against his body for a long moment, inscrutable hazel eyes searching her face. Victoria was acutely aware of the flexed muscles of the arm she had grabbed when he picked her up, of the hard planes of his chest against her other arm, trapped between them. She felt power in his solid frame, and angry energy, wound just beneath his skin. And desire, too—desire for her. It was in his darkened eyes, his tensed jaw, the hardness of his arousal against her leg. Victoria's breath quickened, a hot flush starting in her midsection and spreading to the surface of her body, where it crawled across her skin and left it tingling. She tilted her head back, inviting his mouth to descend on hers, but he shook his head and let her slide the inch to the floor.

"Soon."

The word was so full of promise that it sent a shiver through her. An arm around her waist, Raeburn guided her to the table.

"Sit."

Victoria hesitated for only a moment before sinking down on her pillow beside the table. Instead of taking his place opposite her, Raeburn dropped a second cushion right beside it, shrugged off his waistcoat, and sank onto it. His expression was closed, the furrowed planes of his face unreadable. Whatever he was thinking, Victoria had the conviction that he wasn't finished with their conversation, and the thought of his pursuing it left her full of dread and something like relief. But that last emotion was doubly troubling in its own right.

"The crumble is getting cold," she pointed out nonsensically, more to say something than for any real concern about it.

Raeburn covered the dish and pushed it to the end of the table closest to the stove. "It will be fine for a while yet." He gripped her chin gently between forefinger and thumb, and she thought for a moment that he was going to kiss her again, but he only turned her face away from him. A moment later, she felt his hands in her hair, hunting for the pins that held it in place.

She felt the whorl of hair against the back of her head begin to loosen, and then it slid down across her shoulders. Goose pimples crept across her scalp as Raeburn combed his fingers through it, stopping when his hand caught on a pin he had missed.

"And so I banish the spinster and free the maid," he murmured. She could feel him encircle her loose tresses with a single broad hand and hold them suspended from his fist.

"I am no maid."

"A debauched maid, then. A woman of pleasure, who has shrugged off the confines of ordinary existence to grab at the rich, sweet fruit of life." His fist loosened, and he pulled it softly down the length of her hair.

"Clichés from you? I would have thought you above that." She put as much tartness as she could muster into her voice.

"Sometimes clichés exist because their accuracy is so useful." He grasped her hips and pulled her backward toward him. She came, allowing him to guide her until her back was against his chest, his legs on either side of her. Sitting, she was much shorter than he, and when he coaxed her chin back, the back of her head rested in the hollow of his shoulder. He shifted slightly, so that her face was angled toward his and she could see his expression. "Much better," he confirmed after a moment of critical examination. "You could be naked, but until that hair is let down, you might as well have kept every scrap and stitch of your armor on."

Armor? What armor? Victoria had felt stripped bare long before Raeburn had loosened the first button of her dress. All it took was a look from those eyes, a few words from those lips, and she was reeling, defenseless . . . But she said none of those things; they were far too great a confession.

Raeburn bent toward her slowly, deliberately, so that anticipation formed a hard knot in her center before his breath warmed her cheek, before his lips brushed against hers so delicately there was hardly any feeling of contact at all. But even that butterfly-touch was enough to snatch her breath and send dizziness spiraling through her, and when his kiss deepened, Victoria had the sensation that the world was falling away, leaving nothing but their two bodies, hanging impossibly in a void.

When he pulled back, she opened her eyes to find him watching her intently, a line of concentration between his brows. Without looking away, he bent to the side and gripped the edge of her skirt, tugging it upward to expose the scarlet-clad length of her leg. He glanced down to where the lace-bunched garters encircled her calves just below the knee. Despite the gravity in his eyes, a small smile pulled at his lips.

"They are truly horrible."

"But the corset is worse," she said. "I shouldn't have been so cross, otherwise."

Raeburn dipped his head, nuzzling against her neck even as his hand climbed higher on her thigh. "I shan't give you your old corset back. No, your great and terrible breastplate is mine for a while longer. But tomorrow— no more crimson stockings and garters. Will that mollify you?"

"It will go some way in that direction, yes."

She caught her breath as his questing hand found the slit in her pantaloons. He slipped it through and rested his calloused palm against the upper curve of her thigh, his fingers curling around it, impossibly rough against her heated skin. She shivered as he rubbed his thumb across her soft flesh, a twisting wetness blossoming between her legs as she involuntarily tilted her hips toward his hand.

"Not yet," Raeburn murmured, his lips against her neck. She groaned in protest, but he only tugged lightly on her earlobe with his teeth. He kissed a line down from the base of her ear to the neckline of her dress, each caress leaving her skin burning in its wake. Below, his hand slid across the joint of her thigh to cup her curls in its warmth.

Need tightened hard within her, demanding release, demanding satisfaction. Victoria pushed her hips against his palm, gripping his knees and leaning back into the crook of his arm, but he only kept his hand resting lightly where it was. She shrugged her neck away from the onslaught of his kisses and reached to pull his mouth up to meet hers.

"Now," she whispered into its sweetness.

He took her mouth, but his hand did not move. She pressed her hips harder toward it, but still he let her push him away.

"Why?" she asked against his lips, unable to keep a note of pleading from her voice.

He took her lower lip between his teeth and tugged it gently before speaking. But when he did answer, it was with a question of his own. "Do you want me?"

"Yes," she moaned without hesitation.

"No. I didn't ask if you wanted this. I asked if you wanted *me*."

Even with every sense burning, every fiber straining for release, Victoria stilled. "Why should you care?" she blurted, but Raeburn merely returned her gaze, expression unchanged. "I made no promises of wanting you. I hardly know you, and you ask me if I want you?" What right did he have to demand anything other than sheer organic enthusiasm?

"Yes."

"I—" Her automatic denial died unsaid. She shook her head. "I . . . don't know." And that was the truth. Her mind was torn between delight and dread, between hunger for connection and desire for the wool-wrapped protection of isolation where nothing could ever enter, where no one could ever hurt her again. But her body had no such qualms. It was raging with need.

"I shouldn't care," Raeburn confessed. "I have no right to care. And yet, I need to know." He kissed the sensitive place under her ear, and she shuddered delicately even as she sought to find an answer for him.

"I would not have agreed to the bargain if I did not

find the idea of you giving me this at least palatable. I need not remind you that what I bargained with was my body."

"Is that the only reassurance I will get?" he asked into the hollow of her throat, his breath sending tingles across her skin.

Victoria swallowed. "It's the only reassurance I have to give."

He sighed but raised his head to recapture her lips, and below he found her opening and plunged a finger into her even as he invaded her mouth with his tongue. She gasped and shuddered as expectation unwound all at once, then began to move with the rhythm of his hand and tongue as they stroked inside her. A new, deeper heat coiled in her midsection, winding tighter and tighter as Raeburn pressed on, pulling her with him. She felt every individual hair of his chin rasp against her cheek, every muscle fiber in the arm that cradled her suddenly boneless neck, every nuance of his personal odor, as darkly seductive as the man himself. The knot grew tighter, harder, until she feared she would break. Raeburn held her there for a long moment, at the peak of impossibility, before shifting his rhythm and sending her soaring, plunging over the edge as the fire seared through every nerve in her body, wave after wave. She arched hard against the constriction of her corset and threw her head back, a roar filling her ears until she could hardly hear her own choked cry over it.

Finally, the wave receded, leaving her weak and hollow in its wake. Raeburn slowed, stopped, and then just held her against him for a long moment. Still panting, Victoria closed her eyes and let her head loll in the crook of his arm. It felt good, traitorously good just to lean against someone. Not Raeburn, she told herself firmly.

Someone, anyone—a warm, faceless body that would allow her to abandon her straight-backed self-reliance for just the space of a few breaths and drift . . .

But soon, too soon, Raeburn stood and urged her to her feet, and reality came crashing back with all its doubts and fears. What had she been thinking when she signed that contract? she asked herself as he reached around her and began unbuttoning the back of her dress.

What had she been thinking then, and what was she doing here now?

Chapter Nine

The last button loosened, and Byron tugged the dress over her head, tossing it aside to crumple in a silken puddle across one of the divans. He bent to take her mouth with his again, but he saw a flash of color out of the corner of his eye and looked down, which was enough to make him freeze as if he'd been slapped.

"Oh."

"What?" Victoria followed his gaze downward. "Oh," she echoed.

The corset—Byron's mind shuddered away from calling it *Victoria's* corset—was bared in all its horrible glory, from the red-and-black-striped satin to the hideously extravagant lace ruches at the neckline.

"Now I understand why you were so distraught," Byron murmured, hiding his amusement.

"I wasn't distraught. I was angry."

He returned his gaze to her face. Her expression was tinged with humor but still drawn around her eyes and mouth as it had been all night, and he sensed a tightness in her body that made him uneasy. "And now?" He found himself putting a more meaningful twist to the question than it warranted.

"And now I can regard the mistake with perfect equanimity, for I believe that your delicate sensibilities are far more offended by it than mine ever could be." She gave him a strained smile.

He traced the neckline of the corset, the swells of her breasts warm beneath his finger. She took a shaky breath, her eyes closing to slits at his touch, but still the harsh tension that hummed in every line of her body did not loosen. What was wrong? Surely she expected no more questions—nor did she have the look of a woman with something still to hide. She seemed to be wound up in dreadful anticipation, waiting for a reaction from him. But of what kind?

"My delicate sensibilities might be offended by the packaging, but never the gift." He lowered his head to follow with his mouth the line his finger had just drawn, trying to coax the tightness out of her.

"So I'm a gift now, am I?" Victoria asked unsteadily.

He looked up sharply, stung by her sudden causticity. What had happened between their kiss in the Unicorn Room and this moment to cause that distance in her? "Better than calling you a payment, I should think."

That brought her out of her strange mood in a hurry. Her pale eyes flared, and she opened her mouth—to deliver a scathing reply, he was sure—but her look sharpened and she closed it without emitting a word.

"Nothing to say?" he asked softly.

She frowned. "You have given me nothing worthy of response."

That was the Victoria he had come to know, he thought with some relief. "Well, then," he countered, trying to lighten the tone, "I'll have to find something that is."

And before she could ask what he meant, he dipped his head to her throat and slipped his arms under her, deftly loosening the corset lacings as his lips caressed their way up her neck to her mouth.

Soon, the busk was unhooked, and then Byron pushed the straps from her shoulders and left the corset where it fell.

Damn, but she was irresistible like that, with her hair tumbled down past her shoulders and her chemise hanging from her frame, concealing yet hinting at a curve of a breast, the darker circle of a nipple, the hollow at her waist. And her expression, expectant with a hint of vulnerability behind her guarded eyes.

But the tension was back—in the stiff way she held herself, in the knotted muscles in her jaw, in the tightness around her mouth. What did she want? What did she fear? The thought was not without exasperation.

She met Byron's gaze in the candlelight and held it with her own, searching his face. She seemed to be trying to peel away his skin, invade and examine every private corner of his mind. Byron knew his bland expression had turned to a scowl, but he didn't seem to be able to stop himself.

"What do you think you see when you look at me like that?" she asked suddenly, her voice tinged with defensiveness.

Byron regained his impassive mask and gave a glib answer. "I see what I always have, a desirable woman who has cheated herself of half her life." Her face closed in on itself suddenly, like the collapse of a wall, and the natural mirror of her question rose in his mind. "And what do you see, when you look at yourself?"

The question seemed to take her by surprise, but she answered promptly. "A simpleton who ages in years but gains no wisdom." She turned her head away from him, but not before he saw her grimace as if in pain.

She was still regretting the confession he'd wrung from her that afternoon, he realized abruptly. He had wanted to know her secrets from the moment he'd set eyes on her, but he'd never imagined that it might cost her to tell him—nor thought he'd care if she were hurt.

Why should it hurt her, though? Even if she had been a virgin when she arrived, she was not one now, so the entire story seemed almost trivial. But he had the sudden revelation that it was not the story itself but the sharing that made her so vulnerable, so open to even the most unintentional wounds.

He thought of his own weakness, how it had hurt to confess it into the ear he'd thought the most sympathetic in the world—with what halting, labored words!—and then find himself reviled for his confession. Now, Victoria was braced for the rejection Byron had never anticipated.

Which he had no intention of delivering.

He took her chin in his hand and turned her gently back to face him. Her eyes stayed fixed on a point in the center of his chest for a long moment, and it seemed to take her a wrenching effort to raise them to his face. He could see the strain as she tried to maintain a neutral mask, but the pain in her eyes alone twisted something inside him. *Gently, now,* he cautioned himself. If he responded too quickly to her need and not her words, she might flee from him into some inner recesses of her mind where he could never reach her again.

He could no longer deny that the threat of losing her mattered, so he chose his next words carefully.

"You are wise enough to realize the errors of your past, which is far wiser than many of us ever manage to become."

Her smile was so faint as to be nearly imperceptible, but some of the tension eased from her face. "And you?"

"I like to think that I am wise. Though I know it is a delusion, it's precious enough to me that I pretend to believe it." And now for the heart of it. "Come, Circe. Do not scowl so. Your secret is safe with me, and I find it unfortunate, not contemptible. We are all fools when it comes to the heart." He paused, seeking to smooth away the hurt in her eyes and the furrow between her brows. "A story for a story. I once fancied myself desperately in love with the rector's daughter and behaved most ridiculously on her account. I was older than you when you committed your folly—older in years than your would-be husband, too, I am ashamed to admit, but younger in experience, I'm sure, for I had rarely gone beyond the bounds of my parents' estate. And so, at twenty-two, I was far more a boy than a man, and a fetching black-haired girl with pretty ways and a sweet smile reduced me to a poetry-singing, letter-writing fool."

Victoria's expression eased into a genuine, if small, smile. "I can't imagine it."

"Nor could I, if I couldn't remember it so well." He trailed into silence, and for a moment, the memory of another voice rang in his ears, another laugh, another sigh. Charlotte Littlewood had been good-natured, sweet, and honest, if sheltered and not especially clever. A good match for the boy he had been, though the man he was now would have found her insipid.

"And what became of your raven-haired muse?"

Victoria's question brought him abruptly back to the present. "Her father disapproved because he could not imagine that a future duke would have noble intentions with a rector's daughter—though I assure you, they could not have been nobler—but that wouldn't have stopped me if she'd returned my affections." His smile was bitter. "However, she did not. I could have lived on her smile, but it was never directed at me. I frightened her, and so she could not love me. I left her there when she become betrothed to another man and found my amusement as I could in London." That was true enough, but what it left out . . . He had seen how Charlotte was swayed by his pursuit, how her initial chariness had faded to reserved curiosity, open and ready to be persuaded, if only he'd had the strength to make his confession.

But no, he thought darkly as an even older memory eclipsed the image of her face. He'd made that mistake once, a decade before he had he begun to woo the rector's black-eyed daughter. Once was more than enough. Byron could have lived with her waning interest, with another swain winning her hand and taking her to the altar and out of his reach forever, if only that swain hadn't been the one who had humiliated Byron in the first place. Will Whitford had waltzed back into Merritonshire society with his university degree and charming manners and had swept the simple country girl off her feet. Two thefts, of his pride and the woman he pursued, had been far too much to bear, and Byron had fled to dissipation in London and never looked back, except for the few nights when he had recklessly sunk too deep into his cups.

After a long moment of silence, Victoria took a deep breath, and Byron heard the catch in it. "Thank you for telling me—for giving me something in return." She sighed. "I may indeed be a fool, but if I cannot be otherwise, then I suppose it is as a fool that I believe you. You will not deceive me in this or hate me for it."

Byron smiled, letting the reality of the woman before him chase away the specters of the past. "Believe me however you will, so long as you do believe." And he tilted her chin up with a finger again, but this time it was to meet his kiss.

Her lips were soft and giving under his, eager enough to take his breath away and perhaps just a little desperate, not for the touch itself but for the reassurance that touch brings.

When they separated, she moved her mouth down-ward, across his throat, as she began unbuttoning his shirt. Her lips traced her fingers' progression, across the fabric of his undershirt, until the last button came free.

She tugged up his undershirt and slid her hands against his body, her palms smooth and cool. Pulling it higher, she ducked her head to bring her lips against his bare skin. She teased her way upward, across the sparse hair of his belly to his chest. Byron held himself still under her hands, but his breathing slid out of his control, quick-ening and taking on a ragged edge, and she redoubled her assault.

He pushed her back mutely, shaking his head. He un-fastened his cuffs and stripped in two quick movements, first the braces and shirt, then the undershirt. Victoria reached for his waistband, but he pushed her hands away and tugged her chemise over her head instead. He started to untie her pantaloons, but she stopped him.

"Yours first," she said firmly.

He made a sound of disgust. "Only if those boots of yours come off, too."

"Agreed." Victoria worked at the buttons at her ankles as he stood and stripped off the rest of his clothes. She slipped her second boot off as he tossed aside his draw-ers and looked up.

And froze. It took Byron a moment to realize that she was staring at his erection, directly at her eye level.

"You can't claim you haven't seen one before," he remarked.

Victoria gave him a brief, flat look. "Never so close." She paused. "I should think it ugly, by all rights, but I don't. It's . . . fascinating."

Byron smiled despite himself. "I have heard it called many things, but never that."

She reached out and encircling it tentatively with her fingers. Byron inhaled sharply at the jolt that went through him at her touch.

Victoria's expression turned speculative, almost coy. "Unexpected?"

"My dear Victoria, I have learned that the only thing I can expect from you is the unexpected," he replied through clenched teeth.

She grasped his erection more firmly and slid her hand along its length. He made a strangled sound as the skin beneath her hand slid over the head, sending a surge of heat through him.

Muttering a curse, Byron caught her wrist. "I'd welcome this some other time, my wicked Circe, but tonight, this will be finished another way." He pulled her to her feet and tugged her pantaloons down with the same motion. Two more tugs, and her stockings joined them, and he lifted her up and deposited her neatly onto the pillows.

"What are you doing?" she asked suspiciously.

"Giving you your just desserts."

Byron sat down directly above her head, out of her range of sight, and retrieved the crumble dish from its corner by the stove and uncovered it. He took a fork and speared a single peach slice on the end, then brought it down to Victoria's mouth.

She started when the fruit first entered her range of vision, but her mouth was open by the time it reached her lips. From his angle, her eyes were invisible, only the faintest fringe of blonde eyelashes peeking beyond the curve of her brow. Now they were aimed downward, at the fruit, as her teeth closed around it and plucked it off the tines of the fork. He watched her jaw work once, twice—then a tightening of a swallow. There was something erotic in each movement, something seductive in her simple act of eating. It went beyond deliberate titillation to a deeper level, to the structure of her bones, the blush of her skin, the way the left side of her mouth opened fractionally before the right side. Half-mesmerized, he fed her another bite, and again, she took the peach mutely between her delicately bowed lips, again she chewed and swallowed. Byron speared a third slice, then hesitated a moment before grasping it between his own front teeth instead. He set down the fork and leaned over her, bringing the peach to her lips with his own mouth. Victoria emitted a small sigh, and a moment later, he felt a faint tug as her teeth closed around it. Then her hands clasped his head and pulled it down, and he was caught in an upside-down kiss, sweet and warm, luscious enough to make him drunk, teasing enough to make him crawl half-involuntarily around until he was lying over her, his hips clasped between her willing thighs.

Finally, they separated, and Byron reached once more for the crumble. This time, though, he did not reach for the fork but filled the serving spoon with syrup.

"Raeburn, what are you doing?" Victoria blurted when he brought the spoon within her line of sight. For once, perhaps for the first time since he'd met her, she looked completely uncertain, and the defenselessness of the expression sent a wave of desire through him so strong that he had to grit his teeth to keep from plunging into her right then.

He didn't answer but tipped the spoon so that a thin line of syrup poured down her throat and swirled across her breasts. She gasped as it touched her skin, and her pale eyes widened even more a second later, when it must have occurred to her what he intended to do. Her nipples grew impossibly tight as the line of syrup grew closer and closer on each pass, then finally drowned them in its golden warmth. He filled another spoonful and tipped it to drizzle slowly across her belly, then her thighs, held open by his hips.

Victoria made a stuttering noise, and Byron looked up to meet her gaze. Her hands were bunched around fistfuls of pillow, her eyes disbelievingly wide.

"You're not—" she started. She tried again. "You aren't going to? . . ."

Byron smiled. "Oh, but I am." Her legs tightened around his hips as he reached between them, but his body kept them wedged apart. Slowly, he ran a finger of his free hand in a line from the start of her curls until he found the folds and the opening between. Her wetness slicked his fingers as he parted them, and her breathing grew more rapid. "You can't tell me you don't like the idea."

"Not . . . dislike, exactly . . ." The words were almost gasped.

Byron tilted the spoon, and the last of the syrup rolled off the end, across the separated folds. Victoria inhaled sharply, going rigid, but he was not finished. He turned the spoon on its side and smoothed the line of syrup, first one side, then the other. Victoria's hips tilted toward him, but he set the spoon aside and dipped into the crumble with his fingers, fishing out a single peach slice.

"Don't move," he murmured.

"I wouldn't dream of it." Victoria's laugh came out breathy and strained.

He placed the slice in the hollow of her throat, then others in a line between her breasts until the last lay nestled on top of her curls. Or rather, the second to last. He took one final piece, still warm from the dish.

"Don't!" Victoria said.

Byron looked up to find her watching him down the trail of fruit. "Why not?"

As incongruous as it was, he could have sworn that she blushed, and for a moment, was even at a loss for words.

Byron smothered a smile. "Do you trust me?"

"Should I?" Her expression was unconvinced.

"I promise on my word as a gentleman that nothing will get stuck," he intoned. He paused. "Unless, of course, you're frightened?"

Her eyes narrowed dangerously. "Of course not." The glint in her eyes died as she realized that he was goading her. She smiled slightly. "On this, I suppose I trust you."

"Good," he said, and he guided the last slice between her legs so that it was cradled in her opening. Victoria made a choked sound and arched against the pillows.

"And that, dear Circe, is only the beginning."

And with that, he leaned over her and plucked the fruit from the hollow of her neck with his teeth, licking the pool of syrup clean where it had lain.

The cooling peach slices were cinnamon-rich, but richer was her skin, both firm and soft like the flesh of the fruit itself. He moved erratically across her body, taking up a slice here, kissing away a line of syrup there, reveling in every shudder and tremor that he caused. Some of the pieces he ate. Others, he fed to her with his own mouth—and those were the sweetest, for then the taste of her lingered on his tongue, the feel of her lips burned into his. He took possession of her body with his mouth, laying claim to each flushed inch until she pressed against him, moaning as her hands begged him for satiation. And all the while, his own need thrummed hot and hard in his veins, demanding the release that he could give them both.

When he bent his head to the jointure of her legs and plucked out the last peach slice, she arched her hips hard toward him.

"Now," she said. "I'm ready for you now."

I was born ready for you, he thought fervently, but all he said was, "In a moment. Just one moment longer." And then he bent his head a final time to lick the last of the syrup away.

Victoria lay rigid for the space of one, two, three breaths. Then she sat up, using her hands on his shoulders to push him back onto his heels in the same motion. Before he knew what she was going to do, she was straddling his lap and sliding onto his erection, and it was all he could do to keep from losing himself with the first thrust of penetration.

Her weight on her knees on either side of him, Victoria began to move herself up and down his length, her face a mask of concentrated pleasure. Her hands moved along his back, feeling each rib and muscle, arousing his need as she filled her own. She was perfect like that, in the utter unself-consciousness of ecstasy, with her slick heat embracing him and her breasts rubbing against his chest with each movement. He gritted his teeth, trying to hold on. They moved together, breath spiraling into gasps and gulps as she pushed them nearer, nearer the edge.

God, she was perfect—except for her gaze, which was growing distant, and except for her hands, whose strokes were becoming mechanical as she drew away from him, to some inner place.

"Don't you dare shut me out now, Victoria Wakefield," he ground out.

"Lord spare me—" she gasped, her blue eyes boring suddenly into his face. "I can't!"

And with that, the heat surged up to overwhelm them, and they fell gaze-locked together for a brief moment that stretched into eternity.

In the half-blind aftermath, when Victoria lay limp and panting against his chest, still joined to him for a few breaths longer, he heard her whisper in a voice that was so piteous he could hardly believe it was hers—"Don't leave me alone."

"I won't," he promised, cradling her with his face buried in her lavender and cinnamon scented hair. "Not now. Not tonight."

Not ever.

He rejected the thought—wherever it had come from, it was not his. It must belong to some boyish corner of his mind, still full of the romanticism confused with concupiscence that he thought he'd expelled long ago. Yet another failing, he told himself: the inability to uproot the last dreamings of gormless youth. He was not that boy, he told himself, no more than Victoria was another Charlotte. Yet when he finally disengaged himself from Victoria, it was with the poignant taste of regret rising like bile in his throat.

Victoria woke to darkness and a stirring beside her. She thought she heard a voice—a word or a brief phrase—but it was too soft and fleeting for her sleep-fogged mind to absorb.

"Raeburn?" she asked.

"Who else?" he replied immediately, a hint of humor coloring his voice. She felt his breath, warm and soft, against her cheek, and his hand brushed against her face as he pushed her hair away.

"No one. I didn't know if you were awake—or if you were going back to your chamber."

"Not yet. Not while there's still night left."

Of course, Victoria thought. In the morning, the tower room would be full of light, and Raeburn would slink off into the depths of the manor house, away from it. But why? What was wrong with him?

He must have felt the question rising between them, for he rolled himself on top of her as if to distract her, putting his weight on his elbows on either side of her. "Until dawn, you're mine."

She started to reply, but he caught her mouth half-open in a kiss, and she knew with a drop in her belly that asking would be of no use. There was still pleasure, she told herself. That was what she could have of him. That was what was hers as much as his, and in that she would make herself content.

The room was flooded with steely predawn light when Byron opened his eyes. Victoria had rolled away from him in her sleep, wrapping the blanket around herself so that half his body was bare to the chill air. He had not feared he wouldn't wake; after the one agonizing incident when he was still a boy, he always woke at the first hint of light and fled it long before it could do any harm. If the pain itself hadn't been enough to make him never forget, the memory of Will's reaction certainly would be.

He stood, careful not to disturb Victoria, and dressed stealthily in the grayness. There was no reason for caution, he told himself. After all, it was his manor and his week, and he could come and go and treat Victoria as he pleased. But still he felt like an escaping criminal as he loaded the tray with the dirty dishes, and he hesitated even at the doorway, looking back at the figure sprawled so defenselessly across the mounded pillows. Her white-gold hair puddled around her head like a halo of sunlight, her outstretched hand curved almost imploringly toward him. She couldn't have looked more out of place in his great-uncle's gaudy, exotic boudoir, with her pale English features and an endearing, commonplace hint of damp-ness on one cheek. Byron smiled despite himself at the thought that she could forget herself even in her sleep so much as to drool. He wanted to stay and see her wake, see her expression when she opened her eyes and found him there, waiting for her.

But he knew that was impossible. He *could* wake her and bid her good-bye, but such an action would only be met with confusion and the inevitable questions that he had sworn never to answer again. Meanwhile, the day was waiting for him, the first hour in his gymnasium with his weights and racks and then the accounts and business transactions that seemed to have no end.

Byron shook his head and slipped through the door, but his guilt dogged his heels all the way down the stairs.

Chapter Ten

Victoria awoke bathed in sunlight that poured through the eastern windows of the tower room. She was alone, and she had to suppress a pang of disappointment despite the fact that she had hardly expected anything else.

She shivered, unable to shake the vague uneasiness that had haunted her since the night before. She shouldn't be so disturbed by this situation. After all, she told herself, there could be nothing less complicated than the relationship between herself and Raeburn. It was written in black and white and stored in the night table in the Unicorn Room. A service for a payment, no more, no less. And so she determined to put him out of her mind.

She stretched slowly, her limbs still heavy and sore, before sitting up and searching among the scattered pillows and rugs for her clothes. All of Raeburn's were gone, she saw without surprise. She pulled on her stockings, her chemise, and the awful corset. She could hook the busk closed without assistance, but tightening the laces was a daunting task, and she looked helplessly at the divan where her lavender morning dress lay crumpled. She could never fit into it with her corset loose, and buttoning it alone would be even more impossible. She considered sneaking to the Unicorn Room in her under-things—there were few enough servants that she probably wouldn't get caught—but she wasn't certain she could even find the way, and the thought of wandering the corridors of Raeburn Court half-dressed was enough to make her hesitate.

Her dilemma was solved when the door opened.

"Oh," Annie said, blinking in the sunlight. "I didn't know thoo'd be awake. I ought to have come earlier. I'm so sorry—"

"You've brought breakfast, and that's all that matters," Victoria said reassuringly, nodding at the girl's tray.

Annie stared at it as if just realizing it was there. "I have, haven't I?"

"Indeed." All evidence of the meal of the night before was gone, even the crumble dish. Victoria shivered at that memory, still slightly stunned. She made her voice brisk and practical with effort. "Bring it here, please, Annie."

Annie obeyed, then retreated to hover by the door again. Victoria uncovered the dishes—the expected toast, eggs, and sausage—and began to eat. She glanced at the maid as she took a drink of slightly tepid tea. Considering the girl's delicate constitution, it was curious how unabashed she seemed in the face of Victoria's unquestionably illicit nocturnal activities with the duke. She remembered the hints of stories of his debauched great-uncle and amended that thought. Perhaps it was what Annie was accustomed to.

"Have you worked here long?" Victoria asked.

"Aye, my lady, all my life. I was born here. My mother was a housemaid." Annie's habitual tension seemed to loosen at the innocuous topic.

"You were born *here*? In the manor house?" Victoria repeated.

"Aye." Annie nodded. "My mother died in having me, so I raised myself mostly, but there was always someone to look after me when I was a lass."

Victoria had never heard of a master who would keep even a married servant on, much less a pregnant one. "What did you think of the old duke?"

To her surprise, Annie flushed. "Oh, none of us saw naught of him much, not since I can remember. His grace would sit alone in his rooms with Gregory or Stephen just outside the door, waiting while he needed the least little thing. And Mrs. Peasebody would bring him his food on a tray herself, and that was it." Her expression grew abstract. "I think I had more years of age than times seeing him when he died."

Annie trailed off, and Victoria let her be as she was led away by her own curious thoughts. Her caricatured image of a crazed, randy old man could not encompass this new information. Had all the masters of Raeburn been so convoluted underneath the easy stereotypes, or only the last two? The great-uncle, mad yet merciful; the nephew, playing at iniquity while truly . . . what? Victoria admitted that she still couldn't say.

She wondered how like the old duke the current one was. Strange men with dark reputations, living in the moldering remains of a great manor house . . . In thirty years, would the heir continue the legacy of that dissolute madman, whatever it really was? Victoria shook her head, unable to envision it. Already, her Raeburn was breaking away from his predecessor's shadow, building a queerly beautiful house that could not be more different from Raeburn Court.

Her Raeburn. Exactly how had that pronoun slipped

into her thoughts, and what did it mean? She frowned as she swallowed another bite of eggs. Nothing but that he was the Raeburn she knew, she decided. After all, it could mean nothing else.

And yet she was strangely dissatisfied with that answer even as she took the first bite of the thick, buttered toast.

Victoria walked in the gardens, feeling refreshed despite her sere surroundings. Calling the space "the gardens" was somewhat generous, she had to admit—the tangle of overgrown hedges and half-hidden paths held only a distant memory of its prior manicured life.

She'd come down to the Unicorn Room to find a piping-hot bath waiting for her, and while she had soaked, Annie had whisked away her clothes. By the time she was finished, fresh underclothes were laid out for her, including her own sober black stockings as Raeburn had promised, and her lavender morning dress had been brushed and ironed.

Even if the gardens weren't beautiful, the day certainly was. After drizzling on and off throughout the morning, the afternoon sun had burned away the last of the clouds, and the sky shone blue with the deep bell-like clarity of early autumn. Thrushes flitted among the weeds, and rustles in the undergrowth marked the escape of small animals as she approached.

She might feel refreshed, but she also still felt out of sorts and almost . . . lonely. The garden was causing her odd mood, she decided—it was like a symphony played out of tune, elaborate and abandoned, artificial yet wild. But even as she wandered among the hedges and rosebushes, her mind kept returning to the manor house behind her and the man within.

This time was hers now, a few minutes stolen from the week she had given him. So why couldn't she ignore the duke and all his shadowy secrets? She tried to concentrate on the warmth of the sun against her back, the crackle of leaves beneath her feet, but her thoughts kept going back to Raeburn, wrapped up in some gloomy inner room and shut away from the glorious day.

Victoria squeezed between two wild yews—and stopped dead. Instead of finding herself in yet another tangle of growth, she discovered a small, well-swept clearing defined by the meeting of three brick paths, the hedges neatly trimmed and the flowerbeds mulched for the winter.

But that change, surprising as it was, had not caused Victoria's hesitation. In the center of the space, on a curved stone bench, sat the housekeeper with a tea tray beside her.

Mrs. Peasebody set her teacup down on the saucer she held and stood so hurriedly that tea sloshed over the edge to darken her serviceable gray dress.

"Thy ladyship!" the broad-faced woman exclaimed, the last word ending in a yelp as the steaming tea splashed across her fingers.

"Mrs. Peasebody, please forgive me," Victoria said, covering her own startlement. "I didn't mean to intrude. The day was just so lovely that I couldn't help but go for a walk . . ." She trailed off, realizing the strangeness of apologizing to her host's housekeeper for taking a walk in his gardens.

"It's no intrusion, love." Mrs. Peasebody waved the handkerchief that she was using to dab at the spill across her wide bosom. "It's just that I don't expect naught else out here no more. There's not much to attract folks, I fear, and his grace . . . Well, his grace doesn't go out much," she said obliquely. "His grace's great-uncle was the same way, I fear. Runs in the blood, it does." She plumped down on the bench again.

Victoria was surprised to hear her private comparisons of that morning echoed by someone else, but she held her tongue as the old woman continued.

"Such a shame to see such ailments plague the noblest lines in England." Mrs. Peasebody shook her head.

"Ailments?" Victoria asked. She remembered the rumors of a weakness of the blood and Raeburn's own indirect reference to it the night before. Finally, to have a certain name put to it: an illness, not an eccentricity.

The housekeeper gave her a sharp look. "Now, thy ladyship, I've been a good servant to the Raeburns since long before thoo was born. If his grace is wanting to confide in thee, I'm sure he will, and a better one to tell I don't know if he can find, not that there's been many out to see him. But as for me, my lips are sealed."

"I see," Victoria said, chagrined that the only subject she was interested in seemed to be the only one on which the woman would not speak.

Mrs. Peasebody seemed not to notice her reaction, merely waving to the bench across from her. "Sit thissen down, thy ladyship, and have a little chat, if thoo'd like. I know I get lonely in that old house." She looked at the stained limestone walls fondly where they rose above the growth.

At any other time, Victoria might have shied away from such forwardness, but it seemed ludicrous to attempt to keep up the usual social forms at Raeburn Court. Choosing to indulge her curiosity instead, she sat. "You knew the previous duke, then?"

Mrs. Peasebody nodded vigorously, causing her iron-gray sausage curls to bob where they emerged from her neat little mobcap. "And when I was but a wee lass, the duke before that." Her gaze grew far away. "Aye, those were the days. Half the manor house was no better than it is now, but the gardens . . . oh, the gardens were beautiful. His grace was very par-*tic*-u-lar about the gardens. There was an army of gardeners and boys, and every year there were rounds of planting and fertilizing, pruning and composting. The grounds were famous throughout England, and all the grandest designers did their bit." She shook her head. "But that was long ago, and now I come out here for the memories, silly old woman that I am, and keep my favorite corner as much as it was as I can remember."

"That's lovely. And sad." Victoria was surprised to find that she meant it.

The housekeeper started to pour herself another cup of tea and stopped midgesture. "Pardon me, love. I didn't mean to sit here, sipping afore thee as if I were the Queen hersen."

"Please, go ahead." Victoria motioned to the teapot, and the housekeeper's expression changed from martyrdom to pleasure.

"Thoo is a good one, thy ladyship, if you don't mind my saying." She took a sip from her newly filled cup and returned to her original subject. "Of course, I'm a silly old body, and I like to make it all sound much more romantic than it is. The truth is, the garden's a good place for an afternoon constitutional, and when the weather's fine, this spot is just grand for tea." She switched topics suddenly. "I hope thoo is getting on well with Annie."

"As well as I can, I suppose," Victoria said, slightly bemused, "since she's still half-terrified of me. I wonder at times if I have grown a second head without realizing it."

Mrs. Peasebody waved a meaty hand. "That's just lit-tle Annie's way. Always been a bit queer in the head, but she's a nice enough lass. Her mother was a maid here be-fore her, and her father . . ." She paused and leaned for-ward conspiratorially. "Well, it isn't nice to spread rumors of the dead, but they say her father was the late duke." She sat back with the expression of someone who knows she's just delivered amazing news.

"Oh," Victoria said, at a loss at her frank confidence. "I—I suppose there must be many of his . . . progeny about the place, then."

Mrs. Peasebody grinned. "Thoo would think so, wouldn't thoo? But she's the only one. There was another lass up from Weatherlea, she was here for a week, and four months later, she sent a letter to his grace that she was with child. The duke paid her handsomely, as was his way, but I've seen the child, and bless me if he isn't the spitting image of the young man the lass married only three weeks later."

"I see," Victoria said.

"Now this new duke—he's different." Mrs. Pease-body gave her a hard look. "He's not had a single lass up from any of the villages or towns despite the stories of his London life. He's a deep one, too, deeper than his great-uncle ever was. Thoo should be careful of him, love, be-cause I don't think he knows what he's about." She emptied her teacup with a last swallow, then unpinned a well-worn pocket watch from her bosom. "Why, bless me, look at the time! I do go on forever, don't I, thy la-dyship?" She arranged everything on the tray beside her and picked it up as she stood. "Why, I'd babble half the afternoon away! But my duties call me—and no one would call me anything but dutiful. Good-bye, thy lady-ship, and enjoy the rest of thy constitutional."

And with that, she was gone.

Victoria was left alone in the suddenly silent clearing, her head spinning with new thoughts. So Annie was Raeburn's cousin, in a way. She wondered if he knew. Or if he cared. She shrugged. There was probably a housemaid or two at Rushworth that were her father's by-blows, and she'd intervened between her father and brother on three different occasions when village girls came calling, claiming that their bastards belonged to Jack. It had never bothered her before that half a man's children might be reared in luxury while the other half begged on the streets, but now, it was strangely troubling.

Victoria stood and began to wander slowly deeper into the manor grounds, lost in thought. What did Mrs. Peasebody mean by the present duke being different, and that being dangerous? Surely, if she had been an innocent, there could be no one more dangerous than a randy, callous old man. She shook her head, giving up. It made no sense. Only . . . the Raeburn she knew *was* dangerous. It wasn't physical intimidation or a fear of what he might do to her—if she'd felt either one of those, she'd have been back at Rushworth by now, devil take her brother.

No, Raeburn's dangerousness was of a much subtler sort. Who else could have coaxed the ugly story of the past from her? If that wasn't dangerous, she didn't know what was.

She turned a corner, and the path ended abruptly at a low stone wall where the land dropped away sharply as the garden surrendered to moor. Far below, hedgerows and lanes crisscrossed the countryside, beyond the broken stump of a tower that rose from the top of the manor house's sister hill. The tower was both beautiful and desolate, the afternoon sunlight etching its sharp shadow across the undulating green meadows beyond. It suddenly struck Victoria that there was an answer there, somewhere in the landscape, to a question she had not yet fully articulated, but the more she stared, the more obscure it seemed to grow.

Victoria stood for a long moment, watching a flock of sheep wander across a field in the middle distance as a solitary raven wheeled overhead, before giving up and turning away to work her way back toward the manor house.

She made the final turn along the path, and the back face of the manor house came into view, Baroque giving way to Gothic and Romanesque farther along. Her stomach jolted slightly when she spied an unexpected form by one of the French windows closest to her path. Though she was too far away to make out a face, the sense of size, of coiled expectation, left no room for doubt in her mind.

It was Raeburn, lounging in the shadows of the eaves.

He watched her as she mounted the four steps up to the terrace, his expression unreadable. She wondered what he saw when he looked at her and whether it was a pleasing sight. But there was no answer in the shifting hazel depths of his eyes, and only the slightest detached smile hovered on his lips, a smile that could mean anything.

"I was beginning to wonder if I should send someone after you," he called as she approached.

"Did you think I had run away?" she replied, keeping her tone careless. Despite herself, she felt a slight flush creep up her cheeks as memories of the night before invaded her mind. It seemed impossible that this cool gentleman could be the same man who had tasted every inch of her body only hours before.

He snorted. "More likely that you got lost—broke your neck in the ha-ha or drowned in an ornamental pond."

"As you see, I'm safe and sound," Victoria said, stopping in front of him. She stood in full sunlight. Its golden heat poured across her body like honey, and she drank it in preparation for the inevitable return to the gloom of the house.

"Which is a good thing, because dinner will be served any moment now." He extended his arm to her but did not step out of the house's shadow. "Shall we?"

Victoria hesitated. "Must we eat in your terrible dining room when it's so beautiful outside?" She knew the answer, but the words spoke themselves almost of their own volition. It wasn't the real question, though, and she saw in the darkening of the duke's face and the hardening of his chin that he knew it, too.

Raeburn waved his free hand irritably as if dismissing the silent question, his eyes growing clouded and his brow lowering. "It is my habit to eat indoors. As my guest, you will honor it." His words were so sharp and his manner so daunting that she did not risk more but took his arm in silence and allowed him to lead her back into the cool depths of the house.

The manservant—the footman, Victoria corrected herself, recognizing him from the carriage the day before—was waiting in the dining room as he had the first night, and he first held the chair for her and then hurried around the table to attend to his master.

"I had thought that footmen usually come in pairs," she said as a maid brought the first course into the room. If Byron was going to snap at her like he had, he deserved a little needling in return.

"They do, and Andrew here did, too, once." Raeburn frowned in the direction of the servant, but his displeasure seemed more directed at the situation than the man. "His father died, and his brother inherited the farm and left service some years ago. My great-uncle was not in a position to replace him."

"But surely you are," Victoria objected.

Raeburn scooped a generous bite of rabbit stew onto his spoon. "And I will. As soon as the Dowager House renovations are complete, I shall hire as many servants as I need." He cast a disparaging glance at the faded suit the man wore. "And I shall arrange for proper uniforms, as well."

"What a sight it will be then, I'm sure," Victoria said caustically, unappeased. "Imagine! A duke with a full staff in service."

"Indeed," he agreed, blandly enough that her peevish display made her feel a little foolish, and her ire faded into resignation.

They ate for a moment in silence before Raeburn spoke again. "And so what did you see on your very long walk?"

"What's left of the gardens, mostly. A great deal of local flora and fauna, including Mrs. Peasebody, if she qualifies."

The corner of his mouth quirked. "I believe she would."

Victoria started to ask about Annie, cast a sidelong look at the footman, and changed her mind. Instead, she said, "I saw a ruin, too, just beyond the manor grounds."

"Ah." Raeburn said. "That would be Rook Keep. At a time when everyone is building follies in their gardens, aren't I fortunate to have a real ruin so close?"

"Certainly. To whom did it belong?" Victoria picked at the mushy carrots and potatoes swimming in the stew.

Raeburn shrugged. "To various bailiffs and castellans. It never became a hereditary fief—too close to Raeburn

Court, in my opinion. The old lords wanted to be certain of the continuing fidelity of its master."

"Rather cynical, but I can't say I blame them."

Raeburn raised his glass in ironic salute to his progenitors. "Indeed." He took another bite of soup. "Does it interest you?" he asked suddenly.

"The keep?" Victoria hesitated. "Yes, it does, to be frank." She smiled self-deprecatingly. "I've never been one to go off on the exploratory jaunts that so interest many young people."

"But you wished you were." It was not a question.

"At times, yes. When I'm feeling old and silly."

He raised an eyebrow. "Or young and reckless." His hand reached across the table to take hers and trace it briefly with one broad finger.

Victoria's flush had nothing to do with embarrassment and everything to do with the hungry glint in his eyes. "Or young and reckless."

There was another moment of silence, then Raeburn spoke again. "I shall try to make time to take you if the weather is suitable." He looked up from buttering the thick slab of bread the maid had brought out with the soup. "The riding habit I ordered for you ought to be finished by tomorrow morning."

His tone was too casual, and Victoria knew his offer was not given lightly. She sensed in it a kind of placation, a peace offering in return for his silence over the question she most wanted to ask. "I'd truly like that."

"Good," he said briskly, setting his fork on his empty plate. He pushed his chair away from the table and stood. "Now I have to track down a ledger from the seventeenth century in the hopes of settling a dispute about land boundaries between two of my tenants." He quirked an eyebrow. "It should make for a delightful afternoon. If

you will excuse me, your ladyship." He executed a curt
bow and turned away.

"But of course," Victoria murmured to his back as the
door swung shut behind him, but she couldn't suppress
the twinge of disappointment at his abrupt departure. She
sighed and stabbed at the remains of the rabbit stew with
her spoon, taking out upon it her vague feelings of dis-
satisfaction.

Chapter Eleven

Byron was hot, dusty, tired, and in a foul mood. He'd hunted through every drawer and shelf of the Henry Suite study, the old steward's offices, and even the rooms that had served as the privy closets of the manor's lords in the days of the Lancastrians and Yorks. Nothing.

Now he was in the library, the last sensible place for the records to be, though God knew that few of his predecessors had been known for their sense. He had initially enlisted the help of Fane and a footman, but as the search progressed and continued to yield nothing, his temper grew increasingly shorter until he decided to dismiss them before he started venting his frustration on them.

It wasn't even as if the library were that large, he thought sourly, looking down the musty rows of books. But precious few of the volumes had markings of any kind on the spine, and even fewer were legible. Surrounded by priceless incunabula, all he wanted at that moment was for everything to disappear except the quarto he sought.

A soft footfall behind him interrupted his silent seething, and he shoved a copy of *Temple of Flora* back into its place with rather more force than necessary.

"I asked not to be disturbed," he growled without turning, clutching the tattered ends of his temper.

"You most certainly didn't ask me. Besides, I had no way of knowing you would be here. It's not as if you ever tell me anything." The musical, amused voice doused his smoldering anger as effectively as a bucket of ice water.

He turned around and changed his squat to a sit in the same movement, resting his sore back against the bookcase as he looked up at the slim figure smiling above him. "Good afternoon, Alecto. Come to torture me? I fear I need no heavy rocks to roll or liver-hungry eagles. I have the quest for the nonexistent records book to keep me well occupied."

Victoria raised one finely arched eyebrow, her face set in an expression of false gravity. "I came to find a book to read, if it please your grace. There isn't much else to do while I await suppertime, when I will once again be blessed by the honor of your company." She eyed his shirt, to which he'd stripped half an hour before. "I can see that you're not fit for mine right now, so I shall take myself off to some other corner of the house." She hesitated. "Unless, of course, you'd care for some assistance."

Byron snorted. "I've had—and sent away—my assistance." He balanced his elbows on his knees, allowing his arms to droop between them, and angled his head up toward hers. Her waspish mood seemed to have disappeared with dinner, replaced by playfulness that was perhaps on the caustic side but still refreshing after several hours in the company of his dour steward. And, more importantly, she'd done no more than glance at the tight-drawn curtains that blocked the light from all but one of the windows. No questions to avoid or to cloud the air unspoken between them. "Unless you really would like to help—"

"If I didn't, I shouldn't have volunteered," Victoria returned. "I am hardly overflowing with martyrly sentiment."

With a grunt, Byron stood and brushed off his pants, smearing the marks of dust into longer streaks across the dark fabric. He glared at the shelves. "I am still looking for one of the manor's record books from the seventeenth century. It should be a quarto-sized ledger bound in brown leather, and the Raeburn crest will be on the frontispiece."

Victoria made a face as she scanned the shelves. "Why, then it should be no problem at all. A mere fourth of the books might fit that description."

"Exactly," Byron agreed sourly.

"Well," she said briskly, "I certainly won't go crawling about on the floor. I will take the high shelves, and you can take the low ones."

"Fair enough. I've already checked the high shelves in this bookcase, so you may start with that one." He motioned, and she stepped up to it and began pulling books out with admirable celerity.

Byron turned back to his own shelf, his mood lightened so inexplicably. It wasn't as if he expected her to entertain him, nor had she any secrets left with which to tease him.

He shook his head, pulling another likely looking book from the shelf. To think that all her complexities and contradictions could have a root in something so banal as a lover's death! Byron should have been disgusted at the simplicity and grossness of it, but he was not. Far from it. Instead, he was more fascinated than before.

And he suspected that Victoria was not telling the whole truth. He didn't think she was deliberately lying, though—he just doubted that she was being entirely honest with herself. Fear of ostracism might be a powerful impulse, but it alone could not keep a woman as strong-willed as Victoria under its control for as long as she claimed.

Victoria broke the silence without warning. "Did you know that the maid Annie is your great-uncle's daughter?"

Byron sat back on his heels with the suddenness of the question. "Why do you ask?" he returned, glancing over at her. Or at least, at her legs. She was halfway up the library ladder, frowning down at him with the back of her skirt pushed up and her ankles and lower calves exposed.

"Because I am insatiably curious. Is there any better reason?"

"None that's as believable." He shifted his position slightly to get a better view of her black-clad leg. He'd seen her naked two nights in a row now, but the titillation of unconscious exposure was still worth savoring.

He really should tell her, he supposed. And he would. Just not now. Something about that peek of leg brought back a rakish mischievousness that he had not felt in a very long time.

He continued, "But, to answer your question, yes, I was reasonably certain that she was my great-uncle's. Mrs. Peasebody has dropped a few hints, or at least, what she probably considers hints, and Annie does look remarkably like portraits of my great-grandmother as a young girl."

"Oh," Victoria said. She turned back to her shelf. "Don't you ever think it queer?"

"That my great-uncle fathered a bastard?" Byron

asked bluntly. "He was such a randy old goat I'm only surprised we aren't neck-deep in them."

She leaned forward for a book that was nearly out of her reach, and the back of her skirt bobbed up as the front was pressed against the ladder. "No. That isn't what I meant at all. I meant that if your great-uncle had married Annie's mother, you'd call her cousin, give her a fine dowry, and see that she had half a dozen seasons in London, but since he didn't, she's a chambermaid."

Byron blinked. "Well, does it strike *you* as queer?"

She glanced down at him. "Yes, I think it does."

"And what would you do, then? Send her to London anyhow, so she can be laughed at and snubbed by everyone? Make her miserable by trying to turn her into a lady?"

Victoria sighed. "Oh, I don't know. It just doesn't seem fair somehow."

"We could all give up our titles and inherited wealth," he pointed out. "There's nothing *fair* about my being a duke and . . . and Fane being a steward, if you look at it that way. I've done nothing to earn my birthright."

She made a rueful face. "I think I'm rather attached to my privilege. I'd make a remarkably poor washerwoman."

"There you have it, then. The system propagates itself." Byron slid another book back in its place. "You ought to join Lord Edgington's group of amateur philosophers for a week or two. That would tire you of circular social debates." He looked back up at her. "Honestly, if it makes you feel any better, Annie is walking out with Andrew the footman, as they say, and I've promised her a hundred pounds for her dowry and Andrew the position of porter when Silas dies. I know that allowing my staff to have romantic entanglements is unusual, but considering the circumstances, it seems best to permit it."

Victoria smiled, her expression uncharacteristically free of irony. "It oughtn't, I suppose, but it does. It still might not be fair, but it's better than any 'fair' I could think of." She climbed down the ladder and moved to the next bookcase, starting with the lowest shelf in her section.

Byron began to check the lower books in the case Victoria had just left, but his progress slowed as she climbed back on the ladder, every movement revealing tantalizing glimpses of ankle and leg. By the time she finished her shelves, he had fallen so far behind that it took a full minute of frantic work to catch up, and Victoria was already back on the ladder another shelf beyond. She frowned. "Don't think that I shall help you with your half if you dawdle."

"The thought never crossed my mind," he said blandly, eyeing the curve of her calf.

She snorted and turned back to her shelf, and Raeburn returned to alternately examining the books and her legs.

The easy silence was shattered by Victoria's sharp gasp. "Your grace!" she cried. "You are looking up my skirts!"

Byron looked up from her neat ankle to see her peering down at him, her face a warring mask of outrage and amusement. "Am I?"

She sniffed and settled on an expression of severity, slightly ruined by the hint of a smile that lurked at the corners of her mouth. She climbed down the ladder. "In any event, I've found something." She held the tome in front of her.

Byron stood and took it from her and flipped through the pages. "This is it." He smiled wryly. "I suppose I should be glad, but I would have been glad to find it an hour ago. Now I'm only relieved. And grateful for your help."

Victoria waved away the thanks. "You would have found it yourself in another quarter hour."

"Oh, but by then, my mood would have been irreparably foul."

Victoria grinned, a startlingly impish expression on her usually composed face. "Then I should thank you for allowing me to help, as I would have been the one to suffer from your ill humor. I merely rescued myself."

"Then I retract my thanks." He opened the quarto and grimaced at the faded pages. The dates were right; it had to be in here somewhere. "All that is left is sorting through the records to find the one I'm looking for."

"No problem at all, then."

He sighed. "When I was a boy, I thought that being a duke would be glamorous and exciting."

"We all have our delusions." She shrugged.

Byron shook his head. "There you go again—whenever I am starting to be convinced I am laboring under a unique burden, you point out the universality of the human condition and leave me feeling childish. Why do I allow such abuse?"

"Because you secretly enjoy it," Victoria returned promptly. "Because no one else dares speak to you that way. Don't worry; the novelty will fade, and you will be happy to send me on my way when our week is up."

Byron felt a strange twinge, akin to pain, at her words. It seemed like he had known Victoria an eternity, their three days stretching out to dwarf less significant years in his life, but the four days ahead of them seemed no longer than the space of a breath. He frowned, troubled at the dread he felt at the thought of the end of the week. However interesting, Victoria was a woman like any other.

Why should he care? Surely it was not their nocturnal romps. He'd slept with the best whores in Christendom, and however enjoyable Victoria was in bed, he could objectively state that she hadn't half the sheer energy of most of them.

Nor was it that she was fantastically accomplished, at least to his knowledge. She hadn't sung or played or recited or drawn a thing. He knew nothing of her knowledge of French much less any more obscure area of study. No, she had used none of the typical womanly talents to captivate him. Not that she had shown any desire to—or had any reason.

And yet he was captivated, he realized with a start. He was captivated because—because she didn't try to seduce him with artificial flirtations or to impress him with her many talents. She was in herself seductive, and her very personality was as interesting as the most brilliant accomplishments.

And Byron enjoyed the personhood as much as the womanhood of her. He couldn't think of another female he had thought of in quite those terms; women had always been women, there for his entertainment and amusement and set aside when more serious matters came to hand.

But here he was, chatting amiably with Victoria about his work and accepting her help instead of sending her on her way with a pat on the head and a promise of later attention . . . and it felt *right*. Which was the most disturbing thing of all.

Byron realized that he had been staring mutely at Victoria for nearly a full minute, and she was beginning to frown at him in return, a faint crease of concern appearing between her eyebrows. He shook his head, trying to dispel his lingering sense of apprehension. "It just occurred to me"—and how was he going to finish that?—"that you look quite striking today."

Her concerned expression dissolved into a dry smile. "If it only now occurred to you, I can't look that striking."

Byron raised an eyebrow, relaxing back into the comfortable role of seducer. "Your allure is a subtle intimation, not a flagrant sensuality. It takes a quick mind to realize that it is affecting one."

"And if one never realized it, what would happen?" Her tone was tinged with humor, and he responded in kind.

"Oh, one's days would be plagued with thoughts and one's nights haunted by dreams of you." He stepped forward, trapping her with both hands braced against the library ladder.

She started to lean back but stopped when the bottom edge of the ladder tipped up the front of her dress. Instead, she tilted her chin up to meet his eyes. "Then it is fortunate that you are astute enough not to be so ensnared."

"Very fortunate," he agreed, punctuating each word with a small step forward until Victoria had no choice but to back up, whatever havoc it caused her skirts.

By the time he had her pinned against the ladder, the back of her crinoline was pressed flat and the front stood up, coming almost to her shoulders so that her arms were caught behind its wide circle. Victoria made no sound of protest, only looked up at him in silence, expectation written in her clear blue-gray eyes. Despite the raised hoops and thick corset, Byron could see her breathing quicken, and his own body stirred in response.

He smiled at her hoops. "Confounded things." He reached across and traced the thin, delicate line of her nose from forehead to tip, resting his finger there. Victoria started to reach out, her motion arrested by the width of the crinoline. "But it has its uses, I see," he added.

She tilted her head up at him. "Do you like me so helpless?"

"Indubitably." He slid his hand behind her head, cradling the soft swirls of hair in his palm. Already, her eyes were half lidded, her lips parted in anticipation. A wonderful dark warmth filled him that was entirely carnal and reassuring in its familiarity. But even as he tilted his head down to cover her waiting mouth, a twinge somewhere inside him disagreed.

"Oh, thy grace, I don't know how to tell thee. It's just the most awful thing I've seen in all my days! I never imagined I'd live to see Raeburn Court come— Oh."

Byron pivoted slowly away from the suddenly scarlet Victoria to face the intruder. "*Yes,* Mrs. Peasebody?"

For the first time since he'd met her, the housekeeper was momentarily at a loss for words. "I . . . Why, I . . . I had no idea . . ." she managed. Then she drew herself up, looking, if anything, even more distressed. "But that's not the point, thy grace. I've come to tell thee myseln because I couldn't bear to hear that another brought it." She took a deep breath. "It's the village. It's afire!"

Chapter Twelve

Once again, Victoria found herself closed up with the duke in the windowless carriage. This time, though, the vehicle careered down the drive, and only her death grip on the straps kept her from being flung from her seat as they slammed into a sudden rut, then dropped into a hole an instant later.

Across from her, Raeburn exuded grim tension, seeming to be equally oblivious of her and the nightmarish ride. Until Mrs. Peasebody had made her dreadful announcement, Victoria could not have imagined that anyone could whip an approximation of efficiency from the duke's servants. But scant minutes after Raeburn burst out of the library to thunder down the stairs, shouting orders like a man gone mad, he was swathed in layers of clothing and hustled into the still-moving carriage.

Spurred by morbid fear, Victoria had scrambled in behind with her heart in her throat, and the duke's snapped command of "Shut the door!" was his first and last acknowledgement of her presence.

Another jolt threw Victoria against the straps, and the carriage came to an abrupt stop. For an instant, she feared they had broken an axle, but then the door flew open and the footman's pinched face appeared, haloed by sunlight.

"We have arrived, thy grace," Andrew announced, ignoring Victoria.

Raeburn started up and then collapsed back against the squabs with an expression of excruciating frustration. "I cannot," he ground out. "Go, Lady Victoria, so I may gain what vantage I may from within."

Victoria scrambled down the steps and away from the door. She blinked against sudden sunlight and a wash of acrid smoke and heat. When her eyes cleared, she found herself standing in a bare yard. Directly before her, orange flames tore through a thatched roof and leapt to the sky.

Only one building then, not the whole village—her first thought was one of relief. But the flames were growing higher by the minute, and the wind snatched up embers and rained them on the thatch of the cottage next door, which sat far too close to its own neighbor.

Two boys pumped water into buckets, trying to douse the inferno through sheer energy, but a hiss of vaporization was the only result of their efforts. More buckets lay abandoned near their feet.

The other villagers stood in the yard with the contents of the endangered cottage spread about them, staring bleakly at the fire or glancing without curiosity at her and the carriage. Annie was there, crying and clutching at the collar of a broad-shouldered, soot-stained man who held her, but hers appeared to be the only emotion more intense than resignation on any of the sweaty faces that encircled the scene.

The sound of the duke's voice drew Victoria's attention away from the tableau. She turned to see Andrew leaning into the carriage. A moment later, the footman turned away and shouted, "Where are the ridgepole hooks?"

The soot-stained man rumbled, "They were in the forge when it went up."

A few second's consultation, and then the footman shouted, "Wet down those quilts and haul them onto the roof." The watchers hesitated. "Go on, now! His grace will buy yer more quilts, if he must, and they are a far sight less dear than rebuilding a house."

A red-faced woman standing close by the sooty man gave a small exclamation that ended in a sob, and she ripped the counterpane and blankets from one of the beds that squatted in the weeds and ran to the pump with them. Victoria started forward hesitantly, uncertain if her help would be welcome, but by the time the woman reached the pump, the two boys were there to meet her. A few seconds later, the sopping quilts were in their arms as they nimbly scaled the woodpile on the far side of the cottage. They tossed the bundles onto the roof and scrambled up after them.

Roused from their dull acceptance, the villagers shouted encouragement as the boys reached the ridgepole. One swung his leg over onto the side thick with smoke and ash, but the other grabbed his arm and said something to him. They each grabbed one corner of a blanket and snapped it out over the roof so that it spread out flat before it landed. They repeated the process until that entire side of the roof was covered, then slid down the thatch to arrive blackened and beaming for the cheers and back-thumpings of the other villagers.

Andrew held another quick consultation with the duke, then called, "What are yer staring at? Take those there buckets and wet the ground all around."

The villagers scrambled to comply, and dismissed by

the duke, Andrew took the still-sobbing Annie into his arms and began whispering into her hair.

Feeling superfluous and in the way as villagers dodged around her skirts in their hurry, Victoria retreated to the carriage. She climbed the steps and ducked through the doorway into the shadowed interior where Raeburn stood half-stooped between the seats. He stared at her for a long moment before flopping into his seat with a strangled sort of sigh. Victoria realized that it was the first completely unguarded and graceless action she's ever seen from him, and she paused, weight balanced between the top step and the carriage floor, before taking her seat.

Without acknowledging her presence, Raeburn leaned his head back against the squabs and closed his eyes. At that moment, perhaps for the first time, Victoria did not see a mystery-shrouded duke but just a man, a mere man, tired and frustrated and approaching middle age alone in a decaying house. She took advantage of his inattention to study his countenance. Without the ever-changing glitter of his eyes, his face also seemed lessened. His features were still attractive even etched with weariness, but they looked more worn than rugged.

So this was the real Raeburn, she found herself thinking, without the inflating shadows of intimation and rumor bulking his frame of flesh and bone into something almost titan. Her madcap bargain with him had seemed so daring when she was caught in his glamour. So unreal. But if he was just a man and the ancient hulk of the manor just a run-down house, then her liaison, too, must lose its breathless dazzle, no more fantastic than the hurried copulations of the old duke and the broad-faced girls who gave him a ride for a coin and a new petticoat.

Even as she had the thought, Victoria rejected it. There might not have been anything more in their intentions than a tawdry tumble when she had accepted the duke's offer, but from their first meal together, she had felt a connection that could not be dismissed as delusion and lust.

And she still felt it now. When Raeburn opened his eyes again, she discovered that his moment of weakness—of reality? humanity?—had done nothing to stifle her desire for him. Instead, his exposed imperfection seemed to settle like another layer of nacre on the image she was building of him in a private corner of her mind.

"I will remain here until the fire burns down," he said. "It looks to be well in hand now. If you wish, I can send someone to walk you back to the manor house, or you can go alone."

"I would rather wait with you."

He grimaced. "The pantomime is over. There is no reason for you to stay. For that matter, there was no reason for you to come at all."

"I wanted to. And now I want to stay."

"Suit yourself." He angled himself so he could see the burning smithy through the open door. Already, the flames were getting lower, Victoria saw, but the villagers still passed doggedly back and forth from the pump with their buckets of water, dumping them to form a wide ring of mud around the building. The autumn sunlight poured over the scene like thin honey, the curling smoke more black against the glittering blue of the sky, every fold of the villagers' clothes etched with sharp shadow and clear light. There was something mesmeric about the dancing fire and the steady, circling passage of the men and women in that pale brightness.

But Raeburn did not look mesmerized. His expression had settled back into lines of restless frustration. Victoria knew he wanted to be out there, hauling buckets alongside his tenants, but he made no move to leave the carriage. What was it that stopped him? Mrs. Peasebody had spoken of an illness, and she'd heard that albinos could not see in bright light, but Raeburn was no albino. Perhaps it was something similar. If it damaged his eyes or blinded him when he went outside, he would not dare venture out no matter what he desired.

"The smith is Annie's uncle." He abruptly broke into her thoughts.

"The one who was first holding her?"

"Yes. The men of their family have been smiths here for as long as anyone can remember. The forge burns once every century or so, but it has always been rebuilt." He shifted to look at her. "But Tom Driver has been talking of leaving for Leeds. His son's already there, and there isn't much work for a smith in a town this small. Horseshoes and repairs are all he does anymore, and he prefers the fancywork he learned at his father's knee. I don't know if he could do more than horseshoes even in Leeds, but at least there would be more of them."

"So your smith will follow the weavers?" Victoria asked, remembering their discussion the night before.

"Perhaps." He looked out at the building again, his face inscrutable. "When I was young, I dreamt of what I'd do when I became the duke. I would be fair and just and generous, and the tenants would love me. I would be like a king in a fairy tale, and because I was so good, all my fields would yield double measure and all my sheep would bear twins."

Victoria snorted. "When I was a little girl, I pretended that the Duchess of Windsor had a little boy hidden away a few years older than our future queen and that he would succeed to the throne and marry me."

"You did not dream small."

"Nor did you, to imagine that one pair of hands, however determined, could hold back the tide of time."

A sudden crack split the air, interrupting them, and Victoria started and whipped her head around to see the roof of the smithy collapse, sparks shooting into the air as thatch rained down into the shell of the four walls. The villagers scampered back with cries of alarm. Slowly, majestically, the wall nearest the endangered cottage fell inward, and the flames, subdued for a moment, shot up again twice as high.

Victoria's attention was brought back to the duke by his sigh. The tension in his face had suddenly eased, and she realized that he had been waiting for that wall to fall, for if it had gone outward, it would have taken the cottage with it.

"Andrew!" Byron shouted, and a moment later, the footman appeared in the doorway, the flushed Annie half hidden behind him. "We will go now. But first—first, tell Tom Driver that I will rebuild his smithy if he decides to stay."

"Aye, thy grace." And with that, Andrew swung the door shut, leaving them in darkness once again.

In darkness. Before she could lose her nerve or be interrupted again, Victoria blurted the question she had been wondering since she arrived. "Why do you shun the light?"

Raeburn stilled, and she sensed his sudden strain across from her as the carriage jerked into motion.

"Call it an affectation."

The words were light, but his tone was unequivocal—the subject was closed, and he would tolerate no more questions.

With a sinking in her belly, Victoria leaned back and let the rest of the ride pass in silence.

* * *

"Why did you ask about Annie?" Byron asked.

Victoria stood across from him in front of the door to the Unicorn Room. She had been withdrawn and cold since her unfortunate question in the carriage, and he had been reluctant to allow her to take her leave of him with that edgy awkwardness still hanging between them. So he had taken it upon himself to escort her to her room, and she had voiced no protest.

"Call it an affectation."

Those clipped words came back to him like a blow. Victoria must have read some small betrayal in his face because her own expression softened. She looked uncomfortable. "It's of no importance. Just one of the strange thoughts I've been having recently. I never questioned anything before, I suppose, and now . . ." Her clear gray eyes met his frankly. "Now that I've started, I don't seem to know where to stop." She gave the explanation like a peace offering.

Byron's nod accepted it, and after a moment's pause, he continued his line of speculation. "I asked because . . . well, do you ever wonder what would have happened to your child?" He asked the question softly—after his own reticence, he half expected her to snort and turn away without answering.

But to his surprise, she laughed mirthlessly. "No, because I know too well. Fostered out to a vicar's family, hidden away in the country, or, if that failed, sent with me into exile in Nice or Rome. No, I never wonder, and I am hardly ever sad that it did not survive. It would have been a terrible life for a child."

"And his mother."

"Yes. I admit to that much selfishness." Her look grew far away. "Sometimes—not often, mind you, but some-

times—I look at the other girls who came out the same
year I did, and I wonder which I'd be like, the ones who
hate carrying every child, who call them dirty little crea-
tures and keep them hidden away with nannies and nurse-
maids save for a Sunday pat on the head, or those who
seemed to be transformed from girl-child to matron with
nothing in between, whose worlds are now as centered on
teething and first steps as they had been on day dresses
and dance cards." She shook her head.

"Neither. Those divisions are too simple for you."

She smiled, but her expression had a wistful edge.
"That's no real answer."

"It's the best I can give." He bent down and kissed her
softly, a mere brush of the lips. "I have to meet with Tom
Driver before supper."

She sighed and opened her eyes. "And so you recall
me to my own duties, for I must write to my mother. Until
supper, then, your grace."

"Until supper," Byron murmured. And with a bob of
her head and a swish of her skirts, Victoria was gone.

Victoria closed the door behind her and leaned against
it. She felt emptied as she never had before, and confused. Raeburn was such a frustrating bundle of contradictions that she could make neither heads nor tails of
him. He strove to appear indifferent to everything about
him, but the more Victoria was with him, the more he revealed that he cared deeply, more deeply than anyone she
knew. Duty. Beauty. Even love—she had heard the hurt
behind his jaded bitterness, and though she knew he did
not tell her all, she sensed unhealed wounds festering beneath his impartial façade.

She shook her head free of those fruitless thoughts
and crossed to the night table beside the bed, hoping to

find writing paper and ink there. But when she reached it, she discovered a letter was already waiting for her. The morning post? It must have been, and then taken most of the day to work its way from the porter's house to her chamber.

The handwriting was her mother's distinctive scrawl, beautiful and nearly illegible, but it had an unsteadiness she wasn't accustomed to seeing. Her mother must have been composing messages in the carriage again, Victoria thought as she broke the seal, carrying it to the deep window seat to read in the fading evening light.

> *Ah! My dearest, darling daughter—*
> *How desperately I miss you, and I rue every moment that we did not part more happily.*

Victoria snorted at the countess' usual exaggerations.

> *Rushworth is desolate without you, as am I. I have had to cancel all my engagements in the shire, for I cannot stand to face everyone alone. Lady Bunting was most insistent that I grace her tea— Tea! If such a circus could be given such a dignified name!—but, alas, I had to decline.*
> *I am so desolate without you! Please, hurry back to Rushworth. We all miss you.*
> *Your dearest, most loving*
> *Mamma*

Victoria frowned. The bathos was expected, but the repetition was not. Even more troubling was the reference to Lady Bunting, whoever that was. Old Lord Bunting had been a widower now for three years with no intentions of remarrying, and his son was hardly out of leading strings. Well, whatever was happening back at Rushworth, it would have to wait until the end of the week. Shaking her head, she set the letter aside.

She found writing materials in the night table drawer as she had hoped and began her quick reply. She spoke of negotiations, of walks in the garden, of her maid Dyer— with a fleeting pang of guilt for the lie—and of expectations of returning soon. She finished with a breezy signature, sanded it, and folded it to be sealed later, when she had a candle lit to melt the wax.

Glancing out the window, she saw a slim figure toiling up the drive. Beyond, along the main road, a dark smudge of soot still rose above the village, but Victoria's attention was taken by the walker.

A bonnet blocked her view of the figure's face, but she sensed it must be Annie. Annie, who had somehow made it to the village before the duke's carriage could reach it, who had fallen into her uncle's arms, sobbing, as if he should comfort them both as he watched his livelihood go up in flames. Maybe her tears were meant to give comfort instead of beg for it. If so, it was an expression of sympathy that seemed entirely extraordinary to Victoria. Even accounting for the time it had taken to find Raeburn and rig the carriage, Annie must have sprinted to reach her uncle before Victoria and the duke.

The walker was no more that a few hundred yards from the manor when another figure burst into view from under Victoria's window. This time, the sandy hair and awkward gait left no room for doubt: Andrew. When she saw the footman, the walker sped up, and they threw their arms around each other as they met.

They made no move to kiss or disengage—just stood there, motionless, with their arms locked about each other. Victoria felt a weight settle over her as she watched them, an indefinable sadness that made her feel slow and old—and jealous.

She turned away abruptly, angry at herself that she could even imagine wanting what the maidservant had. She would light a candle and seal the letter now, and then she would find some other occupation for her thoughts. An occupation that concerned only her own affairs.

Chapter Thirteen

"Yet another room?" Victoria asked as Fane bowed her into the study of the Henry Suite.

"I hope you don't mind," Byron said easily, setting aside the quarto. "I decided that you were right. The tower really is too tawdry." He motioned for her to take a seat at the small playing table where supper was spread. "Besides, I was busy with the records. I thought it far more convenient for you to be brought to me."

"Of course." She folded herself gracefully into the chair. "Your taste in women's clothing is quite excellent, it seems," she remarked, motioning to her deep cornflower blue dinner dress. It must have arrived some time earlier that day, but Byron had not received word. No wonder, considering all that had happened.

Byron dismissed that thought. "I can take credit for little more than the colors, I fear." He stood and crossed to her side, judging it with a critical eye. The seamstresses had done well, he admitted. Even working within the conservative constraints of the current dinner fashions, they had managed to create something almost provocative. The bodice was shaped in an imitation of a man's jacket, edged in darker blue ribbon, the deep opening it formed filled by a frilled chemisette. He'd seen a similar style on a dozen other women, but somehow, on Victoria, it had the air of revealing something not meant to be seen. Perhaps it wasn't the dress, he admitted. Perhaps it was the way Victoria held herself or even the way he'd come to think of her.

He shook his head and raised his eyes to her face, surrounded by small, carefully sculpted curls. There was a faint blush on her porcelain skin, and her eyes seemed almost artificially bright, though there was a down-turning of her lips he could not remember seeing before.

"If you were anyone else, I'd say something glib about the gown not being half so ravishing as the woman, but I fear you'd laugh if I were so facile."

Victoria's mouth widened slightly in a small smile. "Oh, no, I wouldn't laugh—but I should be dreadfully disappointed. I thought more highly of you than that."

"Thought? I refrained, and yet I still receive the censure?" He caught her chin in his hand and ran a thumb down the delicate smoothness of her cheek. He did not know why he was so fascinated with the softness of her skin, so different from his own. Had his face ever been unmarred by the hundreds of tiny scars and pits that now covered it? Even at birth, could it have been as sweetly tender as Victoria's still was? He dropped his hand from her face.

Victoria must have seen his frown and misinterpreted it, for she caught his hand in his and looked up at him, gray blue gaze earnest. "I didn't mean to tease. Mirth fits me ill today."

He forced himself to smile down at her. "It wasn't you—only a thought I suddenly had. Mirth seems to have fled me as well."

She laughed, but the sound was hollow. "The fire

punctured the fantasy so neatly. I fear to look at what is left."

Byron took the chair opposite her and uncovered the dishes. "Supper, for one, though I doubt that shall lighten the mood. I'm afraid there are no surprises tonight. Stewed peas, the cook's version of pommes Anna, and leftover cold tongue and rabbit stew." He filled her plate. "You should be flattered. Mrs. Macdougal doesn't take out her fancy French recipes for just anyone."

This earned a freer laugh. "I am duly honored."

They began to eat, Victoria leisurely surveying the room. "Mrs. Peasebody said this is your private suite."

"Mrs. Peasebody is a gossipy old hen," Byron said with feeling. Then he shrugged. "But I can't quite imagine Raeburn Court without her. Like the inconveniences of the architecture, she is both annoying and endearing."

"Indeed." Victoria returned his smile before reverting her attention to the room. "But I would have thought that your own chambers would have something more of you in them."

"What do you mean by that?" Byron asked, stifling his automatic defensiveness as he scooped up a forkful of potatoes. Even with the cook's alternations—was that a hint of pork drippings?—it was impossible to make pommes Anna taste anything but delicious without either undercooking or burning them, and the cook had done neither.

"I mean that I doubt you've done a thing to the rooms since moving in except having them cleaned and rearranging the books on the shelves." She waved to the bookcase behind his desk, overcrowded with records books and ledgers and random scraps of paper that his great-uncle had scribbled notes upon.

"And how would you know that?"

Victoria grimaced. "I've seen the Dowager House, and . . . and I think I can presume to claim that I know you at least to some extent by now. Mangy deer heads, strange little tables crowded with hideous curios, terrible lamps made of all sorts of unspeakable things—it hardly seems your style."

Byron barked a laugh. "I should hope not!"

"I have heard of combining work and pleasure, but it seems that you left pleasure out and simply transported your work into the middle of someone else's room."

"The ghost of my great-uncle seemed to stay my hand any time I even countenanced making a change," Byron intoned. Victoria gave him a skeptical look, and he continued on a more sober note. "These rooms have never seemed like mine. Maybe it shall be different once I begin remodeling the manor house, but I have felt like a stranger in my own house for the past year."

"If you'd at least take away all the extra furniture and bric-a-brac, you might begin to find yourself more at home," Victoria pointed out with crushing practicality. "And then the other changes would come much more easily."

He smiled ruefully. "Too, too true. I suppose I must chalk it up to laziness, then."

She snorted. "If nothing else, this room does reveal one thing about you. Now I understand why you dared me to make the bargain with you."

"Oh?"

"An excess of tedium. This place is layered with it. Every day, nothing to look forward to but another round of expenditures and three-per-cents, musty deeds and sheep diseases. Considering your formidable reputation as a rakehell and a bounder, it is surprising you haven't gone mad."

Byron raised his glass in a mocking salute. "Oh, but I have. The bargain, remember? Twenty thousand pounds for a single week might be a record of some kind."

"Money that you will collect, and with interest, in due time. Money that you could not have collected now under any circumstances. You can hardly call mine an extravagant fee, for I have charged nothing at all."

Byron dismissed her argument with a negligent wave and changed the course of the conversation. "You are calling it 'charging,' now, are you?"

"The word is no crasser than those you have used." She set her silverware down and looked him squarely in the eye, her jaw jutted out slightly. "I whored myself, Raeburn. I've not made pretence of anything more refined. And I don't care because I'm enjoying myself thoroughly and I've spent the last fifteen years caring too much about everything."

Byron looked at her, slightly taken aback by her frankness. He could tell she meant it, meant it perhaps even more than she knew. He wondered if her unconventionality would survive the trip back to Rushworth. After all, habit creates many fetters difficult for even the determined to break, and Victoria didn't seem to realize the implications of her change in attitude. But looking at the set of her jaw and the light in her eyes, he could not believe she would bow back into her old role, whatever happened.

But he voiced none of his thoughts, merely swallowing a bite of tongue and saying, "Eloquently put."

She shot him a narrowed glance. "You would do well not to laugh."

"Am I laughing?" Byron demanded.

"You have that distant expression that means you're hiding something."

"And you think it amusement." He smiled slightly. "Now I am amused. You declare that you've cared too much about what people think, and yet in the next breath, you worry about what I'm thinking."

Victoria sighed, her face relaxing into soft lines once more. "A pathetic start, I suppose."

"Not pathetic. Natural." He reached across the table and took her narrow hand in his. "And I wasn't laughing. I was thinking about what a stir you would cause if you returned to society and . . . and stopped caring, as you say."

Victoria raised her wineglass in a mocking salute. "That would be a sight to see. Me, the talk of London, scandalizing every level of society from Billingsgate to the Buckingham."

He really could go see her, he realized. The idea held a seductive appeal, but the very desirableness made him recoil as if he'd been stung. No, he was finished playing the lord of night and shadows, the mysterious guest, the dark duke. He had no stomach for swirling cloaks and vague allusions anymore, and even less for the whispers that seemed loudest when he tried to seem as other men. His masquerade might have impressed young, fluttery things, but Victoria would give him a single raking stare, snort, and turn aside. And like the proverbial emperor, he would be left naked before the world.

No, better to pass his days among sheep and servants in the country, neither of which would think to question what their master was and what he seemed to be.

"I don't go to town anymore," he said flatly.

That single sentence, dropped inelegantly on the table like a bloodied, feathered game hen, effectively stifled the rest of the conversation until supper was finished. Then they sat, mute and awkward across the table, Byron watching the play of lamplight across Victoria's pale hair as she studiously examined her empty plate, her lips creased in a faint frown.

Finally, Byron broke the silence. "I spoke to Tom Driver this afternoon."

She looked up, her eyes searching his face. "He is going to Leeds."

"Yes."

Victoria's eyebrows rose at the sharpness of his tone.

He sighed. "It seems like they're all leaving. Every few months, another family gives up and goes to Leeds or London."

"They aren't abandoning you." Victoria spoke softly, almost hesitantly.

He looked at his hands, broad and capable as any farmer's, and remembered what she had said about holding back time. A feeling that had been brewing in him for years boiled up, frustration and impotence erupting at the memory of Tom Driver's earnest, agonized face. "I feel like I am failing them. They can't stay anymore, Victoria. Times change, and I haven't figured out how to keep up. Better flocks and new farming methods will make the tenants richer, but it will do nothing for the weavers or the cabinetmakers or the smiths. I can't make this world work for them. I feel like there must be an answer out there somewhere, but I just can't see it." His hands clenched into fists.

"None but the tenants are yours to worry about," she pointed out.

That quiet, practical voice cut across his circling thoughts, and he smiled despite himself. "I sound like a throwback to the days of Edward the First, don't I? The lord who rules his people with judicial disinterest and paternal care. A ridiculous sentiment, I suppose."

Victoria looked at him for a long moment, reading self-mockery and bitterness in his gaze. She kept her expression bland and spoke with careful lightness. "Possibly, but a noble one."

Raeburn blinked, his face going blank, and just stared at her.

"Has no one ever called you that before?" It was Victoria's turn to be surprised.

"I— No. Never." Amusement overcame astonishment in his expression, and he laughed. "Nor have I ever begun to consider myself such except in the most literal, ducal sense of the word."

"Then perhaps you don't know yourself as well as you think."

Raeburn snorted. "When one has as little to occupy his mind as I, one comes to know oneself better than one might like. You have only known me for a few days, Victoria; perhaps I have been on my best behavior and you are the one mistaken."

Inevitably, Victoria's mind returned to the question she had asked in the carriage. "Perhaps. You tell me remarkably little for as much as we speak."

Raeburn's face darkened as he caught her meaning. "Forget it, Victoria," he said softly. "Forget that you ever asked me anything. Most of all, forget there was anything to ask."

Victoria pressed her lips together and shook her head. "I can't do that. You know it's impossible."

She must have betrayed more of a reaction than she had thought because his expression softened slightly. "Will you at least believe that my silence was not meant to hurt you?"

Victoria made her voice go cold. "How could it hurt me? After all, we're the merest acquaintances on all levels but the carnal." She hesitated, but the simmering anger he had roused within her pushed her onward. "And if you thought your choices were to speak or to wound and yet you still chose silence, I do not see why you now seek absolution. You chose the easiest path, believing that you would tread on me to reach it. So what expectations of forgiveness could that wide-eyed insult entitle you?"

Raeburn's mouth tightened. "Once again you cut nicely to the heart of the matter."

There was a warning in his voice, but Victoria ignored it. "I have become skilled at disseminating disillusionment. If you wish forgiveness—since you believe there is something to be forgiven—then there is a solution: Answer my question."

A mask slid over his face, and Raeburn stood abruptly, his chair tipping back with the sudden motion and righting itself with a thud. His eyes never leaving hers, he stalked around the table. Victoria had the fleeting thought that this time she had pushed him too far—this time something had broken within him. He reached behind her and pulled her chair away from the table, spinning it in the same motion until she faced him squarely. She realized she was gripping the arms so tightly that her knuckles were white, and she relaxed her hands with effort, fighting to keep her expression bland even as she felt the blood rush into her face. Even then, though, she could not entirely ascribe her reaction to fear and anger; she felt a second warmth flood across her body that had nothing to do with ire and everything to do with his nearness, the furious heat of his body as he loomed so close over her. She tipped back her chin in defiance, whether at him or at her own reaction, she did not know. Raeburn's face darkened even more.

"You are not the master here." The words were not

shouted as she had expected, but his whisper chilled her more than the loudest roar. Suddenly, all her answering anger flooded away—so uncharacteristically that for a moment she was left mute and reeling. Without that balancing fury, she tottered against the attraction he exerted over her—tottered, and fell.

"I am not," she agreed quietly. His hands gripped her chair back, and he leaned over her so that his face was a scant six inches from hers.

"And you have no right to interrogate me."

"None."

They fell into silence, Raeburn glowering down at her as she battled the lightness in her stomach and returned his gaze levelly. The edge of his cuff slid against her cheek, and she shivered against the prickling awareness that rushed across her skin.

That only seemed to anger him more. "You will not manipulate me. Get up." He emphasized his point by grabbing her arm and all but dragging her to her feet. She gasped at the tightness of his grip, but he ignored her, pulling her across the room and shoving open a door to another windowless room. For an instant, Victoria had the ludicrous impression that she was caught in Bluebeard's castle, but it fled as swiftly as it had come when the light from the front room seeped past him to reveal the shadowed furnishings of an austere bedroom.

She turned toward Raeburn when he released her, but he kept his back toward her as he lit the lamp sitting atop a low bureau. As soon as it was burning steadily, he shoved the door closed. Only then did he face her.

"We had an arrangement."

"I have kept it," Victoria said simply.

"You have asked for more."

"And you haven't?"

His eyes glittered in the orange light of the lamp. "Take off your crinoline. Now."

Now that he was away from her, Victoria could think again, and her irritation sparked anew. She returned his look glare for glare and began unbuttoning the front of her dress, her movements abrupt. She shoved down that other feeling, that weak tenderness, and tried to smother it under layers of ire.

"No. Just your crinoline."

She set her jaw and reached behind her, jerking up her skirt and petticoats so she could reach the crinoline tapes below. She untied them awkwardly, then tugged the hooped skirt down. Raeburn watched her impassively. As soon as it lay at her feet, he closed the space between them, pulling her roughly against him.

"Do you plan on keeping our bargain?" His face was only inches from hers, and she could feel the controlled rage in the force of his grip.

But that touch, as rough as it was, almost undid her. All she wanted in that moment was more of him, all of him, to take his pain and bury it in herself as he buried himself in her. She pushed away those mad impulses, pushed at the rising awareness that skated across her skin and the stirring warmth in her midsection. She forced her chin up and made her mouth speak. "Do you?"

With a muttered curse, he drove her backward, his legs plowing into hers until she fetched up against the wall. Raw emotion spilled across his face, fury and frustration and something almost like grief that twisted his eyes and roughened his voice. She shivered at his touch and the heat of his eyes, and warmth rushed across her skin.

"You don't know what you have gotten yourself into," he grated.

"I know better than you think."

Raeburn let go of her with one hand, reaching for the buttons of his trousers. "This is your last chance."

"I already made my choice." And she realized that she did not want to change her mind. Even then, with his face contorted in directionless anger, she wanted him, and all the quiet, sensible warnings in the world could do nothing to change that. *Come to me,* the wildness in her begged, and when she searched within for the power to resist that urge, the practical, steel-backed spinster she thought she was was nowhere to be found.

He yanked the last button open and tugged at his shirt, and his member pushed free, already swollen. Unceremoniously, he hiked up her skirts, piling them into her hands. She took them, gripped them, hardly able to keep herself from grabbing him instead. He found the slit in her drawers and lifted her up to pin her against wall with the weight of his body. He was heavy against her, his chest almost as hard as the wall against her back. Her hands were caught between their bodies, but even so, she turned them so that she could grip his coat in her fists, pulling him, urging him even closer, if such a thing were possible. His member slid through the opening in her drawers, following the path his hand had made, and pressed against her entrance. She bit back a moan as he slid into her, so hot and hard she feared he would burn her. He drove hard and fast, wrath and passion merged in each stroke, and her own breath came in pants, as if she were the one laboring.

She tried to tilt her hips toward his but the cutting pressure of her corset trapped her. His lips came down hard against hers, shoving her head against the paneling as he gripped her chin and tilted it back to take his kiss. She took him in, accepting, wanting more. Greedy for more. Her skin burned with him, with his anger, and she returned his kiss as hard as it was given.

"Damn it, Victoria, why do you choose now not to fight me?" he gasped, pulling his mouth away even as he continued to drive inside her.

"There is nothing to fight." She spoke against his neck, corded with tension.

Grinding out a curse, he jerked away from her and lifted her in his arms in the same movement. "You are a stubborn, contrary, frustrating woman, and the one time I want you to be difficult, you give in without a whimper."

His arms were strong around her, but even in his ire they were not frightening. Her body hummed in sympathy with his, need and anticipation winding tighter within her. "You might hurt me with your silence, but not with this. I can trust you with this."

He dropped her on the bed and wedged his body between her knees. "You aim to destroy me, and yet you trust me? What kind of madness is that?"

His tip found the junction of her thighs again, and Victoria braced herself, too distracted to answer, her breath quick and short in her lungs.

With a sharp movement of his hips, he was inside her, driving into her until he could fill her no more. She gasped and reached for him, but between his position and her corset, he was out of range, so her groping fingers found only the counterpane. She bunched it in her fists as he surged inside her again and again, his arms hooked under her knees, holding her against him. She knew what he was doing—trying to use her, to make her feel like the whore she'd named herself. But she didn't. She sensed the pain behind the rage, the defensiveness that made him lash out, and it couldn't hurt her. Instead, she rode with him even as he tried to leave her behind, a knot of pleasure bunching in her center so hard it was almost painful.

A moan escaped her lips, and he looked down at her, seeming to see her for the first time since he had dropped her onto the bed, and he gasped out a curse.

And with that, he was on top of her, his mouth seeking hers, hot and suddenly, unexpectedly tender. His hands were everywhere, in her hair, touching her face, popping buttons off her jacket in his impatience to reach her skin. Victoria gasped against this onslaught, far more powerful than his calculated forcefulness only moments ago. Her skin burned with his touch, with desiring him, and anticipation wound tighter within her. She felt the hairs on her arms and legs lift, her entire body prickling as he pulled her along with him, faster and faster.

She gripped his hips hard with her thighs when the wave first broke, shivering out of her core to roar across her body. She threw her head back, panting in the confines of her corset, and her vision dimmed and narrowed until all she could see was Raeburn's face above her, all she could hear was their mingled breaths and the rush of blood in her ears, and all she could feel was him, on top of her, against her, inside of her.

She braced herself against the bed as another white hot wave of pleasure bore her higher, urging Raeburn with her hands and thighs, urging him to carry her even farther, to join her.

And he did.

Chapter Fourteen

Victoria woke to a brush against her cheek and the sudden feeling of emptiness beside her. She fought against the dragging currents of sleep and opened her eyes to find Raeburn at his bureau, lamplight flickering golden across the broad expanse of his back and his tight, narrow buttocks below. As she watched, he drew on his drawers, then balanced with one hand against the dresser as he pulled on his socks one at a time. Still without a glance at the bed, he shrugged into his undershirt, tugging the cloth down to cover his muscled back before pouring a stream of steaming water from the pitcher to the basin and whipping up a froth of soap in his shaving cup.

She held still, naked under the blankets, not wanting to alert him to her wakefulness. She had never seen him thus, so utterly unaware of her. He went about his dressing with the preoccupied unself-consciousness of a man going through the motions of long habit. Each movement was performed with economy, speed, and a kind of fluidity that Victoria had never seen in him before. Usually, there was a restrained abruptness about him, as if every motion were fiercely controlled, constantly checked. Victoria realized that she was seeing him less guarded now than she ever had, but the revelation brought no sense of insight or intimacy.

Instead, she felt a world away, as if she were watching him from the moon through a spyglass. Since their week had begun, she'd shared his conversations, his days, his body, but the part of him that stood now before the mirror, flicking a long razor across the planes of his cheeks and chin—that part of him was not hers to share. That part of him was held aloof, separate, and she had the conviction that it was far closer to the uncomplicated heart of him than anything they had yet exchanged.

She only wished she had revealed so little in return. Raeburn had an uncanny ability to ferret her out, to cajole her until the customs of a decade and a half fell away. He had seen more of her true and hidden self than anyone, maybe even including her. And the deeper he penetrated the barriers between herself and the world, it seemed, the more he insinuated himself behind them and the harder she found it to hold him at arm's length. The night before, when they had roused from their first doze to continue their lovemaking, he had seemed to be everywhere, not just as a man, but as himself, and she'd been powerless to pull away and return their lovemaking to the realm of the strictly mechanical.

Raeburn must have caught a glimpse of her watching in the looking glass, for his posture changed subtly, growing more closed and reserved. He set down the razor and washed the last of the foam from his chin, then spoke as he wiped his face dry.

"You needn't rise so early."

Victoria smiled dryly, trying to shove from her mind her lingering sense of disquiet. "And a good morning to you, too, your grace. What time is it?"

"Nine, or scarcely after."

Victoria shook her head. "Don't you ever sleep? Or is that another of your quirks?"

Raeburn tensed at the reference to his oddities, but he answered easily enough as he pulled on his trousers and fastened them. "I have more quirks than you could dream of. Speaking of which, you still ought to be dreaming now." Two tugs, and his boots were on. "I shall send Annie up later with breakfast. Meanwhile, sleep." He crossed to the door carrying his braces, but he paused with a hand on the doorknob and looked back over his shoulder.

"It was good waking up to you," he said, his voice suddenly soft, but before Victoria could frame a response, the door had swished shut behind him and he was gone.

Byron put away the last of the rosewood dumbbells and chose the two lighter Indian clubs off the wall rack in his gymnasium. He was already damp with sweat and had worked up a pleasant burn in half his muscles. He braced his legs and began to swing the pins in slow, easy motions, savoring the flex and pull of each pass as the weights tugged against his arms.

He loved the hour he spent down among the weights and racks every day, the feeling of control as he pushed himself to his limits. Or at least the illusion of control. Here, at least, he could forget the hidden weakness of his body, how a single, sunny day could destroy him more thoroughly than a fall through a window or kick from a horse. Here, at least, he had power over his body. He could mold it into a machine of lean muscle, bone, and sinew, watch it reshape itself under the influence of his will.

If only his will could heal whatever disease of the blood so crippled him . . .

Victoria would ask about it again. He knew she would, and he knew he could not tell her. A corner of his mind cherished the dream of her accepting his debility without pity, without horror, without scorn, but with sympathetic openness and understanding. But he recognized that picture for what it was—a fantasy, one that could not stand against the test of experience and his knowledge of human nature. Will's young face, contorted in horror, rose without bidding in his mind. He shook his head, dispelling the memory. He should not be too harsh on the boy. After all, Byron loathed the sickness in himself. How could he expect anyone else to do otherwise?

Byron gradually slowed the swings of the clubs, finally letting his arms drop to his sides. He put away the light pair, selected the next set, and began to go through the same pattern of swings, enjoying the heaviness of his tiring muscles and the hypnotic repetition of the forms. No, he would tell Victoria nothing, whatever it might cost him. Then he'd still have the untainted memories of their first days together, and if they departed on strained terms, at least he would not have to carry the memory of her face distorted in revulsion to haunt his nights.

Not that it mattered. He was long past caring what any woman thought. He just saw no reason to expose himself to pointless ridicule.

And yet he had a very hard time convincing himself he believed that.

Victoria frowned doubtfully at Annie's back, holding the candle high enough to shed light for them both.

"You're certain he's in the cellar?" she asked as they started down yet another flight of stone steps.

"Yes, my lady, in one of the cellars." The girl tittered. "There are so many."

"Every day," Victoria repeated flatly. "He spends an hour in the cellars every morning."

"Of course. He's most regular in his schedule, my lady."

"I suppose he is," Victoria said, giving up trying to make sense of it. Every time she thought she was close to the duke, something else would spring up that made her wonder if she really knew him at all.

The staircase gave way to a narrow, stone-lined passageway, the ceiling so low that Victoria had to duck beneath the lowest part of the groin vaults. Annie continued a short distance, then stopped at a low oak door that pierced the blank gray face of the wall.

"Well, here we are," she said. "Does thoo want me to— Shall I announce thee?"

Victoria shook her head. "No need, I'm sure. Thank you, Annie."

The maid hesitated, and Victoria realized that she was carrying the only light between the two of them.

"Rather, I will see if his grace is within, and if he is indeed there and has a light, you may take the candle and go," she amended.

"Thank you, my lady." Annie bobbed gratefully.

There was no doorknob, only a large iron ring, so Victoria placed her hand against the door and gave it a tentative push. It swung open silently on well-oiled hinges, disappointing her expectations of a dramatic groan, and revealed a kind of stoop leading five steps down into a massive, vaulted chamber.

The room was empty except for a tall rack against one wall and Raeburn, who was standing in the light of an oil lamp with his back to her, swinging Indian clubs in a slow, rhythmic pattern. Without looking at the maid,

Victoria passed her the candle. Annie's thanks and departure barely registered, for the duke held all her attention.

He was magnificent. There truly was no other word to describe it. His undershirt was damp with sweat and molded to every contour of his back. He raised the clubs, and the muscles bunched around his shoulders and neck. He swung them down, and the bulge rolled to his back and shoulder blades. Each movement had a poetic, forceful grace, something wholly masculine, wholly fascinating—and more than a little arousing.

Victoria stepped all the way into the room, closing the door of the corridor and descending the five steps to the chamber's stone floor. The flags were gritty under her boots, scattered with fine white sand that had been tracked from the corner by the rack. Raeburn must have heard her crunching step, for a moment later, he let the clubs drop to his sides and turned to face her. He said nothing, merely smiled slightly as if he could read every indiscreet thought that had crossed her mind in the last two minutes. She found herself coloring under his hazel gaze.

"I came to find you," Victoria said to break the silence.

"And why did you think I wanted to be found?"

Victoria snorted at his teasing, managing to be light despite the sense of reservation emanating from him. "And why do you think that I cared if you didn't? The bargain was for a week in your presence, as you so forcefully reminded me last night. There was no mention of me leaving you alone."

Raeburn crossed to the rack and hung the clubs beside a second, smaller pair. "Ah. Only now do I discover my mistake." He took a towel from the rack and wiped his face with it. "I hope that since you expended such pains in finding me you at least enjoyed the show."

"Greatly," she assured him. "To think that I had such an opportunity every morning and yet did not know it! It would be almost worth losing sleep over."

"And thus I am put most properly in my place—ranked right under an hour's sleep."

Victoria suppressed a smile, relaxing slightly. "That should teach you not to fish for compliments."

"I suppose with you I can always expect a shoe on the end of my hook if I do."

"Just so."

Raeburn threw the towel over his shoulder. "Any particular reason you sought me?"

Victoria shook her head. "Ennui. I suspected that there was little chance that you could be as bored as I was."

He chuckled. "I wouldn't know, for how can I judge just how bored you were? In any event, you oughtn't be too bored for the rest of the day."

"Oh?" Victoria arched an eyebrow.

"I've ordered Cook to pack a picnic for us. We'll ride out and eat it at Rook Keep."

"You remembered!" Victoria exclaimed, genuinely pleased.

"And kept my promise. If it suits you, I shall escort you back to the Unicorn Room now and then meet you in the front hall in half an hour. That will give you time to change—and me time to wash up."

"That suits very fine, indeed," Victoria said.

"Well, then, let's be on our way."

Raeburn was waiting for her next to the footman when she reached the front hall. He wore his strange, parson-like wide-brimmed hat and a silk scarf up to his chin, but other than that, he was dressed as any smart gentleman going out for a morning ride. He surveyed her as she approached.

"I have always hated riding habits on women," he observed.

Victoria stabbed the last few pins into her hat as she drew even with him. "Do you feel your rightful place usurped by such mannish dress on a lady?"

He smiled, extending his arm. "I am not so insecure as that. No, I merely find it silly to combine a suit and corset so blatantly. If poufs and froths of lace are a shade over-done, such severity is worse. And as for your hat"—he leveled a disdainful stare at the plumed, feminized version of a top hat that perched on her head—"why, nothing need be said, for it speaks for itself so eloquently."

Victoria took his arm and glanced down across the steel blue expanse of stiff silk that peeked out under her black cloak. It was certainly closer in both color and form to her own wardrobe than either of the other dresses Raeburn had ordered for her. "I rather like it," she said blandly, feeling the obscure need to needle him.

Raeburn just snorted and nodded to Andrew to open the door.

Victoria looked up uneasily at the dark, lowering clouds as they stepped out onto the gravel drive. It seemed more like dusk than midmorning. *So that is why he is willing to go out this day,* she thought. The foreboding in her gut mirrored the shadowed sky.

The groom brought up their horses. Both mounts were spectacular specimens, which didn't surprise Victoria in the least. While Raeburn was not the hunt-mad type— could not be the hunt-mad type—he was fastidious and proud enough to insist that his stables contain only the best horseflesh. But she still raised an eyebrow when she saw that the bay was outfitted with a well-polished sidesaddle.

"Another one of your great-uncle's legacies?" she asked, more to make conversation than because she cared.

Raeburn shrugged. "Princess was intended for Leticia, but he'll suit you well enough, I'm sure."

"*His* name is Princess?" Her disquiet was buried in her surprise.

"Not, of course, his real name. The grooms at Chathamworth dubbed him that, and it was so appropriate it stuck." He grimaced. "You'll see what I mean."

"And the other?" She motioned to the tall black mare.

"Apollonia goes by no other name." He frowned at the groom. "Stephen seems to have neglected to bring a mounting block. Would you like me to help you up?"

"The day I can't mount a horse without assistance is the day I no longer deserve to be called an English lady." She swept by him and swung onto the saddle, her skirts swishing. She adjusted them with a tug and hooked her right leg over the support so both hung down the left side. She took the reins from the groom with a nod. Oh, how she had missed this! The feeling of contained power under her, the swooping freedom of muscle and flesh. It had been not even a week since she had last ridden, but it seemed like a lifetime.

Raeburn gave her an amused glance and mounted Apollonia with light grace. The mare tossed her head, more welcomingly than restively, and he nudged her into a walk. Victoria guided her horse abreast of him, and they started down the long drive.

"Is he always like that?" Victoria asked Raeburn, giving Princess a doubtful look. The gelding was prancing—

no, *mincing*—along the road, neck arched and hooves high.

Raeburn smiled. "And now you know why he's called Princess. But no, he'll tire of it in half an hour, and other than his vain streak, he's quite a steady horse."

Victoria made a face. "I was hardly worried that I might fall off."

"Never been thrown, have you?" Raeburn asked blandly.

"I was practically born on a horse—of course I've been thrown." She smiled. "And kicked, and almost rolled over once by one sassy little mare."

"Quite the horsewoman," he pronounced solemnly. He gave her a narrower glance. "Let me guess—none of the rest of your family rides."

"How quickly you come to the crux of it! No, my mother hasn't been on a horse since long before my birth, my father's gout keeps his range short, and my brother prefers to race light carriages along the back lanes to terrify the local populace. I, however, ride."

"Almost every day," he guessed.

She looked down the slope of the bare hill, stretched out so invitingly below her. "Almost every day, for hours at a time."

They were silent for a long moment as Raeburn led them off the main drive and down a narrow side path. Princess wrinkled his nose and champed the bit at being asked to walk through the grass, but after his initial protest, he went calmly enough, only his ears indicating his disdain.

"Is it only to escape your family?" Raeburn asked finally.

Victoria smiled, a trace of her old trust returning for the first time since their dinner the night before. "I'd be a sad woman if it were, wouldn't I? No, I've loved to ride since the day Father put me on top of my first elderly, rotund pony at the age of three."

"You still remember that, do you?"

Victoria wasn't sure whether he was surprised or not, but she nodded. "Better than almost anything. At first, I was bored and cross because it was hot, the pony smelled bad, and I had a brand new doll waiting for me in the nursery. The groom led me around and around on the end of a lunging line until I was so heartily sick of it I started to develop some plan that would make them take me back inside."

"And then?" Raeburn prompted.

"And then—they gave me the reins. And the groom let go. And suddenly, I was the freest thing in the world . . ." She smiled at the memory. "After that moment, they could hardly keep me away from the stables, and they had to give poor Nurse a stolid little pony of her own so that she could follow me across the grounds. But when I was seven and I got my first governess and Nurse had Jack to watch over, I convinced them to allow me to ride wherever I wanted. No nurse, no governess, no groom, no maids, no mother, no father. Just . . . alone. I could do whatever I wanted, and no one would frown or correct me."

"And what did you want to do?"

Raeburn's question brought her back to herself, and she laughed.

"Run wild like the Red Indians, charge down hillsides until it seemed my heart flew out in front of me. Be mad and reckless, everything a nice little lady is not."

Raeburn's look was meaningful. "You haven't really changed, have you?"

She sobered instantly. "No. I suppose not. I suppose

everything has just dammed up inside until a half hour's dash isn't enough anymore."

That reply killed the conversation for several minutes, and they crossed the moor in silence, heather and furze brushing against their legs, catching at the fabric of their clothes. Eventually, Raeburn looked across at her and gave her a twisted smile. "Surely you aren't opposed to dashes now?"

His attempt at lightening the mood was transparent, but Victoria accepted it gratefully. She threw back her head. "Is that a challenge?"

In answer, Raeburn leaned forward in the saddle, and his mount jumped forward in a canter. Laughing, Victoria followed.

"No fair!" she cried. "I don't know where we're going!"

Raeburn grinned at her over his shoulder. "Not that it would much matter, anyway!" he shouted back.

Victoria gave Princess his head, and the horse galloped gleefully in Raeburn's wake.

An hour later, they emerged from a narrow wooded valley just as the first fat drops of rain began to fall. Victoria had asked why it took them so long to reach the ruin when it seemed so close from the garden; Byron had replied that it was indeed close—if one cared to scramble down a cliff to reach it. For the less nimble, this was the only way.

Victoria looked up. Ahead of them rose the mound of Rook Keep, a long ridge leading up to the broken shell of the old castle. From their angle, she could see that the shape of the hill was too regular to be natural and that the flat-topped ridge was the remains of a causeway.

It was only when Raeburn looked back at her, a smile on his face, that she realized she had stopped.

"Well?" he asked.

"Well, what are you waiting for? Lead on, before it begins to rain in earnest!"

Raeburn nudged his horse into a walk and started across the moor toward the looming black shape of the keep.

Victoria should have felt excited or at least curious, but as they approached, her feelings returned to the apprehension that she had felt the previous day. The keep looked less and less like a building and more like the stump of some great stone tree trunk that had grown from the ground, hill and all. It was blatant in its bulk, yet there appeared to be more shadows among its tumbling ramparts than there should be, more depths and heights than its size alone could account for. Wrapped in arrogant fastness, it seemed to defy her as it defied the surrounding landscape, rearing up against the cloud-tossed sky. Again, she had the strange sensation that there were answers there, among the stones, if only she could understand them. And those stones and shadows called to her even as they rebuffed her.

Her eyes were drawn involuntarily to the stiff shape of the duke, riding a horse-length ahead, and the inevitable comparison arose in her mind. She tried to shut the thought out, but the closer they drew, the more insistent it became.

The horses' hooves clattered on half-buried cobbles as they started up the ridge toward the keep, clacking and sliding across the slick stones.

"It was destroyed during the Civil War, you know," Raeburn said conversationally. "Even then, it had been uninhabited for a century, but since the manor house itself had long been indefensible, my Cavalier ancestors made their stand in Rook Keep."

Victoria said nothing, looking up into the broken shell and trying to guess which of the holes had been made by cannon and which by age.

By the time they reached the top, the sparse raindrops had turned into a steady drizzle. Directly before them rose the square tower, but a little off to the side appeared a second stone structure, low and long, completely hidden from the ground by the curve of the hill. More surprising than the sudden appearance of building itself was the thick thatch that covered half the roof.

"Come this way," Raeburn said as he dismounted, smiling mysteriously.

He led his horse through a doorway in the low building, one of the animal's back hooves thudding dully as it caught on the edge of a half-buried stone. Victoria peered into the dimness, trying to see how large the clear space was inside, but even with the spreading cloud cover, it was too dark within to make out much of anything. So with a mental shrug, she dismounted and followed him in.

Chapter Fifteen

Byron watched from a far corner of the room as Victoria hesitated, blinking, in the doorway. *Never one to leap into the unknown,* he thought wryly as her eyes finally fixed on him and she led her gelding inside.

"I thought you said the keep had been abandoned for two hundred years," she said as she approached, looking up at the sagging roof above them.

Byron took her horse's reins and tied it to a post below his own. "It has been." He loosened the girths and gave each mount a pat on the shoulder. "But during lambing season, the temptation to use this building as a shepherd's shelter must have quickly proved too much." He gestured to the opposite end of the long room, where a burnt circle sat beneath a hole in the roof and a bare cot was shoved against the wall.

"Oh," Victoria said. Her mouth twisted in an arid smile. "I have lived over half my life in the country, and I only now realized that I know nothing of the planting and lambing and calving that is the life of the tenants on my family's estate."

Byron raised an eyebrow, amused at the idea of her running out in her nightclothes to the barn to witness the first birthing of an experimental generation of sheep or getting bloodied up to her elbows in a frantic attempt to save a beloved mare. "Not many ladies do. Nor gentlemen—few who hold more than five hundred acres know in any detail what's occurring on their estates."

Victoria's smile gentled, grew curious. "But you do."

Byron shrugged. "I needed something beyond debauchery to fill my youthful years, and since my greatuncle gave me free rein over four of his lesser estates, I had plenty to divert me." He gave her a sideways look. "Come. You wanted to see Rook Keep, and as yet you've seen nothing but the interior of an outbuilding."

"Gladly," Victoria said, looping the long, narrow skirt of her riding habit securely over her wrist. She followed him across the uneven threshold back into the drizzly day. "If I may be so bold, how many estates do the Dukes of Raeburn hold?"

Byron paused, offering her his arm. "Nine, including Raeburn Manor itself. I own several blocks of London and half a dozen near-worthless Bath town houses, too." She rested her silk-clad arm lightly on his, her soft kid gloves lying delicately on his wrist. "The lands are still extensive, though only five estate residences remain open to me."

"Oh? What happened to the others?" She spoke to him, but her gaze was fixed upon the stump of the tower rising directly before them.

Byron watched her covertly as he answered, gauging her reaction. "One, I demolished. It had little to recommend it if it had been in the finest condition, but as it was, it was not fit for habitation. The second, I let out to a shoe manufacturer from London who wanted a nearby country estate to further his social ambitions. The third is now a boy's school. The fourth has been entirely incorporated into a cheese-making enterprise."

Victoria looked at him then, surprise but no shock written on her face. "I would have thought, with the attachment you have toward the manor house here, that you wouldn't have wanted to let the other residences go."

He stopped and turned to fully face her. "It's all well and good to speak on about fine traditions and family history, but I plan to make my contribution to the legacy a group of profitable estates, not another list of debts." He took up her arm again and resumed their slow walk toward the keep. "Times are changing, Victoria. Fifty years ago, the dukes and earls of England were the greatest men in the world. Now even the richest could be bought several times over by the London businessmen." He smiled humorlessly. "We get our revenge by cutting their sons in Hyde Park and refusing to invite their daughters to our teas and balls, but if the truth be known, we're a little afraid of them, afraid that soon enough we'll be the ones cut from their visiting lists." He gave her a sidelong look. "For all we know, Annie's children will refuse to recognize the next Duke of Raeburn, much to his chagrin."

Victoria shook her head, her eyes bright over windbitten cheeks. "Perhaps that is a balance for the weavers and smiths whose fate you lament. But it all seems too incredible. Even here"—she gestured to the monstrous ruins—"where I should be able to believe most easily in the downfall of our class." She smiled slightly. "But this should illustrate my point as well as your own. No matter how the mighty are fallen, they still retain a memory of might that is greater than the most fantastic achievements of the small."

"So you consign our heirs to decay and dissolution."

He laughed dryly. "I think I would prefer oblivion to that!"

They reached the base of the tower, and Byron stopped in front of a narrow fissure in the stone wall. "This is the only way in from this level. The wooden stairs leading up to the main entrance were lost long ago."

"Well, then," Victoria said, throwing back her shoulders in a parody of bravery, "allow me to lead the way."

She edged through the gap in the wall, then stopped dead.

"Oh," she said, her eyes wide as she looked around.

Byron peered over her shoulder. Even though he had visited the ruins a dozen times before, there was something almost sacred about the space that made him catch his breath. Outside, the wind-swept hill was bare and sere, icy drizzle whipped against the old walls, struggling weeds flattened and beaten even in the lea of fallen stones. But within the shell of the keep, there was a protected stillness, a hush that seemed almost unnatural. They stood on a narrow ledge that dropped away before them into what had been the cellars of the keep. The detritus of two centuries had collected on every flat surface—the treads of a moldering staircase, the decaying arches that had once supported wooden floors, in odd angles of stones that jutted out from the walls. And wherever there was soil, bushes and weeds flourished, forming a strange hanging garden that seemed to wrap the space in a kind of spell.

Victoria cast him a sudden, fey smile and hopped onto one of the tilting blocks.

"Is it safe?" she asked.

He looked up at her. "Not if you go jumping about like that, but last time I was here, it all seemed solid enough. There's a skeleton of a lamb down in the cellars, though—warning enough of what can happen if you aren't careful."

She raised an eyebrow. "I'm as nimble as a goat, not a lamb, but I'll take your warning to heart." A small leap, and she was perched on the bottom step of a stone staircase that wound its way up the wall.

Byron's stomach lurched at the way she balanced on the edge, but there was a challenge in her eyes, and he knew that if he said anything, he'd only provoke her into greater recklessness. So he just leaned against the wall with the best semblance of nonchalance he could manage. Victoria looked strangely at home among the tumbled stones, as if they called to a wildness within her. She would make a good ghost for such a place, he thought suddenly. There was something in her spirit that did not welcome peace.

"Aren't you going to join me?" she asked, her pale eyes bright and her head cocked quizzically to the side.

"As you desire," he murmured in mock acquiescence, shaking off his lingering sense of disquiet. He stepped up after her, his boots scraping against the rain-slick blocks.

She turned away and continued lightly up the staircase. Though Victoria kept up a pretense of carelessness, Byron's misgivings were slightly assuaged by the way she subtly tested each block before committing her weight. Still, Byron made it a point never to be more than an arm's length behind her. If she slipped, he wanted to have at least a chance to catch her.

Ahead of them, the staircase grew less solid. Cracks began to appear in the steps, and farther up, chunks of stone were missing. Victoria paused for a long moment, and Byron was on the verge of ordering her down when she squared her shoulders and took two more steps to draw even with a window slit. There, she stopped, turning

to face out over the landscape. Her expression changed as
Byron watched, her customary guarded impassivity replaced by something more tender and almost awed. Muted
sunlight angled through the window to illuminate her
face, fine features picked out against the gray stone, the
precise nose slightly upturned, the delicate lips relaxed for
once and slightly parted, as if she were drinking in the
wind. She was a creation of porcelain and light, shining
with a vitality that could not be contained by mere flesh.
Byron had a sudden conviction that, no matter what happened in the next three days, this was how he would always remember her—an ethereal creature caught in a
defenseless moment.

Heavier clouds rolled in over the sun, extinguishing
the soft light, and the moment was broken. Byron sighed.
He should be glad, for greater darkness meant greater
safety, but he could not suppress a pang of regret.

"It is very different from the rolling farmlands I'm
used to, but no less beautiful, in its own way."

Byron smiled even though she couldn't see him.
"Soon you'll be echoing the sensibilities of the illustri-
ously monikered Lake Poets."

Victoria snorted without turning around. "If you're too
much of a cynic for the Pre-Raphaelite Brotherhood, I am
certainly too much of a cynic for Wordsworth and Cole-
ridge." She glanced up the stairs. "I should like to go
higher, but I don't dare risk my neck, coward that I am."

"Wisdom and cowardice are too often confused,"
Byron intoned.

That earned him an exasperated glance cast over her
shoulder, but Victoria said only, "I suppose I should go
down. There's nothing more to look at up here. We're
both getting damp through, and it looks like the sky will
let loose at any moment."

Byron reluctantly led the way back down the stairs. At the bottom, he extended his arm to Victoria, and they passed through the gap in the wall side by side.

And as if that were some kind of sign, the clouds let loose and the drizzle turned into a sudden downpour.

Victoria made a noise of vexation. "This will be the second time you're responsible for getting me soaked!"

Then, without warning, she pulled herself free from his arm and made an undignified dash for the shelter of the outbuilding. Before she reached its overhang, though, the sound of her laughter rang out over the hiss of the rain—not a sardonic bark at the futility of keeping dry but a reckless, joyful peal that seemed to surge from some force deep in the earth until it found voice in her throat.

When he ducked through the doorway a few seconds later, Victoria was standing hatless and dripping in the middle of the room, hanging her cloak from a peg on one of the roof beams. Even in the darkness of the rain-lashed shelter, he could see that her hair was completely disheveled, her eyes bright and her cheeks flushed. She shot him a look that he knew was supposed to be reproving, but her glowing face betrayed her attempt at severity.

"I shall be lucky if I'm not ill for a week after this foolishness," she said.

Byron pulled off his own greatcoat and hat and hung them beside hers. "I doubt that you are inclined to infirmity."

Victoria snorted. "You might pretend to be contrite."

"I might if it weren't so obvious how much you enjoyed it." He unwrapped the scarf from around his neck and draped it over the coat.

To his surprise, Victoria actually looked abashed. "You heard me?"

"Like a bell. It was unexpected, to say the least." He

made the last sentence suggestive, inviting her to provide an explanation.

She paused, her expression conflicted, then dropped her eyes to her hands as she slowly peeled off her gloves. "You've caught me out, I see." She laughed, but the sound was strained. "You must think me mad."

"Never." He took off his own gloves and caught one of her hands between his. His were cold from the rain, but hers was icy. He frowned. "Surely there's some firewood in here."

Victoria pulled her hand from his, looking around with more energy than his comment warranted. "Over there," she said, nodding to the corner where the shepherd's cot sat. She hesitated. "But should we use it? I should feel rather guilty if I thought someone else might go cold—"

Byron waved away her worries as he crossed over to the pile of wood, half hidden under the cot. "The shepherds go around to all their shelters a few weeks before lambing to make sure there are supplies. Besides, they aren't supposed to be using this building at all. Just think of it as rent." He looked at the charred spot of the fire circle on the floor, now darked with the rain that had fallen through the roof.

"By the door?" Victoria suggested.

Byron nodded and scooped up an armful of deadwood, carrying to the doorway, where he arranged it to one side of the threshold. He took a box of matches from his coat, and on the third try, he got the fire alight. Victoria drew near as the skipping, hiccupping flames moved from the tinder to catch the kindling, which burned with a steadier glow.

Her gaze slid to the doorway where the rain sheeted down. Byron waited patiently for her to speak, laying out the blanket, china, and picnic luncheon next to the fire.

Finally, she sighed. "Do you ever feel sometimes like there's a . . . a kind of rush in your blood? As if a piece of you just wants to fly away and never stop?"

He thought of the delicate sneer on Leticia's face when she had sat so calmly in her parlor and insulted him, of the insane impulse that had overcome him and driven him north into Yorkshire, riding like a madman—of the urge that had first sent him reeling into society after Charlotte's betrothal to Will Whitford and, even earlier, the fierce resolution to never reveal himself again after Will's display of horror-struck revulsion.

But that wasn't what Victoria was speaking of. He knew instinctively that what she said had nothing to do with that furious tumult of anger and despair that had seemed to wrest sanity from him. He thought of his childhood, of the days spent in darkened rooms when just beyond the thickness of the velvet curtains, there was an entire world of colors that he could only see in stolen glimpses when his tutors and nurses had turned their backs. He thought of how he would steal those looks again and again, drinking in blue skies and emerald lawns long after the sting of his face warned him to stop, how the next day, feverish and aching, the nursery maids would tut-tut over him, wondering how he could have possibly been burned . . . How could he have explained how the lawns and gardens, not even worth a glance to them, seemed to call to some smothered part of his heart? How could he tell them that he would trade places with the gardener's half-witted son just to be able to run barefoot and bareheaded across the grass with the sun kissing his face?

He glared out into the rain, the cloud-swathed sky only a shade lighter than dusk. This was his world—the hours when the sun was veiled by storms, the moments of winter dawns and sunsets when the light was weak and impotent. There was no use longing for sunshine, as that foolish boy had. And yet . . . a part of him still did.

Byron realized that Victoria had been watching him for nigh on five minutes while he stewed and stared. Her expression was guarded, as if she half expected him to make some sort of dismissive response, but there was another undercurrent to it, a flickering of something like sympathetic pain, as if she suspected that there might be more in his silence than repudiation.

"Yes," he said finally. "I think I know what you mean."

She nodded and ducked her head, and for a very long time, that was all that was said.

The rain had lightened from a downpour to a drizzle again. From the doorway, Victoria could see through it to the countryside below the hill, where a few sodden sheep huddled in the lea of a hillock and the smoke from chimney-pots tangled in the gentle wash and was pressed back to earth. The chill air was so damp she could almost drink it, and she imagined that it tasted sweet and brown, like the soil it smelled of. The clamminess that crept along her limbs was almost pleasant, because with only a small shift back toward the fire, she knew she could drive it away again.

"What will you do, Victoria?"

Victoria started, brought suddenly back to herself by the sound of Raeburn's voice. She considered pretending she didn't know what he meant, but that was pointless. "When I return? I will take each day as it comes. What more could I do? You have accused me of being false to myself. How true would I be if I began making plans when I truly have no idea of what I want?"

"Point taken."

Victoria turned to look at him, spurred by the same sense of division, of the distance between them that had been haunting her since she had arrived. "And you—what do you want?"

He smiled humorlessly at her from the shadows behind the doorway, where he had retreated when the rain first began to lessen. His hair had dried in wild tufts that stood out around his head, making his rugged countenance seem almost feral. "I am the Duke of Raeburn. What could I possibly want that I do not have?"

Victoria snorted. "The Dowager House to be finished. Raeburn Court to be habitable. All your lands to be profitable again. Perhaps not Leticia, but a wife. An heir, for you did not build the nursery for nothing. You want what everyone wants—happiness."

His expression darkened. "And you do not think that I am happy?" The words were quiet, but they had a warning tension in them that would have made Victoria change the subject two days ago.

No longer. She met him stare for stare. "No. I do not think you are happy, and I do not think that you ever have been. You're a hurting, lonely man, and the more you do to try to disguise it, the more you betray yourself. You admit that you drew up the plans for the Dowager House for yourself, not Leticia. You designed it on a dream, on an image of domesticity that is so . . . foreign to everything you've ever represented yourself to be that almost no man who thought he knew you could believe you had anything to do with it. You accuse me of robbing myself, but I am nothing next to you."

She stood restlessly. "You've heard my story. But you've kept yours so close to your bosom that I can't begin to fathom it. For three days now, you have asked all the questions. For three days, I have spread myself out bare for you, like an eager cadaver on an anatomist's table. No more." She shook her head. "Only once have I asked you a question of any substance, and that one question you refuse to answer. What do you fear? What has the world done to you—what could it do?—to make you lie and hide yourself away?"

Raeburn stood abruptly, looming over her with his face such a twisted mask of emotion that she thought for a second he might strike her. She recoiled instinctively, then stopped herself and deliberately straightened, lifting her chin in defiance.

"You will not frighten me into silence this time."

She faced his glare without flinching, his hazel eyes burning into hers. His mouth opened, then shut again, muscles bunching in his jaw. For an instant, a mere instant, she thought she saw him soften . . .

Then the moment was gone. He spun on his heel, turning his back to her and striding over to the horses. "The rain has stopped, and it is lightening. We must go." The words were guttural, ground out, and they made Victoria want to scream. But there was nothing she could do.

She sagged against the wall, defeated, as Raeburn tightened the mounts' girth straps. She had no hold over the duke, she realized bitterly. She only had the bargain, that flimsy piece of paper that kept them both at Raeburn Court for the space of a week. She'd allowed him to wrap his influence around her, to tease her secrets out of her, to make her almost believe that he cared . . . And when she asked for something in return, he gave nothing because their week was only a diversion, and he would put nothing into it he did not care to lose.

Fool. She knew she deserved a hundred names worse than that, but that was the only one she could come up with to begin to encompass the enormity of her self-delusion. *Fool.* The bitterness of it made her belly churn. She should have turned her back on the duke when he had first offered her that ridiculous bargain. She should have marched out of Raeburn Court and never looked back.

Why not now? she thought suddenly. Why *couldn't* she leave whenever she wanted? Raeburn himself had pointed her to the truth. She couldn't go on as before, and she had no intentions of it, so why should she stay here? She almost laughed with the freedom of it. Her brother had made his own bed—let him lie in it! As for her, she would leave this tumbledown ruin and its dissolute duke with the next mail coach. She'd leave him, and she'd never, ever look back.

The thought was both heady and sickening. She pushed away from the wall, suddenly lightheaded, and glared at Raeburn's back, still firmly turned against her. Her stomach clenched, and she clutched the door frame for support against knees that suddenly wanted to betray her.

One more chance, she told herself. I have to give him just one more chance.

"I will ask this only once more," she said, her voice trembling despite her resolve. "Byron Stratford, why do you shun the light?"

He stiffened, went utterly still. For four whole breaths, Victoria stood watching him, standing there as if he'd turned to stone. Then he seemed to shake himself, and he turned to face her. Victoria's stomach dropped at his expression, closed and terrible. Never had she seen such a cold light in his eyes nor such hardness around his mouth. Even before he spoke, she knew he would not answer her.

"You know you have no right to ask me that," he grated.

"No," Victoria agreed, her voice cracking on the word.

A hole seemed to open before her, under her feet, and she had the horrible sensation of sliding, falling, all while she was rooted in the doorway. "I have already admitted that I have no right at all, no more than you did to ask me your own questions. I can do nothing but repeat what you said and ask for your trust. After all, what will it matter in a week?" Her voice sounded distant, as if it were coming from someone else, far away.

Raeburn's face contorted. "And like you, I can choose whether to answer. You chose to speak; that is your own affair. I choose silence."

"Then there will be no week!" The words came out half gasped, half sobbed. She launched herself from the doorway and barreled past him, yanking her mount's reins from his unresisting hands and pulling the horse after her. The room seemed impossibly dark, and there was a ringing in her ears. Her breath rushed through her lungs, but she still felt like she was drowning. As she barreled past the pegs on which their outer clothes were hung, she snatched his wide-brimmed hat from the wall.

"Stay here. Cower in the shadows until night falls. But whatever you do, don't you dare come after me."

Victoria barely recognized her own voice, hissing with bile. Raeburn's eyes widened, and he took a step toward her, but by then, she was through the doorway and swinging onto her horse. She kicked her mount into a gallop as Raeburn burst outside behind her. She didn't look back— she would never look back—but she heard him skid to a stop and call after her.

No, she repeated grimly. She would never look back.

Chapter Sixteen

"Damn you, Victoria!" Byron roared. Victoria's only response was to lean forward in the saddle, urging her horse to an even more reckless speed. His black hat flopped from her hand like a wounded bird, and Byron cursed again, ducking back inside to fetch his own mount. He yanked on his gloves and swung into the saddle, sparing only a glance at the emerging sun before urging Apollonia into pursuit. With Victoria's head start, he would barely catch her before she reached the woods. But no matter what, he'd be damned if he'd sit helpless in a shepherd's shelter while she rode out of his life. She wouldn't leave until he was bloody ready for her to leave, and then only with his last words ringing in her ears.

She must have heard the sound of his horse's hooves on the causeway, because her riding crop tapped her mount's side and Princess put on another burst of speed. Byron ground his teeth and followed.

Then time seemed to trip. Suddenly, the horse and rider ahead of him were no longer galloping down the causeway but slipping wildly to the side and plunging down the slope, his hat whirring out of Victoria's hands as Princess lurched. The horse whinnied in terror, his hooves sliding over wet stone. One leg caught, and he pitched to the side. Still holding fast to the saddle, Victoria snapped through the air like the end of a whip. The horse met the ground with a sickening thud, his rider pinned beneath him.

Even from a distance, Byron could see Victoria's body go abruptly limp. He spat another curse, this one with the force of terror behind it, and charged down the causeway after them. He couldn't think—he didn't want to think—

Before he could reach them, Princess rolled to his feet. Victoria was pulled from the ground as her boot caught in the stirrup, but the horse shook himself, and her ankle slipped free. Princess danced away from where she lay sprawled, his eyes rolling.

"Oh, no you don't," Byron ground out, pulling up Apollonia, but it was too late. Princess gave a snort, turned tail, and ran back toward Raeburn Court.

"Hell," he said with feeling. Turning back to Victoria's form, he added, "And bloody hell."

He swung off his mount and dropped the reins, trusting Apollonia to stay where she'd been left despite Princess' defection, and slithered the six yards down the side of the causeway to where Victoria lay.

To his relief, she was sitting up by the time he reached her, clutching her ankle between her hands.

"Are you all right?" he asked as he skidded to a stop beside her.

She let go of her ankle, and the glare she shot him proved that the fall had done nothing to change her mood. "I will be fine." But the words were even more clipped than the glare could account for, and he suspected that the tightness around her eyes was as much pain as anger.

His own anger had been snuffed by the sight of her body flung beneath the weight of the horse. God, he might have lost her— He stopped that thought before it was fully formed, but still his belly tightened churningly, and lingering horror roughened his voice. "Princess is gone. Let me help you to Apollonia—" He started to slip a supporting shoulder under her arm.

"Leave me alone!"

The exclamation was so violent that Byron released her at once, rocking back on his heels as if he'd been struck. There was fury in it, but even more alarming, there was a catch that in any other woman would have made him think that she was dangerously close to tears.

Victoria pushed herself to her knees, then stood slowly, hissing harshly as her right leg took her weight. "I will do it myself," she said through gritted teeth. She took one unsteady step up the slope.

"Victoria—" Byron started, his fear for her changing into irritation now that she was safe. "Your ladyship, do not be foolish. You can hardly stand, let alone climb a hill unassisted."

"I do not need your help," she snapped, but even as she made her declaration, her leg gave out from under her, and with a sharp cry, she fell to her hands and knees. Byron caught up to her as she knelt there, gasping, her fingers digging into the bracken.

"Let me help you up—"

"No!" She pushed to her feet and took another lurching step.

Byron's temper snapped. "Victoria, stop this childishness before you get us both killed!" He seized her elbow to steady her, but she turned, swinging at him, her face twisted horribly.

"Don't touch me!"

Her blow connected with his chest. It wasn't very hard, but between the punch and her turn, it was enough to wrench her elbow from his grasp and send her reeling backward. She put a foot back to catch herself, but the leg crumpled under her, and suddenly her expression turned from anger to fear as she pitched down the slope.

She hit the ground, but her momentum sent her sliding, rolling, tumbling ever faster down the hillside. Byron scrambled after her, heart in his throat, but it was no use. A dozen yards, two dozen—a boulder stood in her path, but there was nothing Byron could do but watch as she hit it, striking it with first her hip and then, with a sickening sound that seemed to crash through his bones, her head.

The breath sobbing in his lungs, Byron half crawled, half slid to where she lay. "Damned proud idiot!" he snarled, unable to coherently voice the fear and rage that tumbled inside him. He didn't know whether he meant her, himself, or both of them.

He ripped off a glove and grabbed her cold wrist, and for a second he couldn't see, couldn't breathe as he felt for a pulse. And then there it was—the faintest flutter under his fingertips.

He let out his breath all at once and sagged down next to her, weak with relief. He pulled her limp body away from the boulder, and his hand met with something warm and sticky. Blood. Her pale hair was matted with scarlet where her head had struck the rock.

Fearing what he'd find, he pushed aside the curls where the blood seemed the thickest. There was a shallow gash with a swollen knot already forming around it. When he prodded it, it was hard and unyielding, not the softness of crushed bone as he had feared. *Thank God*. He cast a glance back at the inviting shelter of the shepherd's building. A fire waited for them there, and shade. He could keep her warm and dry until someone came to find them.

But there was no water, only a little wine left from lunch, and she might die without a doctor. Carrying her unconscious to Raeburn Court might injure her further, but it had to be safer than simply hoping she did not become feverish before help came.

She hung limply from his arms as he levered her upright, and he had no choice but to sling her like a sack of flour across his shoulders, her head and arms dangling down one side of his body, legs down the other. He straightened under her weight. By his feet lay her ridiculous parody of a top hat; his own was nowhere in sight. With the momentum of Princess' fall and the steepness of the slope, it could be anywhere. He looked up at the sun, peering through the clouds, and imagined he could already feel it burning into his flesh.

"God!" The word tore at his throat, half oath and half prayer. But there was no help for it. He had to get Victoria back to Raeburn Court as soon as possible, and so the hat was lost to him. But the blanket—he remembered with knee-weakening relief that the blanket Mrs. Peasebody had packed for their luncheon was waiting back in the low stone building. First, he had to get Victoria back to the road. Then he would fetch the blanket.

Bent almost double, slipping with every step, he struggled up the slope to the causeway where Apollonia waited patiently. His boots found little purchase in the mud, making every step a treacherous, sliding lurch. Stones taunted him with the easy handholds they offered, but he didn't dare let go of Victoria to grasp them. Twice, the slick bracken refused to take his weight and he landed heavily on a knee, and once, he overbalanced and almost pitched backward, but he regained his footing at the last moment, gritted his teeth, and pushed on. It seemed like an eternity before he reached the road again, and when he did, he could only stand gasping stupidly and blinking in the sunlight for a long moment until he got his breath back.

He slid Victoria off his shoulders to check on her. She showed no signs of rousing, but her pulse was steady, though it seemed no stronger than before. There was nothing he could do but get her to Raeburn Court as soon as possible. His impotence mocked him, and it was with almost a physical pain that he left her there for the time it took to dash back to the shepherd's shelter, snatch up the blanket, and run back.

Apollonia shied sideways when he first tried to lift Victoria across the saddle, and he wasted precious time to calm his mount enough to accept the limp, flopping weight across her back. He managed to swing up behind on his second try, then levered Victoria around so she straddled the horse's withers with her face pressed against his chest. He hauled the blanket over his head, wrapping it around Victoria and as high as his own nose, awkwardly shading his eyes. One arm around Victoria's waist and the other holding reins and blanket both, he urged Apollonia into a fast walk, not daring the jolt of a trot.

"Lord preserve us from the stubbornness of women," Byron muttered, but the tightness in his chest was fear, not rancor.

The sun beat down mercilessly. Even with his collar turned up and his head ducked under the blanket against the light, he could feel it searing his cheeks. How long had he been out in it now? Five minutes? Ten? At this rate, it would take two hours to reach the shelter of Raeburn Court. He resisted the urge to nudge Apollonia into a gallop. Once they reached level ground, he promised himself. Even though the sun was drying the cobbles of the causeway, there were too many puddles and too many slick places to risk speed there. If Apollonia stumbled, he could not guarantee that he could keep Victoria from pitching over the mount's head.

Finally, finally, the end of the causeway neared. Apollonia, already restive from her rider's tenseness, sprang forward at the touch of Byron's heels, taking the last dozen yards as a flat run. Byron crushed Victoria against him. Her head flopped against his chest at every stride, and he prayed the gallop was doing her less harm than the increased speed was helping her. Already his face felt like it had been stung by a thousand bees; he could only hope his pain was not clouding his judgment.

Apollonia slowed at the tree line, and they passed through the shaded relief of the woods at a more controlled canter. It was with dread that he saw the bright end of the trail. But there was nothing to be done, so he braced himself as his mount plunged into the light.

The rest of the ride faded into a blur of brilliant agony. The blanket slid again and again, and a mask of fire spread from the skin around his eyes to the end of his nose and the lower half of his forehead, searing and constricting the skin until he couldn't think, couldn't do anything but tighten his grip around Victoria's waist and keep Apollonia pointed home.

After a blazing eternity, he finally spied the bulk of Raeburn Court on its bald hill, but it seemed to hang in front of him like a fevered dream as he rode and rode, never getting closer. Then suddenly, he was pounding around the side of the manor into the stable yard. Through the haze, he saw Andrew look up from his pipe in alarm as Byron reined in Apollonia to a halt and dismounted, pulling Victoria into his arms.

"Find the groom," he rasped at the gaping man. "Tell

him to saddle up Dob and ride to Weatherlea for Dr. Merrick as fast as he can. Then cool down Apollonia and send someone out to find Princess. Lady Victoria has had an accident."

"Aye, thy grace," the man managed, but Byron was already brushing past him, up the steps and into the blessed shadow of the house with Victoria cradled in his arms like an infant.

"Thy grace, thoo really should leave now. We'll take care of her ladyship just fine until Dr. Merrick gets here, and thoo needs to look after that face—"

"No." Byron cut Mrs. Peasebody off midsyllable, his tone harsh enough that she glanced up from her patient for a moment.

Victoria was laid out on top of the coverlet of her bed in the Unicorn Room, Annie supporting her while the housekeeper unbuttoned the back of her riding habit. She still hadn't stirred, and with every moment that passed, the sick knot in Byron's chest grew tighter. His face was burning, and though he refused to glance in the mirror over the washbasin when he paused to splash cool water over it, he knew from experience that it would look as terrible as it felt. And it would only get worse. He hadn't been burned so badly in years, not since that one careless day as a boy that he still remembered in his nightmares . . .

"Thy grace, it just isn't right, and with thy burns—" Mrs. Peasebody began again.

Byron's fraying temper snapped. "Listen to me, old woman. Either you leave me in peace, or I'll dismiss you and tend to her myself."

The housekeeper opened her mouth, then shut it again

without saying a thing and pressed her lips into a hard
line.

Byron snorted and opened the chamber door.

"Where's the hot water?" he bellowed down the staircase, then slammed the door shut before anyone could
give a reply.

"Thy grace, these things take time—" the housekeeper
began, but one look at his expression and she silenced
herself again.

The maid and the housekeeper had stripped Victoria to
her petticoats. She was so fragile-looking, so cold and
colorless that Byron had to fight the urge to snatch her
away from the women and cradle her against the heat of
his own body so that the stir of her breath against his
chest could remind him every second that she was alive.

Instead, he stood with his back to the fireplace as two
kitchen maids entered with buckets of steaming water,
their heads turned away from the ruins of his visage as
they hurried out again. Even these servants, who should
have been used to the sight from his great-uncle's
episodes, were horrified by him.

He glowered as the housekeeper stripped the last layer
of clothes from Victoria and sponged away the mud and
blood from the dozen cuts and bruises that covered her
thin frame. His hands ached almost as much as his face—
he should be the one washing her wounds, they told him.
He should be the one to surround her with warm bricks
and bundle her up in an eiderdown. When Annie lifted
Victoria's head for the housekeeper to begin removing
the hairpins around the gash, Byron could no longer contain himself. He took an involuntary step toward the bed,
his hand extended to forestall them.

The two women looked up, pausing in their work.
Even as preoccupied as he was, he did not miss the

queasy fear on Annie's face as she looked at him. If Victoria woke now, would her expression be the same?

"I—I will do that," he managed. "And I will sit with her until the doctor comes. You are dismissed until then." His voice sounded strange and harsh, as if it belonged to someone else.

Mrs. Peasebody opened her mouth, the look in her eyes one of automatic protest, but she paused and her expression softened, and when she spoke all she said was, "Of course, thy grace. We'll be waiting outside if thoo needs anything."

A moment later, they were gone.

Byron's sigh caught strangely in his throat. He took the comb from the night table, sat above Victoria's head, and began to work his fingers through her hair, slowly, carefully finding each hairpin and pulling it out, setting them gently aside as if they were the most precious things in the world. Once he was certain they were all gone, he unwound her hair and began to comb through it softly, picking out the bits of twigs and bracken that were caught in it and sponging away the mud. It seemed like forever before he reached her scalp, and he set aside the comb and took up a soft cloth instead and daubed it carefully, working closer and closer to the angry gash until he finally cleaned the wound itself.

Victoria groaned and stirred the first time he touched it, her face creasing but her eyes remaining resolutely closed.

"'Tis only I," Byron said hoarsely, a new fear welling up in his throat—this one entirely selfish, a fear of being seen and repudiated.

But he had no reason to worry, for she silenced at his voice and did not stir again, and he returned to his work.

His own pain dulled with the distraction of tending to hers.

Finally, he was finished. He dried her hair as best he could and replaced the damp pillow under her head with a dry one. Then he blew out the lamp beside her bed and sat in the darkness to wait, clasping one of her limp hands between both his own, the burning of his face echoing the burning fear that tightened his heart.

Chapter Seventeen

A sense of speed, a rush, a sudden piercing pain that lanced through her body. She swam up through fog, toward the red-tinted light on the other side of her eyelids . . .

Voices, like birds, chirping incomprehensibly from far away, high and female and nonsensical, and then another, deep and measured—

"Head injuries are tricky things, your grace, and I would not stake my reputation on what she's suffered until I can talk to her, but I shouldn't think that this one will cause any more damage than a blinding headache for a day or two. The ankle, now, that will take longer to heal. She's broken it, right enough, but it seems to be a clean break, and she'll be just fine in six weeks or so. I've bandaged it and elevated it, which is all that can be done for her now."

"Thank you, Dr. Merrick."

That voice—that voice was not like the others. She knew that voice, and it both soothed her and stung her like a whip. She struggled through the fog, but still it dragged her under again, a thousand feather quilts pressing upon her.

"Now, I'll leave these drops with you, Mrs. Pease-body. Put one of them into a cup of beef tea every two hours and dribble it through her lips, if she'll drink . . ."

She fought, but the sounds of the voices slurred, ran together, were lost in the dark pit that opened under her to swallow her up.

She struggled against oblivion—for seconds, hours, days, she couldn't tell. Then—

Red light, flickering, and the sense of confinement. She dragged her eyes open against the weight of her lids. The light went from red to yellow and hammered into the back of her skull. She moaned, and a shadow rose in front of the light.

"Hush, now, dearie. Everything will be fine."

She wanted to shake her head, but it hurt too much to move. The voice was wrong, the cool, soft hand on her head was wrong. The hand she wanted was larger, rougher, and the voice was a soft rumble, not a twitter.

"Where is he?" The words stumbled from her thick lips. There was something important she must remember, before the flight, before the tumble . . .

"Hush, now," the voice twittered again. "Hush, now, and drink this."

A cold edge was pressed against her lips, and warm liquid sloshed against them. She opened her mouth automatically and swallowed when the liquid hit the back of her throat, then swallowed and swallowed again. Her eyelids grew heavier, too heavy to keep open, but she didn't fight them because she remembered what had come before.

She had left. And he would never forgive her.

"I called you here for Lady Victoria," Byron said roughly. "There is nothing your science can do for me."

Dr. Merrick frowned, eyes still flickering over the ravaged skin of Byron's face. "I can make you a plaster and give you some medicine to keep fever at bay, your grace. I *am* familiar with the peculiarities of the condition. Your uncle had great faith in me."

"For all the good it did him. Your plasters only burn." Byron sat—slumped—on the desk chair of the Henry Suite's office. He was tired to his core, more tired than he'd ever thought possible, and his face still felt like a brand had been passed across it. The clock on the mantel declared it to be only just past midnight. But he felt as if the bone-deep weariness of the past two years had been condensed into one crushing moment in which he was suspended. "I will take your medicine, though, whatever it is. There seemed to be some value in that, the last time."

"Of course," the doctor murmured and dug in his small black bag until he produced a green jar of powder. "Dissolve a teaspoon in a glass of water or tea and drink every four hours." He set the jar on the table beside Byron's chair. "And keep cold compresses on your face if you won't have my plasters. They will lessen the pain and the scarring."

Byron stared moodily at his desktop. "Do you think a man could die of it?"

Dr. Merrick paused delicately. "Of your condition, your grace? I do not know. I suppose it is possible, if you spent a very long time out in the sun and got an infection in the burns. But I have seen only one other case of it— your great-uncle's. He was not killed by it. One may argue that it drove him mad, but it did not kill him."

"Pity."

When the elderly man spoke again, Byron recognized the impatience doctors reserved for patients they felt were being self-indulgent. "There is no reason that one with the disease and your wealth cannot lead a long, happy, fulfilled life. If you choose to let it drive you mad, you have only yourself to blame."

Byron turned and leveled a glare at him. The doctor subsided with a murmured, "Your grace," but his expression remained stubborn.

Byron shook his head. "The life of a hermit—yes, that is mine to freely enjoy. Good night, Dr. Merrick. It is late, your room has long been prepared, and you have not had any rest yet. Tell me when you visit Lady Victoria again. Until then, good-bye."

With a small, stiff bow, the doctor left Byron to his black thoughts.

Darkness and light, each with its own pain. Dreams of running, sometimes with the fear of flight, sometimes with the soul-branding terror of the pursuit of something that was lost. And through the mist, his voice, wordless, bodiless, calling her, mocking her, but always, when she stumbled to the place it had been, gone.

"Where is he? Where is he?"

"It seems she's become a little feverish. Nothing unexpected, after what she's been through."

"Hush, dearie."

"Nothing to worry about. Keep the dosage steady, and she should be fine."

"Drink this, now."

"Where is he?"

"Her fever should break soon. It doesn't seem to be serious, but the body frequently responds to such trauma in that way," the doctor said, shutting the door of the Unicorn Room behind him.

Byron grimaced, then regretted it immediately. Despite the hours he had spent with cool, wet cloths on his face, it still throbbed abominably. "Let us hope so. And her injuries?"   ·

"The swelling on her head is already beginning to recede, and her broken ankle is just that. In two months, Lord willing, she won't even have a limp."

"Thank God," Byron muttered, but there was more bitterness than gratefulness in his tone. It seemed so monumentally wrong that she should be injured at all that it was hard to feel anything but anger.

Dr. Merrick took off his spectacles and rubbed them on his handkerchief. "She keeps calling for someone, your grace." His expression made it clear that he had a good idea who she was asking for, though he wouldn't guess outright.

"I know," Byron said shortly. He had not returned to the Unicorn Room since Mrs. Peasebody first reported that Victoria had briefly regained consciousness.

The doctor sighed and replaced the spectacles on the end of his nose, tilting his head up to peer through them at Byron's face. "You should be keeping cold compresses on that, your grace."

"Yes, I know," Byron repeated. "Thank you, Dr. Merrick. Mrs. Peasebody will send for you if you're needed again before morning."

"Yes, yes," the doctor muttered, still examining Byron's face. Then he shook his head slightly and shuffled down the stairs toward the bedchamber that had been prepared for him.

Byron leaned against the door as soon as the old man tottered out of sight. Inside, he could hear the low murmur of voices, Mrs. Peasebody's constant flow punctuated by Annie's more hesitant responses. Neither was the voice he wanted to hear, the one that had last rung out clearly in a rejection of him and everything he offered. *Then there will be no week!*

Could that same voice, laced with fury and bile, be the confused, thick voice that had cried out for him through opium dreams? He shook his head, rolling it against the door. He could not puzzle it out. Not now, with the pain of his face sliding between his thoughts, unraveling them before they could take shape. All he knew was that he could not answer her call. When the fever broke and the drugs stopped clouding her mind, she would issue a second rejection, as clear and cutting as the first had been furious, and he would not bare himself to that. Not again.

He closed his eyes against the burning in his face and deeper, in his gut. No, whatever he did, he could not let her see him.

Nightmares still clung in tatters around the bed when Victoria finally opened her eyes. The room was swathed in darkness, and it was a long moment before she realized where she was. She had a dazed recollection of worried servants, a hoary old man with a thoughtful expression, and warm drinks of beef tea, laced with something more bitter that washed away the pain but sent her into dreams full of confusion. And before that, the shove that sent her hurling down the side of the causeway. *Her* shove. And the expression on Raeburn's face as she wrenched away . . .

She pushed back the stifling blankets, nudging rag-wrapped bricks away from her body and letting the blessedly cool night air caress her naked flesh. Her head throbbed dully whenever she shifted, and there was a constant, warning ache in her right ankle and hip, but her mind was clear if sleep-heavy and her eyes, now that they had adjusted, could make out vague shapes in the darkness, blacker shadows and coal-gray patches that she struggled to reassemble into her memory of the room.

Then it came. That stirring that was more felt than heard or seen in the darkest corner of the room. She strained her eyes, but the blackness swallowed everything. Still, under the scents of camphor, lamp oil, and the ashes of the fire, she thought she caught a hint of sandalwood.

"Raeburn," she said, the name coming out like a breath. "You came."

Something happened in the shadows, a stiffening or cessation of movement so minute Victoria had not realized there had been any movement to begin with. And then silence, stretching out thin and taut.

And nothing more.

For a long moment, she held herself tense, hardly daring to breathe. But there was nothing but the heavy darkness that wrapped around her, pulling her down under its smothering weight. She fought it second by second, but slowly, inevitably, she slid toward the beckoning oblivion of sleep.

On the edge between dreams and waking, though, she thought she heard a sigh and a whisper: "I couldn't help myself."

Dawn found Byron back in the cave of his bedchamber. Exhaustion and pain had finally made him powerless against Mrs. Peasebody's badgering, and he had stumbled back to the Henry Suite, ostensibly to get some rest. But now, sprawled on the bed, he could not sleep. His face stung despite the chilled, wet cloth he had placed over it, but worse were his thoughts. They buzzed through his head like hornets, angry and circling, without respite.

Why hadn't he stayed away? He'd planned to visit her only for a moment, he had promised himself—while Victoria was asleep, when she'd never know. But that moment had stretched into minutes, the minutes into an hour, and she had awoken.

And she had known.

That thought sent a surge of something indescribable through him, some strange emotion that left his senses humming and his mind jangled. She had known, and she had called his name, and he had . . . done nothing. He had been incapable of response. What could he have said? "Yes, I am here, but you have seen me for the last time." And if she had asked why—why he was there, why she would never see him again—what would he have answered then? The mere thought of lying to her made him sick, but the truth he would never confess again. Once was enough.

The honesty of children is a dangerous thing, he thought bitterly. But at least it kept him from having to repeat a lesson that was hard enough to swallow once . . .

It had been a dark and wind-torn day, with just enough rain to stir the trout while not being enough to keep young boys indoors. Just a few months shy of public school—a route only one of them would take, as fate would have it—Byron and William Whitford had made the most of their last days of freedom. Byron's weakness had come upon him years before, so Will was well used to his neighbor and best friend's eccentricities and knew the cloudy day would be one of their few remaining chances to play together outside.

How many times Byron had wanted to confide in Will the exact nature of his disease! How many times he had started to speak and been held back by the memory of the warnings of his mother and nurses! It was well he said nothing, for that summer day would prove that the revelation of his secret was the death of his innocence.

Bundled up to his nose and with a broad-brimmed hat, Byron followed Will to their favorite spot on the stream and settled under the spreading branches of an ancient oak. They played the part of serious anglers for all of half an hour, and when that met with no success, they began amusing themselves around the stream as boys do— wading in the knee-deep current, skipping stones, racing sticks. Byron kept to the shadow of the oak and kept a sharp watch on the sky, but the day showed no signs of brightening. Finally, the boys sprawled belly-down on the wet grass and talked about their plans and expectations for school and cursed roundly their parents' blindness in insisting that each follow his father's footsteps, Byron at Eton and Will at Harrow. Slowly, their talk drifted away into silence, and they fell asleep.

Byron had woken to agony. As he slept, the tree's shadow had moved and the sun had come out, searing half his face, the backs of his calves, and even the soles of his feet. His cry of pain roused his friend, and as Byron tried to explain, words tumbling over each other, Will's eyes got only wider and wider as his face grew tight in a mask of horror until he stumbled to his feet and ran away.

A groom had eventually found Byron wrapped in a ball of misery at the foot of the oak, his face so blistered he could barely open his mouth to speak, his feet too tender to walk. He still had not healed when Will left for Harrow and school began at Eton, but he no longer cared. He informed his mother of his intent to remain at home for his education, regardless of the special precautions

Eton had agreed to take. She had not had the heart to refuse him and had engaged the first in a series of tutors.

Byron never breathed a word of what had passed between him and Will, but it was a breach that never healed. For the next decade that Byron had remained in his parents' house, he and Will met half a hundred times at dances and dinners during the breaks between terms. Always, Will would avoid his eye, slipping to a far corner of the room and pretending to be engaged in animated conversation with some county matron or debutante. Once or twice, Byron caught Will looking at him with an inscrutable look on his face, but they never spoke again. Not even when Will had become engaged to Charlotte Littlewood, the woman Byron had thought he wanted to marry.

Was he foolish? Byron asked himself for the thousandth time. Had he taken the shock of one young boy too much to heart? But Will had not been any young boy. He'd been Byron's closest friend, his only friend, his confidante in almost everything. Will had accepted every oddity of his behavior without question . . . until the moment of discovery. If his closest childhood friend reacted to his weakness with such revulsion, how could anyone else be expected to accept it?

Even Victoria. Especially Victoria, who accepted nothing without turning it, weighing it, picking it apart first.

But still, even with his old shame fresh in his mind, even with the searing pain reminding him every instant of what stood between them, he could not steer his mind away from her.

And when, finally, he slipped into dreams, everyone there wore a mask of her face.

Chapter Eighteen

When Victoria woke the next time, daylight was streaming through the windows of the Unicorn Room and she was wrapped again in blankets up to her chin. She lay staring at the canopy for a long moment, limbs too heavy to move.

The light and the soft, out-of-tune humming that was coming from the hearth told her Raeburn was no longer there, and Victoria couldn't suppress a surge of disappointment. That presence, that voice—had she heard the voice?—they had been enough to make her believe, if only for a moment, that he had forgiven her.

Forgiven her for what? she demanded of herself. She'd done nothing wrong except leave, overstepped no boundaries he hadn't crossed time and time again. Yet the memory of his twisted expression held her answer. She had hurt him. As strange as the idea seemed, she knew it was true.

Yet he had followed her. She clung to that fact. He had followed her despite their argument and his aversion to the sun. A jolt of guilt shot though her. Someone had carried her from the keep to the manor house. It could have

only been Raeburn. Had he found his hat? Were his eyes
hurt? Would he come to her again?

Speculation would get her nowhere. With sudden de-
cisiveness, she pushed all but the bottom layer of blankets off and sat up, wincing as her head protested the
movement and pain lanced up from her ankle.

The humming stopped abruptly, and a moment later,
Mrs. Peasebody was at her side.

"No, no, no, my dear, you can't be getting up yet!" she
protested.

Victoria's bladder said otherwise, and she told the
housekeeper so. In another five minutes, she was back in
bed, this time clothed in her nightdress and propped up
against the headboard. Mrs. Peasebody rang for the doctor and spent the time before he arrived fussing over her
until Victoria wondered how much of her headache was
from the blow and how much from the housekeeper. But
she held her tongue because she knew the old woman
meant well, and the rings around the housekeeper's eyes
attested to a long and sleepless night on her account.

The doctor arrived just as Victoria was finishing the
last of the gruel Mrs. Peasebody had pressed on her. Victoria had never much cared for porridge of any type, and
she had no appetite that morning for anything, so it was
with relief that she set down the spoon as the elderly man
tottered in.

He was, as she had expected, the solemn, hoary-
bearded man she half remembered from the night before.
He showed Mrs. Peasebody out, then ordered Victoria to
lean forward so he could inspect the lump on her head.

He prodded it delicately, occasionally harrumphing.
Finally, he released her and nodded. "Just as I thought,
though it's easier to tell now that the swelling has reduced. Shallow cut, almost certainly no fracture. It will

be tender for a few days longer, but there should be no lasting damage." He peered at her keenly over the rims of his spectacles. "No dizziness, your ladyship? No problems with memory or movement or speaking?"

"I have hardly been allowed out of bed, but there are none to my knowledge," Victoria replied, bemused by his grandfatherly efficiency.

The doctor harrumphed again. "Then let's have a look at that ankle." He unwrapped the bandage and removed the splints that supported it, but he did not try to bend it, merely squeezing it gently with one cool, papery hand as Victoria gritted her teeth against the pain. He made a noise of satisfaction and rewrapped it with practiced speed. "It's broken, of course, your ladyship," he said conversationally. "A simple fracture, so you should stay off it and keep it wrapped for six weeks, and you'll be right enough again. I would, however, recommend against falling off horses in the future."

"A recommendation I fully intend to take to heart," Victoria replied dryly.

The doctor nodded and put the back of his hand against her forehead. "Still a touch of fever, I think, but that should pass soon. If you're in too much pain, I've left opium drops with Mrs. Peasebody."

Victoria shuddered, remembering the dark dreams that had pursued her through the night. "No, I'm sure I shall be fine."

"Then you may begin to resume more normal activities tomorrow, but you shouldn't try to walk for another month. Two weeks more with a cane, and then you can remove the bandages for good." He patted her hand, rose, and turned to go.

"Wait," Victoria called as he reached the door. "How— how are the duke's eyes?"

The doctor looked back at her over his shoulder, surprise written on his wizened face.

"His grace's eyes? His eyes are perfectly fine." He turned away again.

"And where is he now? If I might ask?"

"Sleeping, I should hope, your ladyship," the doctor replied. "He's doing as well as can be expected, considering, but he's as stubborn as his great-uncle."

And before Victoria could frame another question, he left.

Byron knew he would have to look in the mirror eventually, but he could not bring himself to it. He slouched in the chair in his office nearest the grate with a cool cloth across his throbbing face. He would have happily thrown the cloth into the fire if removing it wouldn't make his face hurt worse; he had little faith in its healing abilities beyond the temporary assuaging of pain.

What would he look like after it healed? He remembered his great-uncle's face with a shudder—there was not an inch of skin that wasn't thick with netted scars, his ears and bulbous nose deformed with them. Then Byron would be an exile in truth; he could not appear in society twisted and deformed, confirming all the ugly stories he knew circulated about him. He imagined spending the rest of his days in the Dowager House alone, a monster amid its beauty. He could find no amusement in the incongruity.

Even if he were not so marked this time, there was no guarantee that he would be preserved the next. No, it was best for him to become used to being a recluse now. Perhaps then isolation would smart less when he had no choice.

At least he had sent that damned doctor packing with

his poultices and plasters. The man had made Byron's great-uncle his life study and seemed to feel he had some ownership over Byron because of it. Dr. Merrick was a good man, a compassionate man, but all of his poking and prodding and experimentation—useless, like those of the dozen doctors Byron had seen before him—made Byron want to strangle him. It was bad enough suffering from such a weakness; it was far worse to be confronted with someone who seemed to find it an endless source of fascination.

He had every right to be angry with Victoria. After all, if she had not stolen his hat and then shoved away from him when he was trying to help her . . . But to Byron, her part merely seemed a piece of the greater irony of his life.

Victoria would be all right, Byron comforted himself. Dr. Merrick had assured him of that. Even if Byron would never see her again, he would not have to bear the guilt of sending her away with some injury that would never heal. Will, Charlotte, Leticia. God, did he spoil everything good thing that ever happened to him?

Byron closed his eyes under the cloth and tried to force his mind toward sleep, but it was a long time in coming.

"Tell me more about the old duke," Victoria said, looking out over the front drive and, in the distance, the collection of cottages that was the village and the burnt-out shell of the smithy. Mrs. Peasebody had protested her rising from bed, but Victoria had too much of a headache to read and felt she would go mad if she had to spend another hour staring at the unicorn tapestry while the housekeeper knitted and fussed over her. Especially when her mind kept straying to the warren of dark passages and the man who lurked deep among them . . .

So Victoria had hopped over to the window with the housekeeper's assistance and sat on one of the seats built into the wall, her leg propped on the stone seat across from her. Staring out of the window was an improvement—at least the undulating landscape did not seem so intimately, inescapably a part of Raeburn as every stone of the manor did.

"What do you want to know, thy ladyship?" Mrs. Peasebody asked.

"I don't know." *Anything that will distract me from thinking of his successor.* She shook her head, banishing the thought, and her eyes fixed on the charred remains of the smithy. "Tell me about him and Annie's mother," she said, picking a subject at random.

The rhythmic click-click of Mrs. Peasebody's knitting needles slowed. "Well, dearie," the housekeeper said after a moment's pause, "there's not much to tell, I suppose, and what there is to tell is more than I ought to be telling. Not that I suppose it can do any harm, but it doesn't seem right, spreading stories about the dead. But if thy ladyship wants to know—"

"I do."

"Polly was a chambermaid, of course. I believe I told thee of that."

"You did."

"Well, she was. And I suppose the greatest ambition that ever crossed her mind back then was to become a parlor maid. She'd never hoped to marry, dearie. She wasn't pretty, though I'm the last woman to say an unkind word, as thoo knows. As a matter of fact, most would call her downright homely. That alone would make it hard enough to catch a man, but with three brothers, she had no expectations, and she was a little slow in the head. Kind, mind—let no one say I did not grant her that—kind, but slow."

"Then why did the duke want her?" Victoria asked, curious despite herself.

"Ach, dearie, it isn't the way thoo's thinking—not this one, at least. The old duke left us servants alone and brought up his entertainment from the villages and Leeds. No, Polly became his nurse after the one he hired from London left him. They used to talk for hours, a half-mad old man and a dimwitted village girl, and I suppose after a while, he didn't seem so crazy and she didn't seem so stupid."

Struck by the housekeeper's unaccustomed directness, Victoria looked away from the window to where Mrs. Peasebody sat in front of the hearth, her knitting lying forgotten in her lap. "Did they love each other?"

The housekeeper shook her head. "I don't know if you could call it love, exactly. Not much of my business, anyway. But the duke never did change his ways, and Polly never seemed to expect him to. They were both very lonely people, though, and I think, after a while, they understood each other. And when little Annie came along and Polly died a few months later, his grace saw to it that she was raised and cared for."

"Did she know who her father was?"

Mrs. Peasebody shrugged. "No one kept it a secret, though his grace never said nothing about it. A close-mouthed one he was, if there ever was one! But the day before he died, he saw Annie alone. I never asked her what he said. Reckoned it was none of my business."

Mrs. Peasebody lapsed into silence, and Victoria returned her attention to the window, where she stared out at the slash of the road and village below and thought of the masters of Raeburn Court.

Chapter Nineteen

The light that spilled through the windows of the garden room was still anemic with the early hour, but Victoria drank it in as if it were as rich as treacle. As if its touch could erase the memory of another, more tender caress, as if its warmth could replace the sharper heat of need and skin on skin . . .

Beyond her stretched the terrace, and beyond that the wild gardens she had wandered only three days before. Victoria tried to forget all those things. Her eyes were fixed on the antics of a pert, round robin, but no matter how she tried to set her mind on the tilt of the small, gray head, the touch of the sun across flicking feathers, it always escaped to scuttle back into the shadows of the house to the man who hid there. It was over, she told herself again and again, but each time she did, something within her rebelled, and she knew it was no use.

Though her head no longer hurt except when she touched it or turned too quickly, she felt like it was wrapped in layers of blankets, insulating her from the world, making everything around her seem unreal, almost dreamlike. She leaned against the back of the Bath chair, lying back onto the pillow snugged beneath her

head. The old duke's Bath chair, Mrs. Peasebody had
said. She thought she could still smell the old man on it,
a mixture of stale opium, camphor, and decay clinging to
the wicker as if to remind her that not even that much was
hers.

"My lady?"

Victoria looked up from her sightless staring to find
Annie in the doorway, a piece of paper clutched in her
hands.

"My lady," the girl repeated, "there's a letter for thee."
The maid crossed the room and handed it to her with exaggerated care, as if even such a small motion could
somehow injure her. "I could call Mrs. Peasebody to read
it to thee . . ."

"No need," Victoria assured her. The envelope bore
her mother's hand, and Victoria's fingers clung to that
small proof that the rest of the world still existed beyond
Raeburn Court's walls.

"Does thoo need anything else? More breakfast? A
book?"

"No, Annie. That will be all, thank you."

Annie scurried out. Victoria stared at the letter for a
long moment. Soon, very soon, she would be tracing the
missive's path back to Rushworth. Soon, she would escape the waking dream of Raeburn Court for the usual
round of county parties and then, close on their heels, another season in London. She had spoken only two days
before of her determination not to fall into her old patterns of behavior, but now it no longer seemed worth
fighting. The routines were ingrained with the years.
How much easier it was just to drift along as before.
What was so worth fighting for, after all?

She opened the letter, noting that her mother's handwriting was even shakier than before, and began to read.

My most precious daughter,

How go things in the north? I forgot you were gone this morning and went to look for you, but Jack reminds me of these things, the good boy that he is.

Today I wandered about the garden. I am writing you from the gazebo overlooking the pond. Jack is here with me—he will not leave me alone these days, the dear boy. My headaches have returned, worse than ever, but you mustn't worry about me. Jack tells me you are straightening out some business matter, though what matters you could possibly straighten, I have no idea.

Please come home when you can. I suddenly find myself missing you,

Your loving Mamma

Victoria frowned. If the last letter had been odd, this one was far stranger; it seemed impossible that her mother had written such a rambling missive. Her sense of unreality returned, stronger than ever; there could be nothing beyond the manor house, and her incipient departure would be a plunge into utter unknowable darkness . . .

She sighed at herself, shaking her head at her own imagination, and tried to blank her mind of everything but the pattern of sunlight on the flagstones of the terrace.

Byron stood in the shadows of the doorway. From his angle, he could see nothing but the pale top of Victoria's head above the curve of the Bath chair, her hand lying over one arm with a piece of paper dangling from her fingers. The pale, smooth hair and the white hand drooping like a wilted lily—they were enough to make his chest tighten, so small and lost in the musty old room.

He should go, he knew. He couldn't come to her—not with sunlight streaming through the windows, not with his face still feeling tight and painful, not with the mass of welts and blisters he knew his face to be. But he did not stir. He simply stood and watched as seconds ticked by into minutes. Victoria didn't move, didn't even twitch a finger, and Byron thought that perhaps she had fallen asleep.

Footsteps echoed up the corridor, and he stood aside to let Annie duck past. Victoria turned her head as the girl entered the room, her face still blocked from Byron's view by the high wicker back of her chair.

"I came to see if thoo was needing anything, some tea, a pillow for your foot."

"No thank you, Annie. I'm fine as I am. You may go." Her voice was quiet, but Byron felt a great disconnection in it, as if the woman were speaking from some far away place, and he wondered if she'd been taking the opium the doctor had left for her.

Annie turned back toward him and hurried by in her apologetic way, and he was left alone in the doorway again. For a long moment, Victoria sat as if frozen. Then the top of her head disappeared from view, followed by her hand, and it was a moment before Byron realized that she must be cradling her forehead in her palm.

It was time to either speak or leave, he knew, and he hadn't the strength or sense to turn his back on her then. So he spoke.

"Lady Victoria—my sweet Circe." He hadn't planned what he would say, and the endearment escaped like a sigh.

There was a rustle as if Victoria had stiffened suddenly, and then her voice. "Yes?" The question was soft but incredulous, as if she were doubting her own senses.

"I must speak with you."

"About our bargain." It was not a question. "I understand. I have broken the terms of our agreement, and so my presence here is no longer welcome. I apologize for inconveniencing you, and I assure you that I will leave as soon as I am well enough to travel." The words grew faster as she spoke and ended in a kind of breathless rush.

"No." The word spilled out of his mouth before he could stop it.

"Pardon?" Now there was a new stillness from the chair, tense, wary.

"No," he repeated harshly. "You will not go. The contract is not broken unless I say that you have spent these past two nights contrary to the way I desired you to spend them. I say no such thing. The contract is still in force."

The top of her head appeared again; she had straightened. "But I left, and I have been injured—"

"You attempted to leave. But you didn't. The contract was not broken."

Silence stretched out between them, and finally she asked, in a voice as thin as spun glass, "Why, Raeburn? Why do you want to keep me here? I am no good in your bed now."

Byron scowled, then winced as his expression pulled tender flesh. "Because I've become accustomed to you, I suppose. Because I want the full balance of what you agreed to the day we met." *Because I want you, for whatever time is left to us.*

There was another pause.

"Would you—would you come out where I can see you?"

Byron's heart contracted, and he had to take a breath

before answering. "No. You won't see me again before you leave."

Silence, interminable silence, and then a ragged gasping sound, and Victoria's head disappeared behind the chair back. The sound came again, and Byron realized that she was weeping.

About him.

He had a mad impulse to rush into the room, to scoop her into his arms and tell her she would never, ever need to cry again—

But the sun poured mercilessly through the window, the sun that had seared his face, the sun that would expose him to her for what he was—a scarred monster, a freak—and so he did not move. He did not dare do anything but stand for a long moment, his own rasping breath drowning out Victoria's quiet sobs. Then, unable to bear it any longer, he spun on his heel and strode blindly through the corridors, seeking the oblivion of darkness to swallow him, to wash through him, until there was nothing left but a shell.

He did not know how much later it was when he found himself in the windowless bedchamber of the Henry Suite. He had not consciously sought it out—he had not meant to direct his feet to any place as he paced through the endless, winding corridors, but he arrived nevertheless. The room was pitch black, but Byron knew he was one step to the right of the bureau, three long strides from the bed. His skin burned in darkness in two long trails of fire, one down each cheek, an insistent reminder of the wreckage of his face.

He reached out and found the lamp. His hand hovered a moment beside it before he forced himself to lower it and close his fingers around the matchbox he always kept there. One strike, and a few seconds later, the lamp flickered to life. He watched the flame's dance for a long moment before raising his eyes and meeting his reflection.

From halfway down his forehead to nearly his chin, his face was an angry red mass, welted as if a brand had been drawn across it time and time again, and blisters clustered thick about his eyes. But the eyes themselves were unchanged, staring wetly back at him. Wetly . . . In wonder, he lifted a shaking hand to his cheek, and his fingers came away damp. The salt of the tears still seared the raw flesh, but the pain was subsumed in wonder. He could not remember the last time he had cried. Not for Leticia, not for Charlotte, not even for Will. Then, anger and hurt had balled up so hard in his stomach he thought he would vomit, but he had never shed a tear.

Good God, who was this woman who could do such things to him?

It was late. There was no clock on the mantel, and her watch had been taken away with the rest of her clothing at the beginning of the week, but Victoria did not need those markers of time to know that many hours had passed since sundown. Only the dimmest glow came around the edges of the fire screen, and the sounds of the manor evening had faded long ago. The lamp beside her bed was turned down too low for reading. Victoria did not care; she was in no mood for such distractions.

Exhaustion made the room blur and the shadows in the corners take on strange and dancing shapes, but the ache in her ankle and her head kept her from succumbing to the tugging current of sleep. She closed her eyes, mesmerized by the red patterns of light flickering across her eyelids and the sounds of the wind rushing around the rooftops and towers of the manor house. Her tired mind gave the patterns form, half imagination, half hallucination, and the wind seemed to carry snatches of whispered memories—of Walter, of her fifteen years imprisoned in her own fear, but most of all, of the duke.

She tried to shut them out and think of something else, but the faster she retreated, the harder they pursued her. She fought her way back toward wakefulness, but weariness dragged at her mind and pulled her farther under.

She did not know how much later it was when she realized there was only darkness on the other side of her eyelids. The surprise of that discovery was enough to yank her alert. Her eyes flew open, but in the barely discernable glow of the fireplace, she could make out nothing in the room. Still, when she strained her eyes toward the darkest corner, where she had sensed—or had she imagined?—Raeburn's presence before, she thought she could again make out the hint of a shadow that could not be explained by the intersection of the walls.

For a long moment, she just lay there, watching him. This time, she swore she would not be the one to speak first. This time, he must break the breathless silence—if he really was there.

The coals in the fire grate stirred suddenly as an unseen log collapsed, and Victoria started at the noise. For an instant, a stream of sparks lightened the darkness fractionally, just enough that the shadow in the corner became a vague outline, too solid for imagination, and she knew it must be him.

"You said you wouldn't meet me again," she said before she could stop herself.

"I said you wouldn't see me." His voice, strangely rough but unmistakable, lanced through her.

"And I still cannot." Joy, relief, and fear jumbled in

Victoria's gut so she could not begin to say which was uppermost.

"I know." Raeburn left the corner, his shadowy bulk moving across to her bedside.

Victoria struggled to sit up, but he placed a restraining hand on her shoulder. She gasped involuntarily at that contact and seized it, the first tactile proof of his presence since her fall. His palm turned upward, away from her shoulder, and he wrapped her hand in his. His touch was firm, and some shivering little part of her stilled at its warmth.

"Why are you here?" She wanted to make the question a demand, but it came out scarcely stronger than a whisper.

His hand tightened. "I could not stay away from you."

Victoria laughed unsteadily. "Yet as you pointed out, you have not broken your word. I cannot see you."

She felt him stiffen, heard the minute rustling of his clothes at the infinitesimal jerk. "You asked me why I shunned the light."

Victoria shook her head even though she knew he couldn't see it, her throat thickening, choking her. "What does it matter? I am here for a handful of days more, and then I am gone forever. Why should I want to know?" There was bitterness in her words she had surely not intended.

"You did the day before yesterday."

"Yes." The monosyllable sounded forced in her own ears.

"Do you still?" He continued before she could speak. "I don't ask whether you ought—just whether you do."

Victoria swallowed. "I do."

"Then I will show you."

"Raeburn—" she began, but he had already let go of

her hand, and an instant later, a match flared. "I have given it up. You needn't—"

But then the match touched the wick of the oil lamp. It caught and golden light burst from it. After a moment's blindness, Raeburn's face swam into view, wary hazel eyes, hawk nose, hard mouth . . . and across the middle of his face, cracked red skin and pale blisters swelling and distorting those familiar features into something grotesque.

"My God," Victoria gasped, her stomach lurching. She reached out automatically, jerking back when he flinched away from her touch. His mouth grew even harder, and something flashed in his eyes, something like pain or accusation. "My God. I didn't know, Raeburn—I never guessed . . . this." Her own face seemed stretched tight in sympathy, and she balled her hands into fists and buried them in the bedclothes to keep herself from reaching for him again. "I swear I meant no harm; I swear I never would have done anything to hurt you on purpose."

The duke just stood there, towering over her mutely, his eyes glittering in the flame.

She felt sick—sick at herself, sick at what she'd caused. Still she babbled on, her desperation growing in the face of his silence. "You must believe me. You do believe me, don't you? Raeburn— Damn you, say something!"

An abrupt, shocked silence closed around them after her outburst, the air still vibrating with her oath. Raeburn opened his mouth, closed it, then swooped down so abruptly Victoria had no chance to react. Suddenly, she was in his arms, her head pressed against his chest, breathing in the scent of him as he clutched her to him.

"God, Victoria, I thought you'd hate me," he ground out into her hair.

"How could I hate you? I'm the one who hurt you—"

"You didn't know, and it was my choice. I could have searched for the hat. I could have taken you back to the shepherds' shelter."

She loosened her grip on his coat and pushed away gently, looking up into his face. "But you didn't. You knew this would happen, and yet you didn't stop and look."

Raeburn shook his head and said, "How could I? You were injured—dying, for all I knew."

"But I had left," she whispered.

"You had tried to leave," he reminded her.

"And it didn't matter?"

He pulled her against him again, rocking her gently. "It mattered more than I can express."

Her throat tightened. "Why didn't you just say? Why not just tell me when I asked?" Victoria shook her head, rocking it gently against his chest. "I told you everything you wanted to know, yet you gave me nothing in return."

Raeburn stilled, his hands sliding down her back to her elbows. "And you felt betrayed."

"Not betrayed, not exactly. Cheated, more like. But how else was I to feel?"

He gave a laugh, short, barking, and humorless. "I never considered that, profound egotist that I am. I only thought of what you would think of me—"

"And what would that be?" Victoria looked up into his blistered, swollen face again and saw pain there that had nothing to do with his injuries.

"I thought you would find me disgusting—as unnatural as you told me I was the first day you arrived. I thought you would be frightened, or that you would pity me like a sick pup."

"If disgust is feeling ill and hurt every time I see your

injury because I hate that you are in pain, and if being frightened is being scared for you, and if pity is wishing I could do something, anything for you, then I suppose I am as guilty as you thought I would be." She bit her lip and took one of his hands in both of hers. "You know none of those things are in my character."

"You are a hard woman," he said quietly.

It was Victoria's turn for bitter laughter. "Yes, adamantine. This from the man who first called me a fraud."

Raeburn sighed. "Am I such a fool?"

Victoria bunched her fists in his jacket. "Fool and blind man both, but I forgive you with all my heart, and I only hope you can forgive my theft of your hat and my stubbornness that hurt us both."

"There is nothing to forgive."

They lapsed into silence for a long moment.

"Does—does it hurt much?" Victoria finally brought herself to ask.

"There will be a new layer of scars atop the old, but it will heal. It always has before."

"Is there nothing I can do?"

"You are already doing everything I might ask of you." He frowned down at her, then winced at the movement. "But I am not doing everything I should for you. You should have been asleep a long time ago."

She sighed. "I couldn't sleep. Not truly."

He started to reach for the bellpull. "I can have some warm milk and beef tea brought—"

Victoria caught his hand. "No, no, I'll be fine."

"Is there anything you want, then?"

She hesitated. "Would you stay? I mean, if you don't need to treat your face—"

"There's nothing I would rather do than remain with

you." The words were soft but with an intensity that made her shiver.

He released her long enough to pull off his shoes, then blew out the lamp and slid into bed beside her, silently arranging himself so that her head was pillowed against his shoulder.

Victoria stared into the darkness for a long time, savoring the feel of his body against hers, his warmth and strength, intensified, if anything, by the revelation of his condition. The thought of his sun-branded face made her ache in sympathy, but his confidence in her, his willingness to reveal himself despite how much she realized it cost him—that calmed something that had been twisting within her since their second day together.

How long has it been since he told anyone? she wondered. Remembering his expression, braced and defiant, she could not guess. Her brother Jack certainly didn't know, though he had once been as close a friend to Raeburn as she'd ever heard the duke to have. And yet he had trusted her, the sister of a man he hated, a woman he'd known only for the space of a few days; she had arrived on a Tuesday, and now it was only Sunday night. But despite that short span, it seemed impossible that there had been a time she didn't know him. She felt his chest rise and fall, his breathing steady in sleep. How tired had he been, to drop off so easily? She almost envied him his exhaustion.

Sunday . . . Less than two days left, now. Tuesday's evening post brought her, and it would take her away again. Suddenly, it seemed monumentally unfair, that she should have to leave so soon after she had reconciled with the reclusive duke, so soon after he had bared himself to her—so soon after she was at peace with him and herself for the first time.

But what could she say? That she did not want to go? That their bargain should be extended? She tightened her lips against the foolishness of that thought. Leave she would, whatever she might feel about it, and soon there would be nothing left of the week except her memories of the strange manor house and its dark master.

Perhaps it was the pain of her ankle, beginning to ache again, and the dull headache that still throbbed between her temples, but her eyes began to fill, and even the most determined blinking could do nothing but send the tears rolling more quickly down her cheeks.

Chapter Twenty

Raeburn woke to Victoria shifting in his arms. The curtains were still drawn, but enough light leaked through to bathe the room in a dim saffron glow.

Victoria moved again, murmuring something unintelligible in her sleep and shifting her head in the crook of his arm. He looked down over the top of her hair to see her fine brows knitted and her delicate mouth set in a frown. Carefully, he bent down to kiss her, barely brushing his lips against her hair. An odd sheen on her cheek caught his eye, and he realized with a wrench that tear tracks were dried upon her face. Had he made her cry? The thought was more disturbing than he cared to contemplate.

But she wasn't crying now. She had asked him to stay, and now she was snuggled against him in sleep. He lay for a moment, staring at the canopy above them, and he suddenly wished that the moment could last forever. But the itchy aching of his face roused him, and reluctantly, he eased away from her and slid off the bed. Victoria moaned and rolled into the indention he left in the mattress, but she did not wake.

He poured water into the washbasin and splashed it

over his face, the cold both soothing and stinging the
blistered, itching skin. Running damp fingers though his
rumpled hair, he positioned himself so that he could see
though the crack in the curtains without falling in the path
of the sunbeam that speared across the floor.

The sun squatted on the horizon, weak and orange
with dawn. He watched its infinitesimal creeping into the
steely sky. He loved sunrise as some men loved fire. It
was beautiful and pitiless, rewarding fascination with
pain and so utterly indifferent that his anger and bitterness lost their focus and flew away, if only for a moment.

A noise outside the door made him start and turn to
face it. It opened, and Annie entered with a laden tray in
her arms.

"Oh!" she yelped at the sight of him, blushing furi-
ously. "I didn't know thoo was here, thy grace."

Victoria stirred in her blankets. "Thank you, Annie."
Her voice was heavy with sleep. "Leave the tray on the
night table, and you may go." Then Victoria's eyes found
Byron's, and he nodded in response to her questioning
glance. She added, "But bring another for your master.
He wishes to break his fast with me."

Annie left. Byron returned to Victoria's side and sat
down on the edge of the bed.

There was tension between them, sensuality overlaid
with a new, raw awareness, and Byron tried to cover it by
arranging the pillows behind Victoria as she sat up, feeling oddly nursemaidish as he did. Suppressing that thought,
he settled the tray across her lap, and she gave him an odd
look, as if she felt as awkward about his attentions as he
did. Looking away, she picked up the knife and fork but
paused with them suspended in air.

"I feel terribly strange with you sitting there, staring at
me as if you're making sure the invalid eats as she ought,"

she said. "Share this tray with me, and we'll split the other when Annie returns."

"There is only one set of silverware," Byron pointed out.

She quirked an eyebrow. "That would not have stopped you three days ago. Has so much changed?"

There was teasing in her tone, and wistfulness, too. *More has changed than I could have imagined,* he thought. But he just smiled slightly—carefully—and closed his hands over hers. "I will feed us both, then."

Relinquishing the silverware, Victoria settled back against the pillows and looked up at him through the pale fringe of her eyelashes. He shoveled some eggs onto the fork, fed her, and then took a bite himself. The last time he had done this was with the peach crumble; it seemed incredible that there could be a repetition both so close and yet so different in such a short span of time. As if she, too, was recalling that memory, Victoria blushed slightly and looked away. Neither of them were in any shape to relive that night, and now, over commonplace eggs and rashers, the memory was ungainly and intrusive.

"I feel like a child," she said with a forced laugh before accepting the next bite.

"It was your idea."

And that was the last thing that was said until Annie brought Byron's tray, and then Victoria took back her fork and the strain between them eased.

"I've been thinking about what you've said," Victoria said suddenly, looking up from buttering her toast. "About me, I mean, deceiving myself."

Muscles relaxed that Byron was not aware of having braced in anticipation of her questions about his illness— questions that were not coming yet, at least. "Yes?"

"I thought then that you were mistaken, that you overstated the case in that dramatic way of yours. But now I'm not so certain. Because I've realized something about myself." Her blue-gray eyes met his, solemn and unblinking. "I am a coward. I'm frightened of change, I'm frightened of risks, but most of all, I'm frightened of myself. What Walter and I did . . . that was rash. Stupid, even, in hindsight. But when we were in his parent's back parlor, the garden, the cupboard, the stables—it felt wonderful. It felt *right*. Only a few months later, I knew how stupid I had been, and making a mistake of that magnitude scared me."

"And you never trusted yourself again."

Victoria gave a little shrug. "Oh, I trusted myself when I thought I was being cool and dispassionate. But emotions couldn't be trusted."

"Like when you were feeling wild?"

"I only let myself feel *that* when I rode. Riding was safe enough, I thought. And I felt it when it stormed." The corner of her mouth quirked. "I never could control myself when it stormed."

"You punished and smothered yourself for years," Byron pointed out. "For a girlhood indiscretion, it seems a little extreme."

She shook her head impatiently. "It wasn't that. It was what I might do next. I never could know for sure at the time whether it was idiocy or inspiration."

"Which was our contract?" Byron asked.

Relaxing slightly, Victoria laughed. "Both. I still can't quite believe that I agreed to it. It's so contrary to everything I've stood for—"

"But not everything you've felt."

"No, not that." She paused. "I am sure you wonder now if I regret it. I regret my ankle and my head and your face, but I cannot regret this week."

Byron felt a small lurch deep within him. "If my face is the price for the days we've had together, I pay it gladly."

The customary hardness around her mouth and eyes eased for a moment. "Thank you."

And they finished their meal in silence.

Victoria sat in the window seat again, and Raeburn lounged in the chair Mrs. Peasebody had had brought up. Victoria had wanted to call Annie to help her dress, but Raeburn had insisted on doing everything himself. Somehow, it was so much more embarrassing to have him dress her than undress her, and it did not set her at ease to find him equally competent with both. In the dark, in the heat of their lovemaking, unself-consciousness was effortless. But even the light coming through the crack in the curtains revealed far more than he had seen in any of their nocturnal trysts, and without the haze of passion, Victoria feared that Raeburn would find her bony, aging body unattractive.

But he gave no indication that he felt anything but solicitousness until she was once again ensconced on the window seat, and when he had looked at her then, the muted fire in his eyes spoke of desire rather than distaste.

Abruptly, Raeburn turned to her again and broke the easy silence.

"I thought you would have asked me a dozen questions by now."

Victoria, caught staring, did not pretend to misunderstand. "I trusted that you would finish your explanations in your own time."

"My own time." Raeburn shook his head. "There is not a saint above with enough patience to wait for that."

"You broached the subject last night," she pointed out. "It was your decision. No one could force your hand."

"It only felt like it." A wry smile flashed across his ravaged face. This morning, Victoria found she could look at him without a jolt of sympathetic pain shooting through her, but the sight still left an ache in her center. He sighed. "Not everyone has been as accepting as you."

Knowing an invitation when she heard it, Victoria made an inquiring noise.

Raeburn looked away, staring blankly at the tapestry that covered half the wall. "I had a friend," he said, his voice flat. "His name was Will. We were only boys, so perhaps I should be a little more forgiving. But he knew me better than anyone. I was burned one day in his company. We were asleep outside, and when I woke up, I was"—he waved his hand toward his face and looked at her—"worse than this."

"And he woke up, too, and did not react well," Victoria guessed. Such a sight would be a shock, a terrible shock to a young boy.

"He ran away, even as I was trying to explain. He never spoke to me again."

She looked hard at him for an instant, but his expression remained emotionless and he gave no indication of exaggeration. How could any one incident, however traumatic, cause such a reaction? "Never?"

"Never." His eyes slid away. "The rift is not so dramatic as it sounds. He went away to school before I had healed enough to leave my room."

"Did you ever try to say anything more to him? You said he was your friend."

"My best friend. No. If he was avoiding me—" Raeburn cut himself off with a rough shake of his head.

Victoria searched for a delicate way to phrase her

question. "Did he ever before seem shallow? Or . . . spiteful? Or cowardly?"

"No. He was the truest friend a boy could have." His voice dripped with irony, but she heard the aching honesty behind it.

"Did you never see him again, then?"

"When he was on holiday, and after he graduated from Oxford. We moved in the same circles."

"And he never gave you any indication of—of remorse? Or regret? Or anything?" If they were such great friends . . .

For the first time, Raeburn paused. "There were times that I thought he was going to come over to me, when I caught him looking at me with an expression of . . . I don't know. But he seemed almost sad."

"You said you were schoolboys then—children. Perhaps he knew he had behaved badly and was too ashamed to speak. Children do stupid, hurtful things that they regret yet cannot face even as adults, and sometimes they neglect putting things right so long it seems impossible to speak of them." Surely he knew that—had thought of that in his long days of going over old memories.

Raeburn's hands tightened around his chair arms so suddenly and violently Victoria feared the chair would break.

"He wed Charlotte."

The words came out as a shout, and in the sudden stunned silence, Victoria glanced down at her own hands, embarrassed in front of the welter of emotions that washed across Raeburn's face. "The vicar's daughter," she remembered aloud, hardly a murmur. "Do you really think that he chose her to hurt you?"

Raeburn said nothing for a long time, then shook his

head. "Does it matter? He knew that it would. And if he had cared about hurting me the first time—"

"You think he wouldn't have done it," she finished for him. "I see." She could think of nothing to say to comfort him, and she turned away, gazing at the strip of drive and lawn that was visible through the crack in the curtains.

"I would have lost her anyway," Raeburn finally said. "I thought I loved her, but not enough to answer the question I always saw in her eyes—the one only you have ever been brave enough to ask me. Every day that I stayed silent, she became more distant. Perhaps Will saw that. He loved her, too, that I knew. Perhaps his marrying her when he did was a mercy to me, even if I didn't know it. That way, at least, my courtship stopped dying by stages. I have thought of this, but it is not the sop it should be."

"I'm—I'm sorry for it," Victoria said softly.

Raeburn sighed. "I should have let go a long time ago, but I never could. I thought—no, I felt in my bones— that anyone who was not in my employ could not help but react the way Will did. It might have been wrongheaded, but the conviction was powerful. You have proven me wrong at least in one case, and I thank you for that. But I am not so sure that just anyone—or almost anyone— else would accept me as you do. Still, your acceptance alone has changed my life."

Victoria looked back at him, his form suddenly seeming worn down, tired, less thunderously massive in the confines of the chair. "I never meant to change anything."

He sighed. "Ah, Circe, your touch leaves magic in its wake." He gave her a tired smile, and she returned it, hurting for him. She did not know what else she might do for him, but she touched the cushion beside her in hesitant invitation.

He joined her, and when she reached for his hand, almost shyly, he grasped it firmly and laced her fingers between his. There was no mystery now in his calluses—vividly, she remembered how his shoulders bunched and flexed as he swung the Indian clubs—but they were still reassuring, no less warm and strong for all that their mystique was gone.

"I wasn't always like this," he said. "When I was very young, I didn't burn any more than other children. I can remember standing on the grass of the lawns with the sun pouring down and feeling *good*."

"You can never go out in daylight again? Ever?" Victoria tried to imagine it, an entire life spent in gloom.

"You've seen my limits. When it is very overcast or raining, and when I am extremely careful, I can go out. Dusk and dawn, too. That is all."

"No wonder you never told Charlotte. Even if you hadn't thought she would think you freakish, it would take a great deal of love to want to spend one's life with a man who can never enjoy the day."

"Yes," Raeburn said simply.

They sat together in silence, Victoria wanting to drink his presence, all too aware that every moment spent in his company brought them that much closer to her departure. She wanted to study his face, to memorize it, even blistered and scorched as it was, but she feared he would mistake her desire for macabre fascination. So instead, she fixed her eyes blindly on the bit of drive she could see between the curtains and concentrated on his presence. The feel of him, his warmth, the smell of his skin. She wished she could imprint it all on her mind to take with her when she left.

She did not know how long they sat like that, but a flicker of movement on the drive brought her back to

herself. She watched a small figure toiling closer—
Annie again, but this time she was not alone, for as she
came more completely into the range of view offered by
the slit in the curtains, Victoria realized that Andrew
strode beside her.

Unease tickled her spine as she watched, for Andrew
was gesturing wildly, and Annie was responding with
abrupt shakes of her head.

"Raeburn, can you see this?" She motioned to the
window.

She felt his movement as he shifted so that he could
peer over her shoulder, but she did not take her eyes
from the drama playing out silently below. More waving,
more denial. Abruptly, Andrew stopped and grabbed
Annie's shoulders, spinning her to face him. He talked
more, and Annie continued to shake her head. Finally, he
grabbed her hand and dropped to his knee. She tried to
pull him up, but he remained there, his back to the window. Victoria could imagine his face—determined,
pleading, hopeful.

"He's asking her to marry him!" she said in wonder.

Raeburn grunted. "She does not seem terribly en-
thralled with the idea. I had thought they were all but
promised."

Already, Annie's headshakes were becoming less
vigorous.

"Give him time."

After another moment, her protests ceased altogether.
She stood still while Andrew's head bobbed on, and then
slowly, she nodded.

Andrew bounded to his feet and swept her into a fierce
kiss, lifting her from her feet with the force of it.

Victoria looked back at Raeburn. "I almost envy
them."

"Their youth? Enthusiasm? Optimism?" He lifted an eyebrow.

"Their simplicity. Their naïve courage. So much could go wrong, so much probably will go wrong, but they face it without blinking."

"Once, you did, too, at least from what you have told me."

She shook her head. "I only hope they are not forced to learn the same lessons as I."

"Why not hope that you can learn to forget?" His voice was somber.

Victoria looked back at the embracing couple and felt an answering hollowness in her gut. "If only I could, it might be worth getting hurt all over again."

When Annie arrived with their dinner, she was still blushing and smiling—the latter a rare sight, Byron realized with surprise. She set the tray on the trunk and then retreated toward the doorway, lingering there and twisting her apron in her hands.

"Yes?" Byron said, ignoring Victoria's sideways, amused look.

"Thy grace." Annie blushed harder. "Thy grace, Andrew and me are getting married." It came out in a rush, and she dropped her eyes.

"I promised him the porter's house, but not until old Silas dies," Byron said, keeping his tone carefully neutral.

Annie looked up, her eyes shining. "Oh, I know, thy grace! It's just that, well, it seems that Silas is going to live forever, and Uncle Tom asked me to go to Leeds with him since after he's gone I'll not have no family here no more, so Andrew said he'd be my family." She thrust her chin outward in a display of more spirit than Byron had ever seen. "I hope we'll have your blessing—that we can keep working for you, even though we'll be married. Uncle Tom will let us buy his house in the village, and it shan't be such a terrible walk every day."

Byron looked at her for a long moment before nodding. "You are welcome to stay, Annie—you and Andrew both. And you may have the hundred quid I promised."

"Thank you, thy grace!" Annie beamed. Then she dipped her hand into her apron, looking tentative again. "Afore he died, his grace thy great-uncle gave me this." She held out her hand, upon which rested a long string of pearls with a jeweled pendant and clasp. "He said—he said it was part of what went to the duchesses, but since he'd had no duchess, he couldn't see what was so wrong in giving me one piece to do with as I liked." Her words came faster, tripping over each other. "I didn't take it, understand, he gave it to me. And I've kept it until now, but I don't know what good jewels would do a girl like me—"

"I believe you, Annie," Byron interrupted before she worked herself into a fit of hysterics.

"Thank thee, thy grace." Annie looked relieved. "I want to sell it—not that I don't like it, but I've no use for jewels like this. But I don't know how," she finished lamely.

Byron held out his hand. "If you will give it over to my trust, I will have it appraised by a jeweler and will offer you a fair price."

Annie's face split in a grin. "Many thanks, thy grace!" She handed him the necklace without hesitation and turned away before pausing at the door for a second time. "I almost forgot! This came for you today, your ladyship." She produced a letter from her pocket, set it on the edge of the dinner tray, and left, the door swinging shut after her.

"Mother again," Victoria said, holding her hand out for the letter. Byron gave it to her, but she paused before she looked at it. "That was very kind of you."

He shrugged uncomfortably. "I'd think you'd deem it only approaching justice. She is my cousin, according to you."

"Yes. But most men wouldn't care. I'm glad you do." And with that, she started to open the letter, but she frowned when she saw the handwriting of the direction.

"Is there something wrong?" Byron asked.

"It's from my brother. Jack never writes me." Forehead creased, she broke the seal and unfolded the letter. Her frown grew deeper, then her expression froze, and she sat there staring at the letter for far longer than it would take to read the single sheet of paper.

"What is it?" Byron demanded.

Wordlessly, she handed it to him, and he read.

Victoria,

I know you are certainly engaged in the most delicate negotiations on my behalf, and I assure you that I would not have written except in the most extreme need. Our mother seems to be suffering from attacks of some kind—her hands are unsteady, her speech slurred, and now she seems to be sometimes slipping into dementia. It started the evening you left, and at first, we did not realize it was more than her usual dramatics.

The doctor says that she might yet regain her former abilities, but it is too soon to tell if this is a temporary illness or the sign of a final, precipitous decline. She is asking for you almost every hour

*now, and the possibility that this might be her last
wish is not one Father dares ignore. He has asked
me to request that you return immediately, and for
once, I agree with him.*

    Please hurry,
    Jack

"You must go, then," Byron said, ignoring the sudden
fist around his lungs, squeezing the air out of them.

"Yes," Victoria agreed, her voice dead.

"Tomorrow morning—"

She laughed suddenly, cutting him off. "What a waste!
I break my ankle and cause you to be injured only to default on the last day of our agreement!"

Byron looked at her, and any last lingering desire to
embarrass her family melted away. "Tear up our contract," he said softly. "I will not persecute your brother."

Victoria looked up at him, dampness welling suddenly in
her eyes. "Thank you," she whispered. "I never expected
you to be so kind. I have done nothing to deserve it."

"You didn't need to." He sat beside her again, wrapping his arms around her thin shoulders. "God, did you
think I could be so rancorous now, knowing that I would
hurt you?"

She rested her head limply against his shoulder. "I
didn't want to think." A tear escaped and trickled down
her cheek.

"You will be back in Rushworth tomorrow if you take
the early train. It shall be less than three days since the
letter was written. Surely your mother can't worsen too
much before then."

Victoria laughed again. "Oh, I am a horrible person,
aren't I? I should be crying for my mother—and I am—
but I'm crying for me at least as much."

"You cried last night, too." He carefully did not put a question into his tone.

She didn't look at him. "I thought you were asleep. I hoped you were asleep."

He wiped the tear from her cheek and kissed the dampness from his hand. "I saw the tracks this morning. Why?"

Victoria bit her lip. "You were hurt, and it was my fault. And my ankle was aching, too. And I—I didn't want to think about leaving when I was suddenly so happy."

Byron stared down at her, bewildered. "You were crying because you were happy?"

"I was crying because I knew it wouldn't last." She looked up at him them, her eyes so full of grief and—dare he believe it?—tenderness that he felt the breath snatched from his lungs and his stomach twisted in bittersweet joy.

Victoria was injured and so was he, but suddenly, he didn't care. He couldn't care, not if it would be the death of him. He put his arms on her shoulders and turned her toward him. "Then let us make tonight last the worth of thousands." And he pulled her against him madly, heedlessly, and buried the regrets of the last thirty years in her kiss.

Chapter Twenty-one

"I wish I could touch your face," Victoria said wistfully, twining her fingers in the longer waves of hair at the back of Raeburn's neck. They were lying on her bed, naked save for her bandaged ankle. The first fury of their lovemaking had been spent—and the second. Their supper dishes lay on the night table beside the flickering candle; Raeburn had ordered Annie to leave the tray outside the door and had brought it in himself so they had no need to dress.

Raeburn captured her hand and brought it to his lips. "You can."

She made a noise of exasperation. "You know that's not what I meant."

"In square inches, I am more accessible than you are right now." He waved to her leg.

"But who wants to touch an ankle?" Victoria returned.

Raeburn rolled over suddenly, pinning her to the bed beneath him. His skin was warmer and coarser than hers, and the short hairs of his chest tickled her nipples as he planted his elbows on either side of her head. "Perhaps I do. Perhaps I want to touch every inch of your body tonight and I resent the interference of such things as broken ankles." Against her leg, his member stirred, and a responding heat wound in her belly and trickled up her spine.

"You're a fool." Victoria meant it to be crushing, but his sharp hazel gaze made her dizzy and the words came out with a breathless edge.

"Very likely," he agreed, bending down to tease her lips with his. Foolish or not, Victoria shivered against his mouth. She lifted her head to catch his kiss, but he pulled back, keeping his touch barely firmer than a breath. "Every inch," he repeated, and after a moment more of resistance, she surrendered and tipped back her head as he continued the featherlight caresses down her throat, brushing her skin with every word. "Every fiber, every hair, every freckle"—he kissed the one that hid under her chin— "every scar. I want to mark you, claim you, possess all of you."

"And what do I get in return, your grace? The pleasure of your company?" The words tried to skitter from her thoughts before she could string them together into a coherent sentence, but she chased them down and forced them out.

"And my memory to keep you warm at night." He firmed the pressure of his lips, nibbling the hollow of her collarbone, and she gasped as her too-sensitive skin sent a tremor of sensation across her body. His touch irritated her, thrilled her, made her itch and burn for him at once. She wished he would stop, that he would never stop this slow, torturous covering of her body.

She seized his head between her hands, pulling his mouth up to hers as she trapped his body between her thighs and tilted her hips in blatant invitation. He groaned as his lips met hers, bent his head so the blistered tip of his nose would not brush her cheek, and took every advantage of the welcome of her mouth. Even his tongue was hot, coaxing, insisting, promising, and his manhood pulsed against her entrance, but he did not plunge in to meet her.

It was a repetition of their first nights together, she realized—the teasing, the subtle manipulation, the negotiation of power—but suddenly, she wanted no part of it. Victoria reversed her hold on his shoulders and pushed him away.

"Can't you cease your games just for one minute—for one hour?" The question came out halfway between an order and plea.

The momentum of her shove brought him upright, and he sat there, glowering down at her from the peeling mask of his face. "I thought you enjoyed it." The words were rough with umbrage.

As well they should be, Victoria thought, ashamed of her outburst. "I did—I do—but not now. I can't be transported back to the day I arrived like nothing has happened between us. Maybe if there was tomorrow I wouldn't mind, maybe I would welcome it, but this love play now I cannot abide."

"Then what do you want?" The words came out a demand, but to Victoria's relief, the spark of anger in his eyes died without a flicker. "If it is within my power—"

"It is. All I want is you. All of you." She smiled in gentle ruefulness at the echo of his words, and he smiled back, shaking his head.

"Then you ask no small thing."

"We have all night." She reached her hands out to him, imploring, and with a sigh, he slid back between her thighs. He shifted and bumped her ankle, and she could not help but wince as a dart of pain shot up her leg.

He stopped abruptly. "That has been a nuisance all

day," he growled, and before she could say anything, he pulled back and hooked his arms under her knees, guiding them onto his shoulders so that her ankle hung free of danger behind his back. Then he moved to close the space between them again.

Her body pulled taut in expectation, every nerve humming, wanting. He was true to his word; he did not make her wait but entered her in a slow, even thrust. A twist low in her belly welcomed that first stroke, slick dampness sending a wave of prickling heat across her skin. He pulled back and thrust again, and she emitted a strangled hiss as the movement woke new nerves into trembling awareness, her hands tightening reflexively into fists.

He paused, his expression concerned. "Good?"

"So good," she agreed thickly, a shaky laugh tumbling from her lips.

His eyes darkened. "I'm glad," he said with a force that stole her breath, but she did not respond, for with that word, he picked up his rhythm and her entire body seemed to clench around him. She caught his shoulders again, matching his strokes with her hips. Her body sang with his, a hot pulse that coursed through her, small, promising thrills that built quickly upon each other, wave after mounting wave until she hung, suspended and shuddering. Her breath hissed through her teeth as every individual hair rose across her body.

Raeburn led her, followed her, his weight pressed against her thighs as he drove deeper with each stroke. He rode with her at the edge of ecstasy, and even when her vision darkened with the surging pleasure and her ears filled with the rush of blood and her skin became insensate to the damp, wadded sheets beneath her, he was there—his rasping breath, his straining face, the hard weight of him against her body. He was there, inside her head, filling her mind as he did her body.

And she was glad.

She let go of his shoulders, splayed her hands across his chest so she could feel his heartbeat thudding hard beneath her fingers, and whispered, "Come with me."

As if waiting for those words, his rhythm changed, a deep shudder punctuating the end of each thrust, that small shift enough to send her plunging over the edge. She might have gasped, she might have cried out, but she was insensible to everything but their twining, racing heartbeats and the feel of his skin against hers. Fire tore from her center to lick across her skin; every finger and toe ached with it. Again and again they surged together, let the wave carry them until it crested and ebbed. Consciousness returned as Raeburn's strokes slowed, slowed, stopped. Victoria lay gasping as he pulled away from her. Gently, he lifted her trembling legs from his shoulders and set them on either side of him. Then, still breathless, he slid up beside her and pulled her head against his chest. The bump on her head twinged slightly as it came up against his arm, but she ignored it, laying her head against the solidity of him.

"Is that enough of me?" he murmured into her hair.

"It is a start." She wriggled one arm underneath him and draped the other across his torso.

He sighed, and for a long moment, they just lay there in each other's loose embrace. Victoria emptied her mind and let it drift, only feeling.

Finally, Raeburn stirred. "I'm sorry, but I must wash my face. The sweat—it's burning a bit."

Victoria pulled away immediately. "You should have said. I don't expect you to hurt for my sake—"

He shook his head as he stood and crossed the room. "It was my pride, not you, that kept me silent."

"If you won't be more careful for your own sake, then, remember that I blame myself for any pain you feel."

"You weren't supposed to know that I still felt any." He ducked his head over the basin, splashing water over his face.

The muscles in his back were thrown into sharp definition by the angle of the candlelight, and Victoria couldn't help but notice once again what a magnificent man he was. He turned back to face her, and he must have caught the admiring look on her face because he gave a rueful laugh.

"You shall have to wait a breath or two if you want more, Circe. I am not the youth of eighteen I once was."

"Which is a good thing, for if we had met when you were eighteen, I would have been even younger than you and both of us, I fear, dreadfully shallow." She peered at his face, trying to see if it was any more inflamed than before. "We needn't do anything at all. I'm content just to have you here with me."

"And all this time I thought you were enjoying yourself." He softened as he joined her on the bed. "No, Victoria, I am not so debilitated as you seem to fear." He shook his head. "Was I ever eighteen, or was that another boy whose memories have been transplanted into my hoary head?"

"You were quite the rakehell, if your reputation has any merit."

Raeburn tilted his head to look at her, drawing her against his side. "I did not begin to earn that reputation until I was three and twenty. But earn it I did. I am only lucky that I wasn't struck with half a dozen unspeakable diseases or had my throat cut in one of the seedy judy-houses we used to patronize."

"Idiot," Victoria agreed softly, tracing his lips with her finger. He kissed it. A queer thought struck her. "You never fathered a bastard on one of those women, did you?"

Surprise flickered across his face, followed by consternation. "I hope not. I never shall know, shall I?" He shook his head. "You might think me criminally blithe, but I never even considered it before. I took my pleasure where it was offered . . . and forgot."

"Never considered it? Never thought that your own child might have been left in a doorway or thrown into the Thames?" Victoria stared at him.

"If I had stopped my egocentric whirl for just one instant and thought about anything, do you think I could have still done what I did?" He spoke softly, but the pain in his eyes was sharp, and she sensed that he was asking himself the question as much as her.

"I would hope not."

"So do I." He paused. "If a woman came to me now and claimed that her child was mine, and if it could have been at all possible, I think I would take responsibility. Even if she were lying, the possibility of truth would burden me to act."

"Penance?" She traced her fingers slowly across his chest.

"Noblesse oblige, if you will. I demanded the *droit du seigneur,* and so I should take the responsibility that comes with the privilege."

"Even if the privilege is paid for in coin?"

"Especially then, I think." He looked down at her belly. "And if you should carry one?"

"I pray not!" Victoria burst out. Raeburn raised an eyebrow, and she explained more calmly. "It is very unlikely, but still . . . I may have changed, but the world hasn't. It's no place for a bastard, even a bastard of an earl's daughter. I suppose I would still go to Italy, if I must, for I hate the idea of paying off some poor vicar even worse than my own exile."

"And would you be good then, for your child's sake?"

"I don't know that I could be."

Victoria felt his hesitation, and she gave him a questioning glance.

He took her hand. "If it comes to that, I will make sure that both of you want for nothing."

"Thank you," Victoria said simply. "But now that's the last thing I want to think of. Just kiss me, Raeburn. Tonight, I ask for nothing more."

And he did.

Chapter Twenty-two

Victoria sat on the window seat of the Unicorn Room. The sun was barely over the horizon, but there was nothing left to prepare. An hour before, she had opened her eyes to find herself alone with her valise and trunk sitting in the center of the room as they had the evening she arrived, and with a leaden heaviness in her belly, she had rung for Annie to dress her in her old clothes. She would take nothing home that Raeburn had ordered for her.

Now all that remained was to have herself carried down the stairs, an awkward procedure at the best of times but even worse in her crinoline, which she had no choice but to wear or leave behind. And she was almost as reluctant to leave anything of hers behind as to take something from Raeburn. She only wished she could separate her thoughts as easily as her belongings.

There were hours left before she had to leave, and departing now would not make the train at Leeds arrive any sooner. But the walls of Raeburn Court pressed down on her, smothering her, and the duke was not waiting with her; there was no reason to linger. She yanked the bellpull to call for servants to carry out her things—and herself.

Her eyes felt gritty. Had she slept the night before? Had he slept? Surely she had, at least, if only for an instant, for she could not remember when Raeburn left or when her things arrived.

Her thoughts returned to the duke with inevitable inertia. It was as if he'd opened a funnel in her mind, and no matter what she began to think upon, her thoughts turned upon themselves again and again until she was back to him. Perhaps she, too, had poured out through that funnel, for today she felt emptied out, insubstantial, as if her entire being were filled with nothing more than shadows.

She looked around the room for the last time—at the canopied and plumed bed, its fresh, practical sheets incongruous beneath the faded hangings; at the empty chair in front of the fire screen; at the enormous hanging tapestry. A tapestry that hid nothing but a blank wall. There were no secret passages here, nor were there any monsters. Just a man, a sad man who made her dizzy with missing him already, in a moldering old house.

There was a knock at the door, and at her command to enter, it swung open the reveal the footman and the groom. Even through her hollow daze, Victoria saw the suppressed delight in Andrew's step, the joy on his face that even the most carefully constructed polite mask could not hide.

"His grace ordered us to get thee first, my lady," Andrew said. "Said he didn't want us dropping thee down the stairs because we were tired from lugging that great box of thine." He nodded at the chest.

"Tell his grace I thank him," Victoria replied. It was only the second time she had spoken that morning, and her voice felt high and thin, buzzing in her ears.

Andrew bobbed his head, and the men drew near the window seat, clasping each other's hands so one pair of joined arms formed a seat for her, the other a back. A few seconds' awkward maneuvering and she was positioned in their arms, clinging to their shoulders as folds of black taffeta swallowed their legs.

"Is thoo well secured?" Andrew asked solicitously.

"Yes."

Without another word, the men ducked through the doorway to enter the dark, twisting stairwell. It seemed fantastic, something out of a sensational novel or a fire-side tale, the stone stair that wound down, down, perpetually down into some sort of nether hell. With every step, she swayed in the basket of joined hands, her flattened crinoline scraping her skirts against the stone walls or catching in the embrasure of the occasional narrow window. With every step, she felt herself plunging deeper, away from the light, away from herself, until it seemed that her consciousness was something detached and bobbing on a tether a pace or two behind the two toiling men and the slim black figure hung between.

She was leaving. Leaving Raeburn Court. Leaving him.

The sense of emptiness widened within her, her belly aching from it, her breath coming short as she tried to suck in enough air to fill the vacuum it left. She lurched as the groom stepped unevenly and barely caught her balance in time to keep from tumbling headfirst out of their arms. But she felt no jolt of danger averted, no sudden speeding of her heart. She was numb, too numb to do more than lean back a little more and tighten her grip on their shoulders.

It was with the rushing sense of normality's return that she realized they had stopped—stopped in front of the main door of the manor house, thick and scarred before them. A figure stepped out of the shadows to open it.

Raeburn.

"You came!" Victoria gasped before she thought, before she had time to think.

His smile above his scarf was even harder and more twisted than usual. "I told you I could never stay away from you."

The footman and the groom carried her out the door, but she craned around to keep the duke in sight.

He adjusted his hat carefully and stepped out after them. Following her.

Victoria hardly registered the drizzle that sifted down upon them or the black box of the carriage squatting on the drive until Andrew and the groom maneuvered her inside. She let the men guide her onto the bench, but as soon as they released her, she leaned forward, seeking the duke.

He stood there, filling the doorway for an instant, then he stepped up and ducked inside, settling himself across from her. Her heart jolted, and for a moment, she had the mad fancy that he might be coming with her.

But sanity return a breath later, and that fantasy tattered and blew away.

A minute ticked by, two, but Victoria could find nothing to say. His mere presence seemed to shatter thought, and all that was left was the bold fact of himself, there in the carriage, across from her.

God, how she loved everything about him! His voice, his smell, every sinew and muscle of his body, and, most of all, the intangible essence of him that made him speak as he did, act as he did, that made him grow angry or tender or sad. She didn't want to leave him; more than anything she had ever wanted in her life, she did not want to go.

But she must. Her mother needed her, and however madly selfish her thoughts, she could not ignore that call.

And even if her mother's need did not outweigh her own, there was the matter of the agreement—the promised week that would soon draw to a close. Fleetingly, she entertained the idea of demanding to repay the forfeited time with such interest that she would never be out of his debt . . .

"I didn't want to tell you I would see you off in case I couldn't make it past the door," he said.

"I understand." Victoria glanced out of the carriage into the dim, drizzly morning. "And so I welcome clouds, though we break an axle in the mud."

Raeburn smiled, and this time, there was nothing bitter about it. "But you have always welcomed storms."

"Yes," she agreed. "Though I think I shall never see another without remembering you." *Remembering us.*

Raeburn's eyes closed briefly, and he swallowed hard. "God, Victoria—" he rasped, but he bit off whatever it was he was going to say.

Suddenly, Victoria felt very small and weak and strangely frightened. She was going home, back to her old, familiar role, but the taste of its memory in her mind was alien and angular.

"Please—" she said tentatively. "Would you please hold me?"

Raeburn said nothing, but his eyes glinted in the shadows, and he crossed to sit beside her without a word, his arms slipping under hers and pulling her back against his chest. She laid her head back against him, and he nestled it under his chin. She closed her eyes, emptied her mind, and just took in the feel of his body against hers.

All too soon, they were disturbed by a jerk of the carriage. Victoria opened her eyes to see Andrew and the groom give her trunk a last shove onto the roof. Seconds later, her valise followed, and the groom unwound a coil of rope and began tying the luggage onto the rack.

"I ought not delay them," Victoria said, the words shoving their way up her tight throat.

"I suppose not," Raeburn agreed. His voice was cool, neutral, and she wondered with irrational anger how he could be so calm.

She shifted out of the way, and he stood and ducked out of the carriage, turning back to face her as soon as both feet crunched onto the drive. Her heart tightened as his hazel eyes met hers.

"I expect I shan't even see you in London," she managed, allowing some of the question she wanted to ask to seep into her tone.

"No." He shook his head. "I do not go to London anymore."

"Good-bye, then, Raeburn." She paused. "Byron." All the words she wanted to say, everything she wanted to tell him filled her mind with a raging cacophony until she could manage nothing at all.

"Good-bye, Victoria." And with that, he swung the carriage door shut and was gone.

Byron spun, strode inside, and plunged across the hall into a narrow corridor, his overcoat flapping around his knees. He turned sharply at the first staircase and took the steps two at a time. At the top, he surged forward blindly, across dark galleries, through disused rooms, and up more stairs until he shoved open a final door and emerged in the tower room.

He reached the windows just as the carriage passed the porter's lodge and swung onto the main road, the horses moving lightly at a brisk trot. He stood there frozen, watching the equipage recede into the distance, slowly yet far, far too fast, until it was only a black dot on the road. It dipped completely out of sight over the crest of a hill, and still he stood, straining his eyes for any hint of its reappearance.

Finally, he turned on his heel, half reeling, and collapsed upon the nearest divan.

Gone. She was gone, completely and utterly gone. He snatched up a pillow from the divan where she had rested her head that first night and brought it to his face, breathing against it and trying to sift from its dusty smell any lingering trace of lavender.

There was none. His head tipped against the seat back, suddenly too heavy for him to hold up anymore, and he stared sightlessly over the long, empty road. Until the moment that he shut the carriage door, until the moment the carriage began to roll away, he had not fully believed that she would leave. Some part of him had denied it—had labeled it so ludicrous that it refused to encompass such a thing. But now he knew that he would never see her again. He had told the truth about London—he would not, could not go back. Not when his friends would expect him to play all the old games, not when he could only hope to meet Victoria, at best, across some aging baroness' parlor.

The hand he raised to adjust his hat trembled. It would not be the same, he knew it in his gut, and if it couldn't be the same, he wanted no part of it. If she would not look at him with the same longing in her eyes, touch his hand with the same easy tenderness, speak with the same frankness, and make love to him as truly, then he would rather have nothing at all. As much as he hurt now, it did not compare to what he'd feel to be met with no more than a civil word and a pleasant smile.

He stood shakily and left the room, winding his way

slowly back to the Henry Suite. He lit a candle, stripped off his outer clothes, and dumped them on a chair, sinking into its neighbor to stare into the empty fire grate.

Gone. Gone. Gone. The word echoed inside his head like the toll of a bell. He imagined her, bounced along the road in the dark carriage. She had not wanted to go; if the earth itself started spinning backward, that was the one fact he could be certain of. But how long would her regret last? A day? A week? Until she saw her mother again, or until the first London party? A year? Forever?

As long as he knew his would?

But even if her regret did last, surely time would change her impression of him into something else— something more grand or more noble. Fond thoughts distorted memory, and even if her regard did not fade, he could still never be the man she would think him in two years' time.

Perhaps it should be best if her tenderness did wither quickly—

He did not know how long he sat there, with his thoughts circling, circling until they wore grooves in his mind, but the candle had burned down to a nub when a soft scratch at the door interrupted him.

"Come in," he called, looking over his shoulder, and Mrs. Peasebody entered with a laden tray.

"Thoo didn't break thy fast this morning, thy grace, so I brought thee thy dinner early," the old woman said deferentially, her tone unaccustomedly subdued.

"Didn't I?" said Byron vaguely, turning his attention back to the grate. "Well, I must eat. And this afternoon, have Fane come and see me—I've found some more records we need to go over together."

"Yes, thy grace," Mrs. Peasebody said, and balancing the tray in one hand, she cleared the clutter of ugly orna-

ments from the table nearest him before laying his meal
upon it. Silently, she turned to go. Byron heard the door
open, but it did not close.

"Yes?" he said after several seconds ticked by. He
made his tone flat and uninviting.

"She was a good lass, thy grace; 'tis all I want thee to
know. I did not know her so well as thoo, but she still
seemed a better lass than thoo is likely to find again."

And without another word, the door shut.

Byron uncovered the plate and started to eat, shovel-
ing the food into his mouth and chewing mechanically.
He remembered how Victoria had reacted to the bland
fare, amusement and disdain mingled, and then he remembered her very, very different reaction to the peach
crumble . . .

He dropped his silverware and stood abruptly, making
a restless circuit of the room. Why couldn't he shed her
from his mind? Victoria was only one woman, after all.
He should eat and then review the records he wanted to
show Fane to get everything straight in his mind first. But
he knew with horrible certainty that every entry of every
line would somehow remind him of her.

Damn it, how long would it take for him to feel normal again? His preoccupation swung suddenly to anger,
and he settled into the emotion with something like relief.
He was unused to this aching, unsettled feeling—but
anger, that he knew.

After all, he had a right to be angry. Who did Lady
Victoria think she was, sweeping into his house and turning his whole world upside down? Yes, he'd invited
her—but to his bed, not to rummage inside his head and
change everything around until he hardly knew who he
was anymore. And then to flit out of his life, as if she did
not owe him more than that!

Byron stopped, whirling toward the mirror over the fireplace. That was exactly it. That was exactly what was wrong. She had gone and changed everything, and now she was trying to leave and pretend it never happened. He wouldn't—*couldn't*—let her get away with that.

Some corner of his mind scoffed, telling him that his anger was ridiculous, that it was just an excuse to chase her down and . . . what? He didn't know. He'd know it when he found her.

But he ignored that voice and threw on his hat and coat, winding his scarf around his face as he burst through the door and ran down the stairs.

How long had it been since she'd left? Two hours? Three? No matter. He'd meet her in Leeds if not before.

He thought of how he looked, his red face scabbed over; not the horrific sight of three days before but still bad enough to draw stares and murmurs. His mouth tightened. If she thought even that would stop him from getting his due, she had a surprise coming.

Reaching the front hall, he heard the rain against the windows, dark with the storm. All the better, he thought grimly as he shouted for his horse. An answering cry arose from the bowels of the house, and moments later, he heard the hurried patter of footsteps as servants scrambled to do his bidding. One of the maids, Peg, dashed in from a side corridor, skidding to a sedate walk when she spied him.

"Mrs. Peasebody bids me ask, is there anything more thy grace needs?" she gasped, bobbing.

"Only Apollonia, saddled and bridled," he replied. *I'll fetch what I truly want myself.*

There was no sense of time or distance locked in the carriage's black cab, only a jolting, rocking sway that

Victoria could not translate into minutes or miles. Her stomach roiled in the darkness, and she did not know if it was the movement of the carriage or the lurching emptiness inside her, but it was all she could do to keep her breakfast down.

Every moment, she thought of Raeburn, Byron, *him,* lurking in the corridors of Raeburn Court, growing farther away by the breath. Even inside the carriage with no point of reference to judge their speed, she could not fool herself into thinking—hoping—that she was somehow standing still or going in circles around the estate. No, she was leaving him, even if she could not bear to think of that.

She tried to dredge up the memory of every moment she had spent in Raeburn's company, every word he had spoken, every look, every touch, every kiss. She assembled the pieces slowly, deliberately in her mind, adding layer upon layer until she had a simulacrum so real it might have stepped into the carriage and said her name. She would memorize it, she swore, assimilate it into herself, every flaw as precious as every virtue. Then, perhaps, she could take some little piece of him with her always.

Victoria must have slept, for she opened her eyes with the realization that the carriage had stopped moving. She sat up, smoothing the front of her dress. She didn't even have time to put on her bonnet before the door opened and the steps clattered down. She blinked in the light, as faint as it was, and it took her a moment to recognize the Leeds station, only a dozen feet beyond the carriage. Andrew stood on the pavement, rain dripping from his hat, and beyond, under the shelter of the overhang, Dyer waited with folded hands and a shamefaced expression.

Victoria set the bonnet on her head and tied it with two

efficient moves. With the last quick tug, it seemed as if she were tying up the past week, too, and locking it away, and she felt some quiet part of herself begin to die.

She set her jaw and took Andrew's arm, hopping awkwardly down the steps and using his shoulder like a crutch to hurry through the downpour into the waiting arms of her abigail.

"Has thoo got her, miss?" the footman asked.

"Yes, thank you," Dyer replied.

Victoria ignored them both. A clock stood before her; she had three hours until the London train arrived. Three hours of waiting, and then she'd be hurtling toward Rushworth, every instant putting yards between her and Raeburn Court. Her stomach clenched, and she tightened her grip on Dyer's arm.

"Are you all right, my ladyship? I never would have left if I'd known what would happen—"

"I am fine. Just—fine." Victoria turned back toward the carriage, and Dyer had no choice but to turn with her or let her go.

A curtain of rain hung across the pavement, and through it, Andrew moved, preparing the carriage for its return. He snapped the door closed, raised the steps, and scrambled up to the driver's bench. A hunched shape in his oilskin cloak, the coachman flicked his whip, and the carriage started off, making a wide, slow turn in the road. Heading back toward Raeburn Court.

Heading back toward the man she loved.

"Hold!" Victoria cried. They'd hardly gone a dozen yards, but there were other carriages and horses clattering down the street, and neither the coachman nor footman turned.

"Did you forget something, your ladyship?" Dyer asked, staring uncertainly out into the rain.

"Hold!" Victoria cried again after the retreating equipage, and she pulled away from Dyer's grasp to lurch forward, gasping when pain lanced up her leg from her ankle. She grabbed an iron support post, and Dyer hurried to her side.

"Your ladyship!"

"Stop that carriage!" Victoria ordered. "Whatever it takes, stop it!" Still clinging to the post, she watched Dyer plunge out into the downpour and run across the street, shouting and waving her plump arms. Andrew started and turned, and at his wave, the coachman pulled the team to a stop. Dyer caught up, and lifting her face toward them, she pointed back at Victoria at the edge of the overhang.

Slowly, slowly, the carriage turned, coming back toward the station, and once again it stopped. Victoria glanced again at the clock. It was enough time. It had to be. And if it weren't, then a few more hours of waiting for the next train couldn't hurt that much, could it?

She sent a silent message to her mother, begging her forgiveness. Then she squared her shoulders and turned to face Andrew, who swung down from the bench and gave her an inquiring expression.

I'm coming, Byron. I'm coming to tell you what I should have admitted days ago.

Noon. It was almost noon already. Where had the time gone?

Byron tucked away his watch as he swung past the porter's lodge and up the road, wishing he dared ask more than a canter from Apollonia. But there were forty miles between Raeburn Court and Leeds, and there was nowhere to change horses along the way.

If Apollonia threw a shoe, if the weather cleared suddenly, if the road got worse . . . Fear wriggled its way into his brain, but he ignored it. He would not even think of failing.

He ducked his head against the cold rain as it slanted into his face, eyes on the mud-churned road and the deep, fresh ruts that led him like a promise. *Follow, follow.* Apollonia's hooves threw up clods at every stride, splattering her black flanks and the tail of his long gray coat. His legs grew numb with cold, and water dripped down inside his low, soft shoes not meant for riding.

Weatherlea—he hardly registered the turnoff and the pale, startled boy who jerked away from the horse's thrashing hooves as he surged by. Now he could not feel his hands, for the kidskin had soaked through miles before, nor his face—a good omen, he had the presence of mind to think wryly before he turned his attention back to the road.

He did not know how many miles he went, his path stretching out in a long brown blur. He did not want to consider failure, so he filled his mind with the rhythm of Apollonia's strides and the two square yards of mud under her hooves, and the seconds and minutes blurred until time seemed to stop.

Suspended in that interminable moment, he almost lost his seat when Apollonia suddenly shied sideways and his numb legs refused to keep their grip. He scrabbled at the pommel with one hand as he brought Apollonia around with the other. She danced in a tight circle, head tossing and nostrils wide; as they passed, he caught a quick glimpse of a black carriage stopped on the road, its door finishing an abrupt swing open, and then he was facing the road again. But that instant was all he needed to take in the faces of his footman and driver, and he bit back a curse as he wheeled the horse around to face them.

"Where are we?" he demanded, unbuttoning his great-coat with cold-stiffened hands to find his pocket watch. "And how long ago did you leave Lady Victoria?" He could have sworn he should not meet his carriage for another half hour—and that he should have met it much farther up the road. Had that much time passed? Was he going that slowly? His fingers closed around his watch, but a voice arrested them.

"They did not leave me."

His stomach lurched, fear and joy and anger surging up until all he could manage was a strangled, "Good God." Disbelief struggled uppermost in the welter, but it was shattered by the pallid, narrow face peering out of the door.

"You should not have followed. It could stop raining at any moment, and you're still burned." Victoria's fine eyebrows knitted under her hideous, hateful black bonnet.

The absurdity of her reproach made him blink, and then his irritation blossomed into ire. "You left me. What was I supposed to do, sit and twiddle my thumbs after you got into my head, under my skin, and then ran away as if it didn't matter?" Byron swung down from his saddle, ignoring Apollonia as she sidled away, blowing. He glared up at Victoria through the rain, one hand braced on either side of the doorway.

Two spots of color appeared high on Victoria's cheeks, but almost as quickly, they disappeared. "You idiot. You damned, blind idiot." She spoke softly, shaking her head, and Byron abruptly felt like a scolded schoolboy. "This isn't how it's supposed to go." She looked up at him, her gray eyes damp but clear. "I love you. I know that, somehow, you must sense it, but that isn't enough. And I couldn't leave without telling you so."

"You can't leave at all," he said roughly, forcing the

words past the constriction in his throat. "I won't let you. Not now that I know . . . I want you with *me,* not scandalizing London or shocking your priggish parents. Ride the moors like a madwoman every day; develop a passion for small, obnoxious dogs; take to reform dress and open the manor doors to every Chartist agitator—I don't care what you do. Just don't leave me again. God knows I have no right to demand this"—his voice roughened— "but I can't stop myself."

"What are you saying?" Her voice shook, but she collected herself and tilted her chin up. "My mother is ill. I must go to her."

He clenched his hands into fists. "I'm not talking about visiting your mother, dammit. Can I make myself any clearer? I can't live without you. I don't know what to call it, but if it isn't love, I don't know what is. So stop looking down your prim little nose at me and say you'll marry me so I don't have to kill myself." The last words pulled out of his control, wavering with emotion instead of cool with dry humor as he'd intended them to be.

Victoria just shook her head, gaping at him, the edge of her ugly hat dripping with rain where it thrust beyond the carriage roof's edge. His importunate agitation faded in the face of that mute response, his gut plummeted, and he was beginning to fear that was all the answer he would get when with a strangled cry, she lurched to her feet and threw herself at him from the doorway.

The air rushed from his lungs at the force of the impact, and he reeled backward and pulled her against him to keep her from sliding into the mud. Her hands were clasped behind his neck, dislodging his hat and forcing his head down, and it wasn't until her lips found his that he realized what she was going to do. Impetuous, demanding, searing his mouth with her need. Dazed, he surrendered to her assault, opening his lips under the pressure of her tongue as she tasted him, teased him, loved him, an answering if confused passion heating his skin and tightening his trousers across his groin. Finally, she broke away, tipping her head back to the sky and letting loose a wild peal of laughter, looking younger and more striking in her mournful weeds than any woman had a right to look.

"Is that a yes?" he demanded.

"Yes, yes, yes!" she cried, turning her rain-wet face back to him. "It is the most foolish, impractical thing I have ever done in my foolish, impractical life, yet I doubt I shall ever regret it."

A shard of sanity broke into his wash of exultation. "You know there is no cure for my condition." He voice was thick with the pain of that admission. "I will let Merrick plague me with a thousand of his useless cures for your sake, but hope is faint, very faint. You will be consigning yourself to a life of darkness."

"No," she said, cupping his still-tender cheek in one hand, keeping the other wrapped around his neck. "Thick curtains can be opened as well as drawn shut. But even if what you said were true, I wouldn't care. You are all the sun I need."

Something dark and terrible within him broke then, something so deeply rooted in its old, hard bitterness that he had not felt it as separate from himself until the moment of its shattering. And a sense of sweet solace washed into the emptiness left by its passing, snatching the breath from his lungs and tightening his throat in wonder.

"And you are mine, Victoria. Always mine."

He kissed her, pulling her to him and drinking the raindrops from her lips, that dampness soon mingling with the saltier moisture of tears that could have come from him or her or both. He didn't know. He didn't care.

He nudged her lips open to trace with his tongue the almost imperceptibly uneven line of her teeth. He would never tire of her teeth, he thought, giddy disbelief bubbling through him. Her mouth was hot, welcoming, insistent, so gloriously and uniquely Victoria that he could get drunk on the taste of it. Her fingers twisted in his hair, and his own ached to bury themselves between her legs and smear their wetness across her belly until the air was heavy with her dark smell. Then he would kiss her, taste her damp flesh, tear out her hairpins and let the pale waves tumble across him, his alone . . .

The bump of her bandaged ankle against his leg brought him back to himself, and he drew away with a sigh. "Our betrothal does not end your mother's need for you."

"No, it does not," she agreed, sobering. Her pale, clear eyes met his. "I must still catch my train. But I swear to return the earliest moment that I may, pausing only long enough to write ahead so that you may round up the local parson to await my arrival."

The thought of letting her go even for such a short time ached sharply, but he suppressed it and replied in the same light vein. "If I even begin to suspect that you are gone a minute more than you must be, I will chase you down and demand you fulfill your promise at the nearest chapel—be it dissident, Quaker, or Catholic."

"Even in London?" She quirked an eyebrow, a smile playing at the corner of her mouth.

He tightened his grip. "Especially in London, Circe. Especially in London."

Epilogue

April 1866

Dusk came, setting the spent storm clouds afire in a blaze of orange. In the shadows of the shepherds' shelter, Victoria leaned against her husband's chest, loosely grasping the letter that Fane had brought to her as they mounted for their rainy ride.

According to her mother's missive, she was still doing well, having swiftly recovered from the fits that had slurred her speech and made her hands and mind unsteady a year and a half before. As usual, she was also in a tizzy about Jack's latest escapade. Victoria couldn't find it within herself to care. She loved her brother—as strange as it was to realize that—but Jack was old enough to make his own decisions and suffer the consequences of them, however it might besmirch the family name.

"So, what has the reprobate done this time?" The vibration of Byron's voice through his chest was as soothing as it was familiar.

Victoria laughed. "You know my mother too well, and you've only met her once."

"I don't need to know her. I know your brother." Byron snorted.

"He is facing charges of some sort for importing French pornography. That's what I think, at least; it's hard to tell from the letter exactly what's happened."

"Do you think he might go to gaol this time?" There was a hint of wistfulness in Byron's tone.

"Are you still hoping to get your revenge?" Victoria teased.

"No. I have everything I want right here." His voice dropped.

Victoria craned around to catch his eye, and she didn't need more than a year's marriage to him to know what his expression meant.

Gladly, she dropped the letter and turned in his arms, sighing in pleasure as he kissed the sensitive place on her neck and skated one hand down her still-flat belly toward her thighs.

That reminder made her stiffen slightly, and Byron, almost more aware of her body than she was, broke away and opened his eyes.

"I started my courses this morning," she said. She knew he read the rest in her face—her awareness of her age, the fear that she could never produce the heir he needed. The child she wanted.

Emotion flashed in his eyes, regret and acceptance mingled with pain for her. "It is not your fault, Victoria. Perhaps it would be best, after all, if the family debility were to stop with me."

She lifted a hand to his lips to silence them, and he kissed her fingertips. "Do not say that," she told him, even as she shivered at the little trills of pleasure that traveled up her arm. "It is rare, even in your family."

"Yes, it is," he said against her hand. She dropped it,

and his expression turned wicked. "So we might as well try, try again then, hmm?"

Victoria sniffed with feigned derision. "I couldn't get pregnant *now*."

His chuckle was throaty. "Practice makes perfect, or so they say."

Helplessly, the last of Victoria's tension dissolved, and she laughed, too. Then she took his face in her hands and pulled his lips down to hers.

Unheeded, the red sun finished sinking below the horizon, dragging the veil of night behind it across the moors.

Read on for a preview of
Lydia Joyce's next novel

The Music of the Night

Coming from Signet Eclipse
in November 2005

The ferry dipped and rocked on the choppy waves, its movements more queasily abrupt than the graceful rise and fall of the steamer they had left the day before.

Sarah Connolly stood at the rail between Lady Merrill and Mr. de Lint, straining through the mists for her first glimpse of Venice as the lady's granddaughter chattered with her friends, their backs to the gray view of the Adriatic.

Venice. The name was pregnant with promise. Of Trieste, she carried only an impression of stuccoed houses in failing light as they were driven from the steamer to their accommodations, and their hotel had been disappointingly similar to the one in Southampton. But Venice—surely Venice would not, *could* not disappoint. Her imagination had feasted on the promise of La Serenissima since her employer first stated her intention of spending spring in that city, and Sarah's quiet, half-desperate gratitude for such an opportunity allowed her to bear the delicate tortures of Mr. de Lint with greater composure then she had thought she possessed.

Sarah stared at the low smear of darker gray that stood as a divider between the undifferentiated expanse of sea, land, and fog. Finally, she saw a break in the land ahead, and a few minutes later, the ferry was sliding between the narrow arms of two barrier islands.

Now they were within, and Sarah strained her eyes for the first hint of the glorious city. Hummocks, hillocks, and sea reeds thrust through the silty water everywhere she looked, and between them hundreds of wooden posts were sunk into the lagoon bottom in a baffling pattern. In front of the ferry, sleek black darts pierced the fog, shallow boats sliding among the more wide-flung isles.

For a hundred heartbeats, that was all, until finally, a bone-white mass detached itself from the unquiet waters in the mist-shortened distance, resolving as they approached into blocks of towers and colonnades in pale marble and red brick, cut through by avenues of the brackish lagoon.

"Isn't it a sight?" Mr. de Lint said with a display of heartiness that Sarah couldn't quite believe was sincere.

She did not know whether he was addressing her or his mother; he had used that trick before to embarrass her, so she simply nodded slightly, keeping her eyes fixed on the white buildings that marched down to kiss the sea.

"I'd bet you never pictured yourself here," he continued in the same too-easy tone.

Sarah looked up sharply to meet his amber gaze. Eyes that color should not be able to look cool, but his did, and they had a glitter that made clear that the reminder of her origins was neither accidental nor careless.

"I am pleased to go where Lady Merrill wishes, sir," she said softly through the rising heat of impotent humiliation.

"What virtuous meekness," he murmured, those hard eyes scouring her face, picking out each pock-mark that welted her skin with an expression that was almost hungry.

She jerked her head away, the deep brim of her unfashionable bonnet shuttering his view.

"Sarah is quite the perfect companion," Lady Merrill said, oblivious to the tension that thrummed in the air. She patted Sarah's white-knuckled hand on the rail next to hers.

"You are easy to please, your ladyship." Still rattled by Mr. de Lint, Sarah knew her words had a hollow ring. But it was true; Lady Merrill, for all her faults, was a remarkably undemanding mistress. Sarah would be more than happy to spend the rest of her life as a lady's companion if she knew that all her future employments would be as pleasant as this one. The lady's flighty granddaughter and her fluttering friends Sarah could bear with equanimity. If only it weren't for the lady's son . . .

"Would you like to see the carnival, madam?" Mr. de Lint asked over Sarah's head, dismissing her as if she had ceased to exist the moment his attention turned elsewhere.

"The carnival?" Lady Merrill asked. "Why, that's three-quarters of a century dead!"

Her son laughed. "Oh, it never truly died, and with Venice's glorious liberation from the greedy Austrian oppressors—" He struck a pose. "—certain elements of the Venetian youth have decided to revive its more notorious elements year-round. In private, of course, and with far more taste and discretion than was displayed in times past." From his tone, Sarah could not tell whether he thought that was a good thing. "You would make a stunning houri in any of their masques, Mother. If I might be so bold." He adopted a tone of wild flattery.

Lady Merrill laughed merrily. "Oh, those days of mine are over. I am done with shocking society! And besides, Sarah might die of humiliation if she were dragged along in the company of a seventy-year-old odalisque, never mind what Anna and her young friends would think."

"What is it, Grandmama?" Lady Anna asked, turning

from her conversation with the Morton sisters at the sound of her name.

Sarah said nothing as Lady Merrill explained, hoping that the girl's interruption would deflect Mr. de Lint's attention. But almost immediately, she felt his eyes light upon her again.

"Our Sarah might just enjoy the opportunity to hide behind a mask and veil," he said, ignoring his half-niece. There was no edge in his words, but Sarah could feel their malice biting into her.

I don't care, she told herself. But she did, and he knew it. No matter how many years stood between her and the filthy streets of the rookery, she would always carry the evidence of her origins on her face, bare for everyone to see. Her speech was now flawlessly correct, her education—if not her experience—as good as that of many peeresses, her bearing and etiquette without fault . . . but nothing could erase the smallpox scars that disfigured her cheeks and forehead.

A century ago, those scars would have merely made her plain. But by the time of her birth, all but the poor and a few objectors whose wealth protected them were inoculated, and now that every child in England was required to be vaccinated by law, it marked her as one who had slipped through the cracks—who had origins such that it was possible for her to be invisible, and who had received none of the doctors' various concoctions or treatments for preventing scars when she contracted the disease.

Quite simply, she wore her life story on her face.

And so she would never be more than a lady's companion, and she was remarkably fortunate to have been elevated to that position. It was far more than she had once dreamed of and far more than anyone of her past deserved, and so, she told herself, she would be content.

Resolutely, she shut out Mr. de Lint's continuing acid-laced commentary and turned her eyes to the palazzos that rose from the murky waters like a pale dream.

*　　*　　*

It was he. There had been no mistake.

A black anger filled Sebastian as he stood in the shadows of the doorway of a draper's shop near the Ponte della Verona, wrapped in an amorphous cloak and in the swirling fog that now rose from the canals faster than the wind could tatter it. Three crowded gondolas and half a dozen wider *batèle buranele* rested in the oil-smooth water at the canal door of the palazzo, the wallowing *batèle* nearly gunwale-deep under the loads of boxes, trunks, and servants.

Under the first gondola's black hood, de Lint sat with another passenger, his head bare and his chin raised with conceit that radiated across the water. Sebastian watched as the man leapt nimbly to the water stairs, much to the irritation of the gondolier, who cursed him roundly in the Venetian dialect as the boat rocked with his jump. His cloaked companion pressed her hands against the sides of the hood and said nothing.

It was obscene that the man could stand there, smiling down like a benevolent deity upon the gondolas that floated at his feet. Even through the distorted lens of Sebastian's vindictiveness, de Lint looked every inch the gentleman, from the top of his perfectly smoothed hair to his shining short boots. Nowhere did the filth lying under that veneer betray itself; he was a picture of refinement and moderation, and Sebastian's hands balled into fists at the very sight of him.

Ignoring both his companion and the gondolier, de Lint shouted at a servant who had issued a challenge from an upper window of the palazzo. As the great wooden doors were opened in response to his reply, he waved his boat away and ordered the next gondola up, holding out his arms theatrically to a white-haired woman within—Lady Merrill, Sebastian saw when she turned toward him, recognizing her through the twining mist. He allowed himself a surge of dark satisfaction; his sources had proven correct thus far.

The lady flashed her son a dazzling smile and allowed herself to be helped up, laughing as he fussed over her extravagantly. As soon as she was shooed within the palazzo's tall carven doors, he turned back to assist the second passenger. The pretty redhead was exactly whom Sebastian had expected, one who was as essential to his plan as Lady Merrill or even de Lint himself: Lady Anna Dutton, de Lint's half-niece.

The girl and the gondola were dismissed, and the final boat slid into place. Two more young girls—Melinda and Euphemia Morton, his sources had told him, friends and distant relatives of the family—were swiftly assisted out, followed by a third woman who had "governess" written in every line of her stout body. That conveyance, too, was rowed away, and Sebastian was about to turn aside when the first one pulled up again and de Lint held out an imperious arm.

It was only then that Sebastian realized that it still carried de Lint's slender, cloaked companion. And no surprise that he had forgotten; as the woman stood, it became apparent she was a creature whose very meekness made her small body seem even smaller. Hunched shoulders, ducked head, all clad in a discreet black linsey-woolsey that completed her air of utter insignificance.

And yet . . . His eyes were caught by the tension that radiated through that frame, more like the string of a bow than a lute, threatening danger rather than breakage. Despite the servility of her posture, there was still something—in her movements? her posture?—that spoke of strength and a deep, burning anger that was kept in check only by such elaborate displays of subjection, and Sebastian found himself wondering what would happen when that control finally snapped.

She hesitated, standing in the gondola and radiating uncertainty. The deep poke bonnet that she wore was twenty years out of date, and it hid her features as effectively as a wall.

Until she looked up as if seeking an exit from de Lint's too-pressing offer. Then Sebastian has a brief impression of a narrow, pale face before her incredible dark eyes lit upon him, capturing his own gaze with their force and sending a jolt of—what?—surging through him. It wasn't alarm, exactly, or lust . . . something more like recognition, which was strange because he could not think of a single person who resembled that slender, tenuous girl in even the most remote way.

Sebastian realized that he had been unconsciously leaning out from the doorway in interest; now he jerked back, but it was far too late to hide in anonymous shadows. Those eyes, darker than any shadow, followed him, touching every line and plane of his face that was visible beneath his hood.

For an instant, he felt as if some sort of link formed between them through that intense scrutiny, boring into him and forging a connection by the sheer force of her gaze. Then she looked away, distracted by something de Lint said, and the illusion snapped. Released from the spell of her eyes, Sebastian saw for the first time the scars that marked her face.

Another shock went through him, this more identifiable—mixed of vindication, fury, incredulity, and an in-

stinctive sympathetic pain. The nurse's wail when he had
burst into the nursery echoed in his head: *It was that
pock-faced strumpet! She told me I was needed!*

And now here was de Lint with just such a scar-faced
woman in tow. The marks were not very deep nor were
they truly disfiguring, but they were clear enough that
there was no room for doubt. Sebastian brooded as the
man picked her up by the waist—to the gondolier's further curses—and swung her around once, acting for an
instant as if he were going to tip her into the canal. Her
hands tightened so convulsively on the man's arms that
Sebastian could see the knuckles standing out from her
flesh, but if she uttered a sound, he could not hear it. Finally, de Lint set her down. He was laughing. But when
the woman turned back toward the gondola, not a trace of
levity showed on her face.

Two scarred women. Chance? Unlikely. Yet there was
nothing of a whore in her expression as she looked at de
Lint. She only looked frightened, shot through with an
abiding anger that was so hopeless that Sebastian felt a
mixture of pity and fascination without meaning to.

Then her head came up: She was looking for him
again. Wishing to avoid that disturbing gaze, he gripped
the doorknob behind him and pushed, ducking into the
draper's shop behind him.

"Posso aiutarlo, signor?"

All your favorite romance writers are
coming together.

SIGNET ECLIPSE

COMING MAY 2005:
Fire Me Up: *An Aisling Grey, Guardian, Novel*
by Katie MacAlister
Seeing Red by Jill Shalvis
Lady Midnight by Amanda McCabe

COMING JUNE 2005:
Beyond the Pale by Savannah Russe
My Hero by Marianna Jameson
The Chase by Cheryl Sawyer

www.penguin.com

Penguin Group (USA) Inc. Online

What will you be reading tomorrow?

Tom Clancy, Patricia Cornwell, W.E.B. Griffin,
Nora Roberts, William Gibson, Robin Cook,
Brian Jacques, Catherine Coulter, Stephen King,
Dean Koontz, Ken Follett, Clive Cussler,
Eric Jerome Dickey, John Sandford,
Terry McMillan…

You'll find them all at
http://www.penguin.com

*Read excerpts and newsletters,
find tour schedules, and enter contests.*

Subscribe to Penguin Group (USA) Inc. Newsletters
and get an exclusive inside look
at exciting new titles and the authors you love
long before everyone else does.

PENGUIN GROUP (USA) INC. NEWS
http://www.penguin.com/news